The hospital erupted with chaos.

First, I heard a lingering howl of the siren letting everyone know that there was an emergency. It was unfortunately just when I'd almost laid my head on the pillow! Clenching my teeth, I peeked out of the staff's lounge and moved down the stairs, deciding that the elevator took too long to wait for. When I stepped out to the first floor, I stopped, petrified, watching the reception room doors wide open, ambulance cars crowded outside, flooding half of the floor with the sinister flickering of the red lights, staff running around the entrance with stretchers.

"What happened?" I exclaimed as I came closer to the reception desk, carefully looking at the hall.

"A massacre in the center," the nurse on duty spluttered. The whole floor was full of the doctors' shouts and the victims' cries. "You better get out of here, Thea…"

I took a deep breath and pressed my lips together, not allowing myself to start ranting as the advice wasn't so bad after all. Only it was already too late.

"Simon, you take these!" the head doctor's voice miraculously came through the chaos. How did he appear here in the middle of the night? "Gordon! Bring this woman to the OR. Ten minutes for you to get ready!" It seemed like he wasn't even breathing, shouting orders. "Thea!" I shivered. Exactly at this moment, the staff brought new stretchers to Dr. Close. Bending over them, he raised his head in just a few seconds. "Thea, this one to the ER."

I nodded nervously, swallowing. Why the hell did I have to come down here?

"Fast!" Close shouted, and I made a rapid movement, showing the way to the paramedics.

On the way, I realized I forgot my radio! I had no idea how to prepare the ER without it. When the elevator doors closed, I felt deaf.

"Is he a dead man, that one?" one of the paramedics asked.

I automatically looked down at the stretchers, realizing that I would have to get the body out of the blood-soaked hoodie with the hood covering half the face. It seemed like the man liked to work out — when the sleeve lifted, I couldn't help but notice a strong muscular forearm. Black lines of a tattoo were intricately placed on it, but it was impossible to guess the pattern.

"I don't know," I answered and frowned, thinking that this half-corpse's life was now my responsibility. Maybe it was all just a dream? Although it looked much more like a nightmare.

Quickly getting out of the elevator, I sped through the hallway to the ER and grabbed the landline phone. Paramedics rolled the patient in but let go of the stretchers as soon as they were in the room. They then rushed back towards the elevator.

It was impossible to get through to the centralized emergency room. I, getting more and more nervous with every second, was trying to call all of the numbers, glancing towards the dreary image near the door — a body with a hand tragically hanging from the stretchers. That wasn't something I had seen before. I had just started doing three hundred hours of community service ordered by the court, and the first night, it felt like, would certainly cost me several years of my life.

"Just pick up the phone, for fuck's sake!" I turned to the landline, almost howling. Was it possible that the hospital was not able to handle all of the injured? If that was the case, it could cost lives! I hung up and walked up to the stretchers, confused.

"And what the fuck should I do?" I swore, clenching the side of the stretchers.

The man's chest didn't indicate breathing. Leaning closer to him, I pulled the hood up to try and find any signs that he was still alive. Under the hood, there was a mask, black, glossy, covering everything, but his lips and chin. I didn't think much when I firmly grabbed it, and then two things happened in such a short moment that I hardly noticed them. First, there was a late observation that the hand, previously hanging from the stretchers, did not do that anymore. Second, this exact hand suddenly darted to my neck so quickly I didn't even have time to get scared. The man opened his eyes and pulled me closer by the neck.

Looking at my reflection on the glossy surface of the mask with its owner staring hard at my face was not very pleasurable. I saw lively flames in the brown pupils. An animal-like growl came out of his throat, and I finally shook off the dazing sensation and started moving, grabbing his wrists with my palms. It left no effect on him. He sat up sharply, not letting me go, and glanced around.

In the eerie silence of the ER, my fast ragged breaths and cries were deafening.

"Let go," I gasped, "I didn't do anything to you!"

He stopped looking around and focused his unwanted attention on me. The hair on the back of my neck stood up as I started to understand who he was. The man's nostrils flared as he breathed in the air like an animal, a predator, and squinted at the badge on my chest. When his hand disappeared from my neck, I felt a hot drop sliding past my collar.

"Where's the exit?" he growled, and I flinched back, painfully hitting the corner of the table. He didn't let me fall, pulling me closer by the hand, almost dislocating it. "I asked where the exit is!" he angrily repeated through clenched teeth.

A beast…

A person with genetic deviations (or modifications — there was no way for us, common people, to know that for sure) who everyone in the city has only heard about from the news. They warned us to be on alert as the mutants were among us. There were mangled bodies found, strange men with glowing eyes and fangs out caught on cameras in the city... These urban legends disturbed our society for no less than several decades, but no one knew where they came from.

"There," I motioned to the exit with my trembling hand.

"Lead the way," he pushed me to the front.

"There are many wounded in the hospital," I babbled haltingly. "They're not going to notice you..."

"Sure," he said and chuckled; his voice was almost human. "Lead the way!"

We rushed through a labyrinth of corridors to the stairs, but when I was about to push the door the beast pulled me close and pressed his palm against my mouth, listening carefully. There was a commotion on the stairs and the sounds of several male voices.

"Where to hide?" he snarled in my ear and scratched my cheek with his claws.

"Th-Th-There," I motioned my head and lost a breath from the rapidity of his movement as he held me closely and lunged in the pointed direction.

A small and stuffy storage room smelled of stale clothes and antiseptics. The beast jammed inside, pressing me into himself almost to the point of my ribs cracking. The door closed. The floor was full of shouting and movement, but I didn't understand a word. His heavy breaths were all I heard. I could smell blood. He held me tight by the neck, his hand on my mouth. Pressed against his chest, I could hardly reach the floor with the tips of my toes. His fast inhales pushed all of the air out of my lungs and I felt like I was suffocating. Without thinking, I started to adapt to his rhythm. I couldn't get enough air and fell into a weird trance caused by the rush of adrenaline.

The beast inhaled sharply and suddenly held his breath. I froze too and trembled when he touched my temple with his nose and slowly moved down my neck.

My brain continued to drown in fog. I tried to sober up, biting my lips under his palm, but it wasn't working. It seemed that the smell was not that of blood anymore but of something hot, spicy, burning, spine-tingling, and body-warming. I felt drunk. When the man's hand suddenly grabbed my thigh and pressed it onto his tense groin, I squeaked into his palm. I felt my neck burning, and my legs buckled.

He bit me!

I put my hands on the door, scratching it with my nails and slowly falling into madness from everything that happened next — I thought I was going crazy...

The beast touched my neck with his tongue.

It was rough, trailing across every pore, and from his movements, I felt something down my stomach tighten more and more. My body was in his power as a puppet was in the power of its master, and when the man pulled my robes up to my belly button, I just shook my head, unable to object. It was like I was disconnected from my mind, destroyed to dust by fear. Somewhere inside the remainders of common sense were alerting me to run, free myself, fight, but those cries sounded like a faraway echo. A brief sound cut through as he unzipped his jeans. The sound hit my nerves like a hammer.

"No," I whispered with the last bits of energy, but I couldn't move to get out.

"Yes, Thea," the beast growled into my ear, "it's a fucking 'yes.'"

He tore my robe, got under my bra, and cupped my breast. His scratching whisper made goosebumps travel down my body, and a moan came out. His hand wasn't covering my mouth anymore, he lowered it and pushed it inside my underwear. I should've screamed but I moaned, tilting my head back and placing it on his shoulder. My breast pushed further into his palm all by itself, and he squeezed one of the nipples, simultaneously pushing his fingers between my legs.

How could I ever describe this? Since when a storage room was a way to my personal nirvana? What did this beast do to me? Was I now poisoned?

My body was not interested in answers to any of these questions. I arched my back, asking for more, and he didn't make me wait for it for too long…

When I felt a sudden pain below my stomach, I was almost happy, hoping that it would help me to sober up. As soon as he pushed his dick into me in a single motion, I moaned again, accepting my defeat. I couldn't resist him. I thought it was his poison breaking my will, making me feel things that were not true — wild pleasure and arousal. His hoarse moan fueled the madness, and I moved back and forth as much as I could in his tight grip. He murmured something approvingly, sinking his claws into my skin. I took it for granted. His every move made me submit to him more. Concentrated pulsating pleasure spread through my body. I wanted this beast like I had never wanted anyone. I wriggled and moaned in response to his movement.

He pushed faster and harder, making me go crazy from the firework of emotions and feelings in my body. I didn't have any doubt that I was going to die. A human can't survive having sex with a beast. I felt my chest tense, my thighs cramped up sharply as unknown and scary anticipation pulsated between my legs, tightening something inside. I moaned and cried when a wave went through my body, and I trembled at the spot where we connected, unable to stop. I wanted to break free and wake up, but he wasn't letting me, continuing his tough movements to his climax. The beast's hand went back to my neck, the second one clenching my hip…

I felt like I went over the edge the second time, now with him. I was shaking, my legs buckling, while he was hoarsely growling into my neck, trembling. When our agony slowly started to decline, I felt tears trickle down my cheeks, but the beast couldn't care less.

He squeezed my neck with his fingers as he snarled into my ear, "No Plan B or police involvement, got it?! You show yourself to them and end up in a place no one returns from. Got it?!"

His harsh request made me flinch, but he just pressed me harder into himself, reminding me that he was still inside of me.

"You got it?" he demanded, and I nodded nervously. "There are no cameras in the corridor," he continued, "tell them I almost choked you and you ran away."

I continued to nod obsessively, ready to do anything for him to leave me alone.

"Good girl," he praised. He then added suddenly, "And remember — you're mine now. You get under someone else, and I'll kill you."

He didn't wait any longer. He slid out of me, zipped his jeans, and fixed my robe as if it could cover what he had done to me! He had to carefully open the door and exit with me after checking that there was no one outside. Dim lighting blinded me in the first couple of seconds, and I blinked, wiping the tears away. When my vision came back, the corridor was empty…

***

Even if I met someone on my way to the staff's lounge, I wouldn't notice and wouldn't be able to explain anything. I couldn't even explain it to myself! All I needed was to get out, get further away even if I had to crawl. It felt like the beast tore me to pieces inside and out. Everything hurt. My mind was bouncing, searching

for an explanation to whatever had happened and finding just one
— the poison. The beast bit me, infiltrating my blood with it, making
me submit to him. What for? And why? He was about to run and
wasn't hiding for no reason — the men on the staircase were
looking for him... Did he decide to have some fun while waiting for a
good moment to dash?

"Bastard... What a fucking bastard..."

Tears went down my cheeks, blinding me, as I put my
tracksuit pants on. I felt pain, itching and pulling between my legs. I
wanted to scratch my skin away with his sperm on it! I wanted to
scratch all of it, only to stop scenting his sickeningly musky smell. I
suppose I went mad, but it just felt like I got dipped into mulled
wine flavoring or, even better, marinated in spices!

Covering my face with the hood of my tracksuit hoodie, I ran
across the hallways without anyone noticing and dashed as soon as I
was outside. I should've called a taxi, but I wanted to let out some
of the adrenaline, burn down any remains of the terrifying delirium
because I still sensed the man as if he was inside of me. I rushed
through the dark streets, desperate to run away...

When I got to my block, the sun was rising. I was walking,
my steps fast, for about half an hour, surprised at the calmness that
took the place of nervousness. There was no fear, no pain, no
bitterness. There was nothing a victim of an assault would probably
feel. I was so calm that it was frightening.

When I entered my silent flat, there was a loud bang in the
bedroom and Bunny slowly crawled out under the dim light. He was
wearing funny acid-green PJs, his light hair spiking out. Who would
believe that this creature was a high-paid and sought after model?

"Bitch, you almost gave me a heart attack— Thea, what the
fuck?!"

My friend's sleepy eyes went wide as soon as I took off the
hoodie.

"A beauty, am I not?" I said and grinned angrily and went to the kitchen, unperturbed. I threw the hoodie, pants, and T-shirt into the trash bin. "Bring the medical kit and some bandages, I'm off to the shower," I said as I walked to the bathroom naked.

"What happened?!" he screamed. All gays are such drama queens in these situations!

"Stop panicking! It doesn't make me feel any better. Who's the man here?!" I said, not holding back.

"You are!" he replied without a second thought, following me. "Are you going to explain?"

"First I'll take a shower, you'll disinfect the bites, make some coffee..."

"BITES?!"

"Get out!" I ordered and closed the door right in front of his face.

I stood near the door, listening to him muttering to himself in the kitchen, opening the cabinets in search of the medical kit. It was terrifying to take a step and look at myself in the mirror, and I kept staring at the stone-cut basin... It's pretty. It was one of the reasons Bunny and I rented this flat. We could afford it. We worked day and night as our lives depended on it in several modeling agencies, but we could afford to live in a flat with a basin like this one.

And then the devil brought me to the hospital!

I took a breath and stepped to the mirror. There was a red and blue bruise on my neck from the bite on one side and scratch marks from the claws on another. The back of my head hurt, dried drops of blood going down my spine. I was looking at myself in the mirror, blinking fast. My hair was a mess as if I participated in the show of a loony fashion designer all over again. I couldn't grow my hair for a year after that... My eyes were red, skin looked almost greenish in the light.

My wounds stung in hot water, making me notice a couple more on my hips. I stood under the shower, fighting fatigue and lack of desire to grab a washcloth and scrub the skin to wash away the feeling of the events... The murmur of water, firm drops hitting my skin, painfully swollen nipples... His hands everywhere...

The feeling between my thighs was so sudden that I screamed and opened my eyes. I didn't have to persuade myself to wash anymore — I got to it with eagerness and enthusiasm. When will this fucking poison stop? That's just craziness! This bastard fucked me against my will, and I... I... What about me? Should it destroy me? He'll get no such pleasure from me! It had happened, and now I need to fix the consequences. I'm lucky to be alive.

Self-persuasion didn't help, and even clean and wet I could smell this scent... Although now there was something bitter about it...

"Can you smell anything strange on me?" I asked as I stormed into the kitchen, naked and wet, to face shocked Bunny sitting on a barstool with his legs up. He looked at me as though I was out of my mind.

"What the fuck happened?" he repeated through clenched teeth, his eyes glowing dangerously.

"A beast fucked me?" I replied indifferently, putting a towel around myself.

"A beast?!" he cried. He seemed to get even more flustered. "Where were you, a zoo?!"

"In the hospital! I'm doing three hundred hours of community service for saving your ass!"

"And I'll always owe you for that," he muttered. "And what kind of beast, according to you, you got fucked by?"

"You... You don't believe me?!" I exclaimed and pushed my shoulder into his face, showing the mark. "What do you think this is?"

"I don't want to think!" he said and jumped from the barstool. "I want you to explain it without acting insane!"

I slowly took a deep breath and got some air into my lungs, pulled a cup of hot coffee closer — Bunny was good at following orders even in stressful situations — and told him everything.

My friend went silent, staring at me for a very long time.

"Help me with the wound," I forced quietly. "I want to sleep."

"You need to see a doctor," he protested emotionlessly. "And a policeman."

"Police isn't going to help. They never do…"

I didn't have any faith in this system anymore, and I never will. I learned not to do that when I was running around a supermarket parking lot with my bleeding brother in my arms, screaming for help, asking these badge-bearing fuckers to come closer and do something, anything… Life is an impatient and cynical teacher.

No, fuck the police. Those bastards will have their hell to enjoy, and I'll burn in mine.

"He forbid me," I explained as the memory of the beast's threat sent goosebumps down my spine. "Hinted that he'd put me away somewhere with no way out."

Bunny rolled his eyes and said, "Thea, if he is who you think he is…"

"Police will do nothing to him…"

"He came in you."

"I know."

"And?"

"I'll figure it out tomorrow."

Bunny snuffled and stood up.

I was melancholically drinking my coffee while he was looking through antiseptics and bandages.

"Thea..."

"Don't..."

I knew what he wanted to say. Bunny and I were so close that thoughts occurring at the same time were not unusual anymore.

My contract with *Dew Corporations* — one of the most elite and expensive jewelry manufacturers — was over. The shoot would be the day after tomorrow. The fitting was today. This contract could be my breakthrough moment. And now everything went to shit.

"Can you hug me?" I sniffed.

"Come here."

Bunny helped me to put on my PJs — everything from neck to shoulder blades hurt. He then placed me on his bed and hugged me carefully.

"Thank you," I whispered, "you're the best."

"So are you, and that's why we're together."

I grinned sadly.

"He was the first man who got me there," I whispered into his shoulder.

Bunny nodded.

"We'll figure it out, Thea. I'm here."

"I know."

***

That morning Bunny's harsh whisper woke me up.

"Thea, the breakfast is on the table. I have to get to work."

"Hmmm..." I mumbled. "Thank you. Bye."

When I finally was awake, Bunny was long gone. I looked at my phone and sighed — it was past noon. The good thing was that I at least got enough sleep.

I expected not to be able to turn my neck. I expected it to be sore, but to my surprise, I didn't feel even a slight bit of discomfort.

On the contrary, as soon as I stretched, my eyes were wide open with no help from coffee, and my body was warm and energized, ready for the day. As soon as I saw the list of the calls I missed, it became very clear where all of this energy was going to go. But not before the intercom rang, making me drop my phone.

"Who's there?"

"Miss Melory, Inspector Cavien speaking," he said, showing his ID into the camera. "Let me in, please."

I swallowed and started to run around the room. I didn't come up with anything better than quickly getting into Bunny's PJs. It was the only clothes with a hood to help cover the bandages on my neck. I did not doubt that showing the beast's marks to the police was not a good idea.

Inspector's eyes narrowed as he saw me in my unusual outfit, but he quickly pulled himself together.

"Hello, Miss Melory."

"Good afternoon," I replied, inviting him in.

Inspector, who was a middle-aged serious-looking man, entered the hallway.

"Yesterday you disappeared from the hospital," he stated, turning to look at me.

"Yes... I got scared and I ran away," I said, watching as he clenched his teeth and sighed slowly, staring at me intently. "The man attacked me," I started nervously. "No one came to help; everyone was so busy..."

"Did he hurt you?" Inspector Cavien frowned.

"He grabbed me by the neck," I nodded, showing him the bandage on my clavicle.

"Yes, we saw that on the cameras," he noted politely. "What happened next?"

"He ordered that I show him the exit and then... He ran away," I replied. "He scared me," I sniffed to make it all more believable.

"Did he... Did he say anything?" the Inspector's voice was calm and confident. It seemed like my act had worked.

"No, almost nothing..." I said, pretending to remember. "He said he'd kill me if I move, and I..." I continued and looked the man straight in the eyes.

"Got it. But why didn't you ask doctors for help?"

"You must be joking. I couldn't even call anyone into the ER," I said and grinned, leaning against the wall as if all strength had left me. "And, as you probably know, I'm doing my community service there so there is not much trust from the staff."

"Well..." he sighed, pulling down the mask of a serious detective, "sign here, please." He handed me a clipboard.

"Sure," I said and shrugged, doing as asked. "This guy, is he a criminal or something?"

The man looked at me as he stood at the door.

"Yes, and you're very lucky. Good day to you."

"To you too," I mumbled under my breath. "Lucky is not quite the right word."

After the policeman left, I spent an alarmingly long time standing next to the door and listening. I tried to persuade myself that everything was fine and they had nothing on me. It was not surprising that I was flinching after everything that happened, because there was no one to protect me. That bastard was right after all. I should keep a low profile and tell no one the truth. No one except Bunny.

I sighed and went to the bathroom where I had a sudden realization. The lack of pain in my neck, which I found suspicious earlier, had a simple explanation. After I took off the bandages and dropped them on the ground, I discovered that the inflammation was gone! Where previously was a deep wound, there now was nothing but a thin pink scar, which looked like a dotted line with occasional shades of red in it! Heck, I'd even call it artsy!

I clenched my teeth and finally let myself descend into desperation as it was now so painfully clear that my hopes had no chance to come to life. This shoot was something I could only dream of, and now I should just forget about it.

"Why me?!" I muttered. It didn't make it better, that my face looked amazing today like I spent the past week on a holiday — eyes glowing, skin tanned, and no bags under my eyes. That's some bullshit! Or maybe the poison was truly magical. "Why some people get everything, and others get nothing?! Me and Bunny worked so hard on all those shoots and shows... Why me?!"

A phone call disturbed the silence of the flat.

"Thea, are you alright?" Bunny asked, breathing heavily, probably on his way back to the shoot from a smoke break.

"I'm okay. The police were here."

"And?" he asked, his voice tense.

"Asked me some questions."

"Good," he sniffed approvingly, "that's the right thing to do."

Oh, he thought that I had told them the truth. Sweet, but not if I could help it. Although it's better if he thought that way for now, and we could talk about it tonight.

"Are you sure you're okay?"

"Yes," I said and I didn't lie. "Your miraculous work with the wound worked — it's almost healed. Was it some new medicine?"

"No, just a normal antiseptic, T."

I sighed, walking around our only bedroom.

"Well, then it's even better that I didn't go to the doctor because it healed all on its own."

"T..."

"Bunny, don't," I said, biting my lips.

"I'm not going to work for *Dew* without you."

"Shut up. Don't even think about it! Don't make it worse than it already is," I snapped. "Get to work!"

When he hung up, I felt angry tears go down my cheeks.

***

I moved to Cryton-City five years ago. Capital had so many opportunities, and it was the only chance for a girl from a single-parent household to achieve something. In the beginning, even a cup of coffee instead of cheap tasteless tea was a success. I worked night shifts at the supermarkets, going to casting calls during the day. With my nocturnal lifestyle and dark circles under my eyes, I was only good for some alternative designers, but it had given a start to my career. I became a favorite model for some of them and left my night job, got rid of the circles, and started to take care of myself, getting my stimulator-pills addiction under control. I got healthier, gained some weight, stopped looking like a skeleton. I couldn't be the alternatives' muse anymore, but *Dew Corporations* showed some interest...

It was meant to be my golden ticket into the world of elite modeling, the world of high fashion photography. This new ad campaign for a jewelry collection should have been the most important event in my life...

I exhaled smoke into crystal clear air. Our apartment's balcony had a view of a picturesque park, which looked like a colorful plate with warm fall adding shades to it. The smell was incredible. I felt like going down to the pond, stepping on the leaves under the big eucalyptus, and drinking coffee from "Spicy Meadow", letting my desperation take over.

There were only a couple of hours left until my meeting with Dewman. Those hours were all I had left before I was going to go back to where I had started. Or maybe even further. I wasn't sure I'd be able to get back up there so easily, not right away anyway. I would prefer to lay in silence and misery, but even this I had no chance of doing thanks to the stupid hospital community service!

I have to survive this… Just maybe not now, later.

It took almost half a day to get ready for the meeting as I thought about whether I should cover the scar. The realization that there is going to be a permanent mark caught me on my way from the bathroom to the kitchen, and I slowly sank to the floor, grabbing the wall.

"Shh…" I whispered to myself, trying to calm down desperate screams and cries inside my head.

I crawled to the cigarettes and by the time of the meeting, I smoked about five of them.

The mirror, however, was on my side today. I looked in it and saw a supermodel wearing jeans and a blouse and black high-heeled pumps, red lipstick on her lips. I smiled at her, at myself, and decided that if I got to go, I might as well do it in style! I decided not to cover my neck, just hid the mark with the bandage. It's difficult to see under the hair anyway.

When I got into the taxi, it was already dark outside. My blood boiled expectantly, awaiting the night, the time I loved the most. I first saw Cryton at night and it was forever in my heart — full of life and sounds, a living creature, so promising… It seemed that it kept all the promises it had given to me, but it also punished me for some things…

My agent was waiting at the door of the *Dew Corporations*. He was a tall charming dark-skinned man with dark eyes, wearing a fashionable suit and a shirt with top buttons undone. He opened the door and held out a hand for me.

"Babe…" he greeted and grinned.

"Looking good yourself," I replied with a smile, looking at him from below.

Cave Malter and I first met when he walked up to me after one of the fall collection shows, which showcased… my naked breasts. Not a great message or something models are proud to have in their resumes, but this show was great for me after all because I met Cave. Unlikely that he did it because of my cleavage, but since then he made enough money selling it.

"Let's celebrate tonight," he said, taking me by the arm. I held my breath. "How was yesterday?"

"Not great," I admitted and squeezed his forearm, throwing a look back at a busy street. "I really want a drink."

"A drink? You?" Cave asked, observing me intently. I hurriedly pressed my hair against my neck, even though he was on the opposite side. "This hospital is doing you no good. Listen… We should talk about the bail again."

"Maybe later," I replied and shrugged, "when we're sure about *Dew*'s creative director's opinion of me."

"What do you mean?!" Cave exclaimed and frowned. "Babe, he chose you already! I went to the bitter end and not for nothing I must say! We are about to walk into the fitting of some of the most expensive jewelry in this city! Are you wearing good underwear?"

"Who do you think I am? Of course, I am."

I felt like I was walking on hot chalks. Cave was full of anticipation of success. He believed in doing work first, getting paid later, and this motto never let him down before until tonight. I thought of talking to him but quickly decided against it.

I was determined to go all the way.

And so I went.

*Dew Corporations* building looked like one of the crystals in their jewelry. Its spire was striking through the sky, and the building itself was shining so bright you could see it from any part of the city center. Transparent doors slid open, and Cave walked me to the reception desk.

"Okay, look, Dustin Dewman is not an easy man, but you definitely should not try to flatter him, smile for no reason, and especially flirt. Well, not like you are skilled in any of those anyway..."

"You can count on me," I reassured and grinned at the receptionist sitting at a fine desk. "Good evening."

The receptionist responded with a wide smile and invited us to follow her to the elevators down the hall.

"The plan's simple — try on the jewelry..." Cave continued, "but he can... ask you to show yourself in full glory."

"Underwear at least?" I asked, tensing.

"Let's see how it goes?"

"Cave, I don't get naked in public anymore," I replied sharply.

My eyes were locked on the elevator, which looked like a big jewel. It shimmered slightly as it went down from the very top of the building.

"I'll be there," Cave said, leading me inside.

"Are you kidding me?" I asked and turned to him.

"Listen, less than a year ago you went all out with your amazing boobs on Swarlock's show, and it was fine..."

"You know that it's something we both should leave behind and never come back to," I said, irritated.

"I'm not coming back to it," he told me and leaned closer, staring at me with firm determination. "This is a new step for us. I'm not telling you to open your legs up for Dewman, I'm just saying that if he asks to see you topless with the jewelry on, you shouldn't start any fuss! It would mean nothing, but his desire to be sure he made the right choice, and, well... see the full picture."

I went out of the elevator, feeling much more nervous. Cave caught my hand and led me through the hall past all of the pricey designer-made jewelry-encrusted paintings. As I was staring at our surroundings, my agent was already speaking to some pretty girl.

"Would you like anything?" the girl chirped.

"Whiskey for me and coffee for Thea."

"I said I want a drink too," I commented reproachfully. "You think it's easy to show off my boobs sober and somehow manage to overshadow all this luxury?"

"I don't doubt it's manageable. Why do you think I chose you?" he noted and smirked. "Let's go."

Stylish metal doors opened in front of me, and we entered an unusually matte room. I felt lost for a second, my eyes desperately trying to find something to stop at. It didn't last for long, only until the owner of it all stood up to greet us.

The moment our eyes met I felt like an incredibly strong magnet pulled me closer. He was a brilliant man with no reflection. Even the cufflinks peeking out down the sleeves of his obsidian-black jacket had no shine to them. He didn't need it. He had a handsome manly face and deep dark eyes, which looked intently at me. His stiff lips had an anticipating grin on them.

I clenched Cave's hand even tighter, but he suddenly left me alone. I turned back to him, but he just gave me an encouraging nod and made even more steps back.

"Good evening, Miss Melory," the man said. His god-like voice pulsated somewhere in my chest.

I had such a strong desire to kneel before him that it took all of my self-control to shake my head and feel normal again. It was almost impossible to not recoil.

"Good evening, Mr. Dewman," I replied, almost whispering, clinging to my suede clutch.

"You look great," he complimented and made a step towards me, but this moment his nostrils moved and all the friendliness in his face disappeared. His dark eyes flashed with anger, and he suddenly was so very close to me. I couldn't even blink when he pulled me closer by the neck and ripped off the bandage.

"What are you…" I squeaked, trying to break free.

Cave was near us in a second.

"Mr. Dewman…" he started, but stopped abruptly, pale as snow when he saw my neck. "What is that?!" he demanded. "Thea, fuck, what happened to you?!"

"Leave us alone," Dewman ordered with power in his voice.

Although it was a strange request, Cave and I didn't object. When my agent was out the door, Dewman looked up at me and I met his gaze flashing with the familiar glow.

My legs betrayed me for a moment as I tried to break free and scream, feeling like it was a dream. I watched him walk around me as if in slow motion, looking like a wild beast, which caught his victim.

"I did everything to make you come to me willingly," he said. His voice had a growling feel to it, and my body shuddered strangely. I closed my eyes as if I didn't need vision, as if it only made it harder to hear this strange vibration. "When did this happen?" he spoke with an obvious distaste.

"I don't know what you're talking about."

"Another beast marked you if you're not aware," he explained coldly. "When?"

I swallowed slowly and licked my dry lips.

"I…" I started nervously, but he interrupted.

"I had a contract for you," he said loudly, "which cost more than all of the jewelry for this shoot combined."

"I don't understand," I muttered, frowned, and looked straight at him. "What kind of contract?"

He was silent for a long time, observing me and wrinkling his nose in his disaffection. I could swear his eyes started to glow dangerously.

"Who fucked you yesterday?" he finally asked through clenched teeth.

I inhaled noisily.

"Who are you to ask?"

I was quite fed up with the demanding way he spoke to me. I was never scared of people like him, not even millionaires and billionaires! I was surprised to see Dewman grin suddenly. "Sassy," he licked his lips. "What are you even doing here with a fresh mark?"

"Where should I be?" I hissed, although he was not as discontent with me as earlier.

"With whoever marked you..."

"Well, he is very busy," I replied. "Between pretending to be a bleeding corpse and running away from ER he only found time to grab me and fuck me in a broom closet..."

"Pretending to be a corpse?" he said and leaned forward, frowning.

"They brought him in last night, bleeding."

For some time Dewman seemed to be deep in his thoughts, touching his chin and looking at the floor.

"Time of beautiful courtship is over," he finally said. "What a pity though... Although I must admit that it is better to fuck someone like you in a broom closet..." he stopped for a second as my palm hit his face but continued after an impressive pause paired up with a killer glare, "so that no one else can get you."

He continued staring at me as he touched the corner of his mouth with the tip of his tongue.

"You have no idea how hard I have to try to stop myself from taking you and making you mine..."

I recoiled, my hands on my neck, and it seemed like this sobered the man up. He sighed, taking a step back.

"Alright then, let's get to the fitting..."

"What?!" I exclaimed, still trembling. "The fitting?!"

"Yes, the one you came for," he declared imperturbably and walked to the table. "Sure, it's not the nicest feeling to desire you and have no right to touch you, but we have no way out of this situation. You're mine according to the contract, and until whoever marked you buys you out, it is to stay this way. If he does."

He smirked gloatingly but was still somehow very attractive to me.

"You're sick…"

This moment the knock on the door interrupted us, and the pretty girl from earlier flew in with a tray. The smell of coffee brought me back to reality.

"Sit," Dewman demanded, loosening his collar.

My legs barely held me up, so I gladly obeyed him. I walked to the nearest armchair and took a cup off the tray.

"You don't want to upset Mr. Malter, do you? This contract is important for both your careers."

"You said that you bought me."

It was difficult to suppress the desire to stand up again to be on the same level with him. I felt like this beast was a hyena in a human form and that when I sat down I was not an equal counterpart to him anymore.

"Anything can be bought," he replied and shrugged.

"And what exactly did you buy?"

"All of you."

"If I weren't… marked," I muttered, unable to believe things I was saying, but it was about time to start, "what would have happened then?"

"It would be like any other normal couple," he bared his teeth. "Dinners, gifts…"

"A bite mark on the neck?"

"It's something one should prepare for," he confirmed and stopped grinning. "I would prepare you though, no doubt."

"Why me?" I asked the most worrying question because it seemed like the whole world focused on me.

He sighed deeply thinking for a couple of seconds.

"We don't have enough women. Or, should I say, women, who are born from a man and a woman of our kind, are sterile," I raised my brows in surprise, "and we have to search for someone like you."

"Someone like me?"

"Fit for creating a good match. I'm not going to go into the genetics of this, okay? There are not a lot of people like you..."

"Was I auctioned?"

He smirked and replied, "Something like that."

I had chills crawl up my back.

"Then why did this," I asked and touched my neck, "happen?"

Dewman sighed heavily and squinted at me as if looking at the fire.

"Blood loss makes us lose control," he finally replied. "In this state smelling a woman who is a good match is similar to a feeling a junky has when he finally gets a dose. No chance of resisting, no "STOP" buttons. You were just unlucky."

"I'm not some object," I hugged my arms.

"Of course," he said. His voice was emotionless. "And now, take your clothes off and don't stop thinking about that," he concluded and grinned angrily. "You're going to be a star of my new collection."

"Then what?" I closed my eyes, knowing I can't say no.

"I'll expect compensation. And revenge..."

This meeting took an unexpected turn, but I still had an offer for a shoot of a lifetime and there was nothing else I wanted to think about. All I could do was work this contact and make Dewman choke watching me.

***

It took Cave an hour to organize the shoot. He was a real professional; he got everyone he needed to be involved in this huge project. Those who could come at short notice replaced those who couldn't.

Dewman's office became my private dressing room, and the whole shoot would now take place in a big hall, which was an art piece itself. Stylists were running around, the smell of coffee and pizza lingering in the air, something falling on the floor, people screaming and phones ringing.

Bunny came in about thirty minutes.

"What happened? What got into Dewman?"

"A wild hyena, I'd say," I told him and turned away from the window.

"Did he like you?" Bunny asked when he got closer to me, trying to catch my gaze.

"I'm… going to tell you late," I muttered and turned back as I saw Cave at the door.

"Did he say something about the scar?"

"That's the thing. He is also one of them…"

Bunny's eyes widened, and it was the first time I thought that it had been a bad idea to tell him all of it in the first place. I had no idea how dangerous this knowledge could be.

"Bunny," Cave said as he approached, "what are you doing here? You should be at the stylist station! Go!"

When my friend went to the opposite side of the office, Cave held out a cup of coffee for me.

"What happened? You look like you saw a ghost," he said, cautiously trying to look me in the eyes.

I was wondering what stopped him from approaching me straight away. My face likely didn't change much in the last hour.

"You're only asking now?" I mumbled and hid my nose in the cup. "Nothing happened, Cave. The shoot is on, and it's the most important part. Let's not sabotage each other's work moods."

"Hey," he called and grabbed my chin with his fingers, making me look straight at him, "just say a single word and I'm going to end this whole shoot if you want me to."

My eyes widened as I looked at my agent. Was he really ready to say no? My lips curled in an angry smirk — yeah, sure he was! He brought all those people here and only now came to me to put all the responsibility for the events on me.

It was a long time since I felt so lonely against the whole world…

"It's okay," I replied and shook his fingers off my face. "We are pros and let's do everything to make Dewman shit himself from joy."

It was almost impossible to fit all the thoughts I had for the past hour in my head.

So, beasts just casually walk among humans and buy those of us who match them genetically. Well, Dewman at least has a lot of power and money if he could afford to buy me. The price was impressive. I wondered if all the potential matches were as expensive.

What should I expect from the beast, whose mark I bore on my neck? Who even is he? I would hope he died from the blood loss, and I was somehow lucky to not become Dewman's new purchase.

According to the collection owner's behavior, I was more in a "spoiled goods" category. He emphasized it with every word and every action during the shoot. He made me feel like a pet he could ask anything from.

He chose underwear I looked naked in. Beige lingerie had no seam and was so skin-tight that it would be easy to make it disappear at all in post-production. Dewman asked for a lustful slut look with drops of water down my body, wet hair, and open lips. And I gave him what he wanted, enjoying the angry filthy glow in his eyes.

"Alright, prepare the black diamond set," he ordered after some time.

The atmosphere in the room was hot as it would be during any shoot, but I wasn't melting from the lights and found no help in cold water sprinkled on me.

When the guards entered with the new set, Dewman was near.

"I made the right choice," he whispered and smiled suggestively, lifting the jewelry from the tray. "None of them outshone you…"

It would've been a nice compliment, but I remembered all too well that this man bought me, according to him. Every time I thought that this was all crazy and not real my fingers found the bite mark on my neck, bringing me back to my absurd reality.

I was never interested in stones and jewelry, but when a white gold choker with a black diamond in the center wrapped around my neck, I lost my breath. This diamond had such strong energy, almost living, almost like… a beast. I felt like his hand was holding me by the neck, and all my confidence disappeared, my breaths became heavy, and fear started pulsating in my chest…

Dewman's eyes were glowing brighter. For the first time I thought that he might not let me go after the shoot. What's next? How will he expect me to pay the bail?

As if he heard my questions, Dewman leaned closer.

"I'm not going to give you to him," he whispered in my ear, sending goosebumps down my skin.

My legs almost collapsed when I looked at the door. I didn't fall with the heavy diamond on my neck only because I felt like a steel pin in my spine.

I didn't know how but I knew it was him.

A man stood at the door. Even the diamond on my neck couldn't compete with him. No, he wasn't shining, but the energy he had drew everyone's attention to him. The crowd suddenly fell silent when he arrived. Black suit and sharp look in his eyes. I didn't see the color of his eyes, but the way he looked was enough to stop breathing.

He was about thirty-five with short fair hair and lips... Lips that were impossible to forget when they were the only thing I could see because of the black mask. When he approached Dewman and me I thought that my heart stopped beating.

"Mr. Dewman," he greeted and smiled, staring at me.

"Mr. Houwer," Dewman turned and replied, noticing the guest, "what a surprise."

The men exchanged a handshake, and I licked my dry lips. It felt like the diamond on my neck was reaching out to whoever resembled him and I was following.

"Yes..."

My legs tensed from this 'yes', and I felt dizzy with fog before my eyes.

"Anything I can help you with?" Dewman was not very happy to see the other man, but perhaps even the beasts had an etiquette like the one humans have.

"I need something special, Mr. Dewman," he told his opponent as his eyes went back to my face, going lower, to my neck, "for a very special woman..."

"I heard you're getting married," Dewman commented and smiled stiffly. "Congratulations."

"Thank you..."

I felt his gaze on me, but I wasn't able to return it anymore.

"Excuse me for invading," the man called Houwer continued, "but I was told you're at work, and I just flew in from Apollynis…"

"Shoot for my new collection," Dewman explained and gestured towards the lights, "but I'm always free for you. Coffee or maybe something else?"

"Coffee is fine," he said. I felt him smiling. "Am I interrupting?"

"No, no, Aaron, please…"

Aaron.

Now I knew his name.

"Continue!" Dewman ordered, leading the guest towards the sofa. Cave suddenly appeared next to me with a hairstylist and a make-up artist. All of them were around, creating action, but I was in a different universe.

I was staring at the beast's back and shivering.

I don't know why but out of these two I knew that the beast was the one who left the mark on my neck. Dewman stood next to him, they were talking, but I could see so clearly that he was not on the same level as his counterpart. The difference between them was the same as between the diamond on my neck and a cheap glass from a painting in the hallway. Yes, it was well-lit and looked good and expensive in a certain setting, but in the end, it was just a piece of glass.

Dewman's guest moved with out-of-this-world grace, nearly flowing through the room. His every move awakened a stream of pulsating emotions inside of me. Why is he here? And if he is here for me, then why all this masquerade?

"Babe, we're on," Cave called.

The next half an hour was the hardest in my whole career. Every flash felt like a bullet. I felt the beast's eyes on me, and I wasn't playing a slut anymore. I was one. The mark on my neck was pulsating with soft warmth, trying to satisfy its owner. I was ready to rip it off with my skin.

When Cave finally gave me a break, I thought I'd collapse. I was about to turn to the exit and find some fresh air when Dewman's voice hit me.

"Theana!"

I turned around and glanced at the sofas. The beast didn't look at me, and it was the only reason I did not run away.

Even in my head, I couldn't call him Aaron. He was Beast to me. I didn't even get too close when Dewman grabbed my hand as though I was his possession.

"Mr. Houwer wanted to take a closer look at the diamond. Here you go…"

I glared at Beast. His face looked slightly different from what I saw half an hour ago before we were divided by several meters and camera flashes. He looked at me from below, not standing up, and I thought I could see the expression of surprise in his eyes. His features went sharp, his eyes darkened.

"It's perfect," he said, his voice hoarse. He looked back at Dewman and spoke again, "I'm taking this rare beauty from you."

This moment Beast's eyes flashed with crimson and his face moved. He was beautiful, cold, and burning at the same time. He was a real predator, the one you can look at but can't touch because he is going to kill you.

"Great choice," Dewman exclaimed. He seemed surprised. "It's a very rare stone."

His customer wasn't talking about the stone.

"Is your fiancee going to wear it?" I asked and smirked, looking directly at Beast.

"She is."

If he told me that moment that parallel lines meet, they would do that, sending a shower of sparks into the air.

"I feel sorry for her…"

I felt high on emotions. I suddenly felt a need to lean to this bastard and kiss him to make him stop staring at me with his wild eyes full of hunger.

"My girl is quite cheeky," Dewman noted and smirked, embarrassed, as he pulled me by the arm.

"She is not yours," Beast stated and stood up, now standing in front of me. "The mark on her…" he started as our eyes met. He looked at me as if he had just claimed me for himself as if the mark was not enough. This collar-like choker felt very appropriate. "...Is not yours." He gave Dewman a quick glare and spoke to him, "Was nice to see you, Mr. Dewman." He looked back at me and called, "Thea…"

I watched him leave and felt that I couldn't bear it anymore. The pin in my spine disappeared and my legs started shaking. I would have fallen if Dewman hadn't caught me.

***

"Bunny, it was him."

We were sitting in our kitchen, which I honestly thought I'd never see again, and drinking coffee. The sun was rising outside, the new day started, but I was still living in my nightmare. Dewman sent me home almost instantly when Aaron Houwer left. I was exhausted from the meeting with Beast just as I would be from two days of work. Bunny was looking at me with his eyes red from the lack of sleep and cigarette smoke and holding his large mug in his hands.

"How do you know?"

"I just do. And these lips, they were the only thing I saw in the hospital."

"That's some wild shenanigans," he said as he stood up and walked up to the window.

"Well, maybe you should send me to an institution then," I admitted and rolled my eyes, "if you think I'm out of my mind."

"First Dewman, then this…" he sighed and turned sharply. "Do you think they're walking around us all the time?"

"They aren't just walking around; they're ruling over us."

I did some research and had already found everything I could on Aaron Houwer. He was thirty-six, single but engaged to a daughter of *Central Cryton Bank*. One could probably compile a book out of all of the magazine articles about their engagement. Aaron Houwer himself was a CEO of *Black&Gold Industries*, the son of its owner Denver Houwer, a petroleum tycoon. What did this billionaire do, covered in blood in a suburban hospital?

"I could accept the fact that you were attacked at night in the hospital by some masked dude… But I find it hard to believe these guys in suits are the monsters…"

"Maybe we should move out?" I said and hugged my knees. "I worry about you."

"No, Thea, you're in all this shit because of me," he countered and ran his hand through his hair, "so don't even think about this."

I smiled. Bunny was always so unapologetically himself. He was so scared but still didn't give up. That's exactly how we used to take agencies by storm when we were just starting — I was in the front, and he was in the back, but he was always ready to give me a little push. But not this time…

"Well, that was fun," I said and smirked. "You looked great in that shirt with the black diamond clip."

He smirked back, worried.

"Let's leave. Just take everything and go to the coast."

I thought about that, but Dewman quickly dispelled all my hopes to run away from him.

"...with this salary, we'll have enough money to hide for at least half a year," Bunny continued.

"His guards are at our backdoor," I exhaled heavily.

It seemed like there were no places I could go to but Dewman. His promise to not give me up to the other one wasn't a good sign.

"What?!" Bunny exclaimed and ran to the window. "Where?!"

"Black limo that drove us here."

"Fuck!"

"You're not the smartest," I told him and shrugged.

"Is Dewman trying to take you from that... that man, who came there yesterday?" Bunny asked as he turned to me.

"I don't know," I replied and shrugged again.

Powerless anger boiled inside of me. Who are these monsters to decide what I should do and who I should be with?! They are not only non-humans but also very powerful ones. How unlucky! Well, the misfortune hadn't even started in the hospital, although there too. All this time I thought I was the mistress of my fate, worked hard for a chance to eat croissants and bacon in the morning, but my fate was decided on a very different level, almost on the godly one. No wonder *Dew Corporations* looked vaguely like I imagined office buildings in heaven would look like.

I was wondering about this Aaron Houwer... why did he come there? Why didn't he say that the mark was his? Or was it that polite beasts don't run around at night wearing masks and don't get to hospitals half-dead? In that case, sure, he would be interested in covering the circumstances of how his mark appeared on a woman who doesn't belong to him. And Dewman... How is he planning to not give me up? And what was that strange mood change? He was ready to wait for the bail-out but he then changed his mind and decided to leave me for himself.

"Let's go to sleep," I decided and shook my head.

I needed to save some energy, although everything around seemed like a dead end. Well, at least I can get on these guys' nerves and for that I need rest.

"Go, I don't want to," Bunny said, looking out the window with worry in his eyes.

I felt broken and exhausted. I fell asleep as soon as my head touched the pillow.

***

I was woken up by a phone call. Not understanding where I am and what's going on, I accepted the call.

"Hi," he said, and I was stricken by a familiar voice.

I jumped in bed, looking around. It was dark outside, I had a headache, and my body hurt as if I had a month worth of training in the gym.

"It's around five now," Beast told me, not waiting for my reply, "you have a dinner with me at eight."

I blinked and repeated after him, "Dinner? With you?"

"You're my smart girl," he praised, and I heard him smirk.

"I'm not yours," I replied. "I was bought if you're not aware."

He went silent for a little bit.

"In my world, Thea, the one who has you is whoever put the mark on your neck."

"Dewman would disagree. His guards are outside my house."

"Well, I talked him into it..."

I got up and, tumbling, went up to the window. There was no limo outside.

"I'll pick you up around eight."

My phone went silent, only long beeps left. I threw it on the bed and rubbed my face. What the hell is going on? No, I wasn't worried about whatever Dewman and Houwer decided among themselves, I was worried about getting out of it.

"Bunny!" I called, but he didn't respond.

After not finding him in the kitchen, I went to the shower. Is it possible to make a deal with Beast? What does he want from me? Maybe we could discuss getting rid of the mark? According to Dewman, Houwer didn't want this to happen; it was against his will. If I understood correctly, blood loss left him with no choice. But maybe now, after he seems to be okay, we could talk? He has a fiancee after all, and a random model would be a dirty spot on his reputation. Good logical conclusion.

I decided not to think about Dewman. Good enough that he cleared his guards downstairs. I felt almost calm standing under hot drops of water.

The apartment door was slammed shut, and worried Bunny ran into the bathroom.

"Thea, Dewman's dead!"

Reaching an agreement with Beast didn't seem like a possible option anymore! He was lucky he didn't call me now, because I would certainly not agree to see him!

"Fuck!" I muttered and almost slipped in the tub, falling from behind the shower curtain straight into Bunny's arms. "When?! How?!"

"He was found in his office," my friend babbled, putting me down, "with his throat slit! What did we get ourselves into, Thea?" He started whispering desperately, trying to hug me, but I freed myself from his grip and exited the bathroom after putting a towel around my body.

"Can you make coffee and something to eat?"

Unfortunately, Bunny in his shocked state was not much help. He broke my mug, burned himself with hot coffee machine steam, and dropped the sugar bowl. I was done with it and sat him down.

"Calm down!" I barked. I hated this hysterical behavior, especially from men. "We have no options. I have a meeting with Houwer now."

As soon as I said the name, Bunny paled even more.

"Why?" he whispered.

"Well, you know we were planning to die young," I tried to joke.

Although why did we? We stopped overworking and had a relatively healthy lifestyle. I even almost quit smoking... I would've if not for that night in the hospital.

"I changed my mind!" he barked back.

"Where were you by the way?"

The cup of coffee and bitter smell brought some life back into me.

"In the store. That's where I've heard the news," Bunny told me and automatically took a cup from my hands. "Police suspect some of the people Cave found for substitute. Dewman was in such a hurry for the shoot that he broke all of his own security rules. They didn't check people who had to be called in an emergency, and Dewman let it go. Now, according to the police, the CEO is dead, and one of the collection pieces of jewelry lost."

"Shit..."

"They will get to all of us," he muttered and closed his eyes.

"And what?" I growled. "Let them do that! One interview isn't going to kill you!"

"Do you know how the police treat gays?" he asked and arched his brows.

"Oh, shut it!" I rolled my eyes. "You don't have it written all over your face."

I wasn't worried about the police. I was almost certain that it was Aaron who dealt with Dewman. Seemed like he was quick to solve problems. Now I just had to figure out if he considers me one of them.

***

Bunny was sitting on his bed in his neon green PJs, holding a bowl of ice cream and almost shivering. I kissed his forehead and ran out of the apartment. I got a short notification on my phone that someone was already expecting me near the elevator.

"Miss Melory," a dark-skinned man in a suit said as he stepped through an open elevator door, "good evening."

"You too," I muttered.

"I am Claud Knife," he introduced himself, giving me a polite nod. "We'll meet quite frequently, so you can call me Claud."

This promise gave me hope. It meant that I had a chance to not end up on Houwer's death list.

Houwer didn't send a limo to pick me up. A practical, but expensive sedan kind of reminded me of Beast himself — it didn't need to show off to attract attention. As soon as the driver started the car, it roared approvingly, leaping straight out of the apartment complex and onto the highway.

Although I was invited to dinner, I had no idea what to wear. In the end, I wore black jeans and a blouse with a jacket. I didn't know how to do my hair so I just left it naturally wavy. When we stopped near the *Grand* hotel I felt extremely underdressed. A dress and some heels would definitely be more appropriate for this place.

"Miss," Claud called, holding a hand out for me.

Is he nice to everyone or did he have some specials orders regarding me? Something like "be polite to her, I'm planning to kill her myself." Entertaining myself with such silly thoughts, I tried not to shake as we walked through a shining hall straight to the elevators. It was crowded, so I was almost calm, but when the elevator doors opened on the top floor, dark and empty, full of dim light, I was startled again. The host brought us to the second level, where it was even darker and quieter. I was ready to run. Claud was walking behind and left only when I was pierced by Beast's cold and calculating glare.

He was standing near the corner table. I didn't want to be stuck in a private lounge with him, and it calmed me to know we would stay in a public area.

"Thea," he greeted and nodded slightly as soon as I approached, still looking at me. "Sit down."

"Mr. Houwer…"

It was ridiculous how official it seemed. These beasts were almost like humans: suits, restaurants, bodyguards…

"What are you drinking?" he asked and stepped to my left to pull the chair out for me. I suppressed my deep desire to run to the exit. I wondered how far I would get and would he be offering me a drink in case I did try to make a run for my life?

"I don't drink," I replied as I sat down.

"I know…" he noted and sat on the opposite side of the table. "I know everything about you."

He had no shame. His glance was calm, confident, just heavy enough not to leave me broken in pieces… The situation was more than simply unfortunate for me…

"Will you kill me?" I whispered, tired of being nervous.

I felt a drop of sweat slide down my back when his face didn't express even the slightest bit of surprise. I licked my lips, feeling helpless. There was an unpleasant heaviness in my chest. Once, when I was a young girl, I'd had this feeling. It was when I stole a chicken from our neighbor. His older sons caught me in the corner of their property. I had no doubts then that they'd kill me.

"No," he replied. He blinked and added with a slight bit of disappointment, "I can't."

"Sorry about that," I commented sarcastically. "Don't like easy ways out?"

The man's lips curled into a satisfied smirk and his eyes flashed.

"This time my whole life experience just failed... When I saw you yesterday... With him..."

"I think I need a drink after all," I admitted. I wanted to celebrate the cancellation of my own death order.

He nodded understandingly and ordered some wine. He watched me with interest, his eyes squinted. I was shaking inside from his attention. He really thought about getting rid of me, and if something didn't change his mind, I would... I would not be here.

"Shit," I said through clenched teeth when the waiter filled glasses with wine.

"Drink," he ordered. His voice was like metal. I realized the whole danger of this situation.

I drank up. The drink went down my throat, my eyes watered.

"What's next?"

"Next we have dinner."

"Are you fucking kidding me?" I exclaimed and looked up at him. "Do you think all of this is so easy for me? Do you think I am some stupid girl you found in the hospital? You think it's easy to realize I was an inch away from being another corpse, just like the one everyone's talking about on TV right now? Really? I mean, also..." I shrugged and continued, "It's not too late for that..."

"I'm sorry," he stopped me suddenly. I was so surprised I blinked and shut my mouth. "I'm sorry for what I did to you in the hospital. I lost control."

"Dewman explained," I spit out, and his tense glance really made me feel stupid for saying that.

"Yeah, it was quite a rare coincidence, not something anyone can predict," he muttered. He seemed very disappointed, but then looked back at me. "Do you feel the smell?"

I was almost used to this deep flowery aroma, which followed me like an expensive perfume. Bunny and I figured out that I was the only one, who could smell it. I didn't think much about it then. I had bigger problems than that.

"I do…"

Aaron frowned, and my mouth suddenly dried.

"People of my race have three levels of partner compatibility," he started. "The first one is faint; partners only feel similar emotions sometimes. The second one includes a shared smell, and it's just the beginning…"

The last one I didn't want to know.

"It's rare to have matches higher than the first level. One couple out of a hundred," he concluded.

"And?" I asked. Alcohol almost made the fear disappear. The courage was slowly waking up inside. Quite successfully, I must say. "Why didn't you buy someone like Dewman did?"

Beast didn't reply for a while. He poured himself some wine and took his wine glass into his hands.

"A contract for someone like you is a luxurious pleasure. I thought that I didn't need luxury…"

"What do you mean by a luxurious pleasure?" I muttered. My voice went hoarse.

Beast took a sip and brought his glass up to his eyes.

"Special emotions, feelings, which are only available if one has a connection with someone like you…"

His eyes flashed red, reflecting on his glass, and his lips curled into an almost invisible smirk.

"Dewman is not here anymore," I stated. My hand went up to my neck. "What happens to the contract now?"

"I've bought you out."

He put his glass back on the table, showing me that the discussion was over. I was about to throw my own glass at him.

"It's an unforgettable feeling to transform from a free human into an object which could be sold," I forced myself to speak, grinning bitterly.

He squinted inquisitively.

"What is freedom, Thea?"

He sounded as if he was actually interested.

"My job, decisions about how to spend a night, a week, life…"

"Job is not freedom, it's a way to get by," he argued.

"Maybe, but it's also self-development. I need to achieve something in life."

It was a bizarre conversation. I just found out I almost lost my life and now I was debating Beast on the issue of success and self-realization.

"Okay, let's say, it is. Haven't you ever thought of finding a man who could take the responsibility for making money?"

My eyes widened and I laughed. I laughed loudly, throwing my head back, and when I calmed down and sat up, I realized he was looking at me with an unexpected and unfamiliar expression in his eyes. They were sparkling. They weren't flashing with poisonous red but were similar to the fireworks in the sky. His lips didn't show any sign of amusement, but it seemed somehow that he was smiling.

"No, I haven't," I replied after I finished laughing. I shook my head and looked at the glass reproachfully. "Usually men need something in return, and I'm not a fan of bargaining."

"Unfortunately, you'll have to become one now," the stars in his eyes died away, and his eyes went dark. "You're mine now. Legally."

I snorted scornfully.

"What if I don't agree with that?"

"We have a problem then."

"It's dangerous to have shared problems with you," I noted, taking a sip.

"That's an understatement," he accepted. "But you're a special case. More wine?"

"I suppose."

We separated this first part of the evening with a few minutes of silence and wine drinking. I didn't want to talk anymore. I wanted to celebrate this night because it wasn't my last. I'm definitely giving Bunny a royal breakfast tomorrow.

"Where can I study your laws?" I interrogated. I sat back on the chair, relaxed.

"Why?" he questioned and looked at me, frowning.

"I want to know," I explained, returning the look. "I want to know my rights."

Beast suddenly grinned, his grin wide and dangerous, showing his snow-white teeth and sharp fangs.

"Thea, we have nothing to split yet."

"I understand that my freedom is not something quite important to you. I don't want to be sold like an object. If you think I should belong to you, I want to see the contract that says so. Responsibilities of the parties, penalties, early termination options..."

"Oh, this will be a precedent," he said with a chuckle. He was so obviously enjoying me trying to find my way out of it.

"I doubt you'd be satisfied with a quiet piece of wood, Mr. Houwer," I challenged, clinging to my chair. It was easy to see the interest in his glare. Two glasses of wine down my empty stomach told me that I might find a way to turn this all around. "Or at least I'd hope so."

"I'm not planning to take everything you're used to away from you," he assured and finally looked away, letting me out of the captivity of his gaze.

I drew a quick breath, feeling dizzy.

"Can you elaborate on that?"

"We'll have dinner first. I had a difficult day," he declared and gave a sign to a waiter, throwing me a quick glance.

I ordered a meat plate with cheese and fruit, and Beast was very trivial with his order of rare steak.

It was so hard to be calm around him. I ate a little bit of meat, simply because I felt drunk from such little alcohol. Even that didn't help. Beast also didn't rush with his food, looking intensely at me and at his glass of wine.

There was also the smell. It became brighter, almost so bitter that I needed to drink it away.

"I want to go outside," I mumbled and stood up. "May I?"

Aaron stood up next and nodded, taking a step in my direction, but I recoiled.

"Can I be by myself for a minute?!"

"No," he growled, took me by the arm, and walked me to the transparent doors with a beautiful view of the night Calvais, an elite district of the city center. Doors opened, and fresh cool air touched my hot cheeks. Beast dragged me through the terrace until we reached the fence. He pushed me against the fence and pressed his body into mine, causing me to twitch. His rough strong fingers squeezed my ribs, and I grabbed his hand and tried to break free even harder. Beast pretty clearly showed me that he wasn't happy with me putting up a fight. He grabbed me by the neck, pulling me closer.

“Stop it,” he growled into my ear.

“Fuck you!” I hissed.

“Be careful, Thea.”

“You shouldn’t have worn a suit, your hospital wear suits you much better! Blood, a mask, sperm gushing…” I whispered. The wine was boiling in my blood, finding all of the courage I had in me. “You think I will be crawling at your feet?! Well, think again.”

“Oh, you will,” he told me, and his voice vibrated with an animalistic growl. He suddenly squeezed my neck even tighter, pulling me closer, and touched the mark with his rough hot tongue. At that very second, my legs buckled and all of the air left my lungs. Sweat ran down my back. With a small movement of his tongue, I felt a pulsation down my stomach. My world spun around and suddenly disappeared. There was only the sensation of his tongue against my skin, every inch of it driving me into my personal wild nirvana. Every breath into my neck felt like his cock thrusting inside of me. It was rough, painful, almost to the point of screaming. And so I did when he bit sensitive skin right near my jaw. I screamed… and came. My fingernails sank into the man’s wrists; my body shook as if his hands were bare electrical wires; I fell into his arms, exhausted.

***

I curled into my seat, not able to pull my head up. The car was slowly moving through the traffic, and I didn’t want to think about where it was heading, even if it was a dumpster where I find my final rest…

“Where are we going?” I asked, not recognizing my own voice. It was hard not to stay silent.

“To your house.”

Beast’s voice sounded hollow and desperate. When I heard it, I felt a wave of goosebumps march down my skin, and my body trembled with the memories of the incident on the terrace. Everything inside felt like jelly, unable to gather itself but shaking at any vibration. It gave me no chance to think straight.

"The wine was good, I can't pull myself together," I whispered and smirked.

"It's not about the wine."

I turned my head and looked at his profile. In the dim light, it looked even rougher, really wild and animal-like.

"What's next?" I asked indifferently.

"We'll see."

It sounded as if he was on edge. It was easy at that moment to push him down, but I didn't have the guts to do that. I felt frightened.

"I would like to know what to do," I whispered, but he heard me nonetheless.

He turned to me, and I shuddered and squeezed my legs together. I was terrified of the reactions of my body but didn't feel like thinking about it right then. I tried to take his glare and make him understand that he underestimated me and my weakness. Yes, I was weak, but I also had a line, and I wasn't afraid of the unknown behind it. I had been there before.

"You just live your normal life," he instructed and tried to grin, but it looked like a painful wince, "until I call you."

"So, that's how you want me to live now?" I questioned. My eyes narrowed in fury.

"I said that we will see how it goes," he said bluntly. "And don't go to the hospital anymore, all charges are dropped. And Thea… don't show the mark to anyone and don't tell anyone that Dewman had bought you. You mustn't do that."

I kept silent, turning away, although I wanted to say something that'd sting him.

When we arrived at the house doors, Aaron got out of the car to open the door for me. He held his hand out, but I ignored it and was about to enter when I heard his steps behind.

"What else do you need?" I asked. I didn't need to turn to look at him — he was already beside me.

"I'm walking you to the door," he explained. He didn't glance at me and pressed the door handle.

"Thank you and goodbye."

Beast followed me to the foyer.

"Not this door."

"Can I at least go and throw up in the bathroom by myself?" I asked and rolled my eyes.

He smirked.

"Thea," he called suddenly. I looked at him. "I'm not guilty of what happened to us."

"Doesn't make it better for me," I admitted and stepped into the elevator.

"It will never be better now," he confessed and followed me in. He pressed the button. "Both of us are going to be in our own versions of hell."

"It would probably be easier to shoot me," I told him and started shaking again. I didn't understand him and didn't want to understand.

"Maybe, but we'll never know now."

"Everything can be fixed, and you're quick to fix problems."

"I'm not going to do that," he interrupted calmly. "I made my choice, and there's no way back."

It was the first time I regretted getting an apartment so high up. The elevator was moving so slowly as if it was stuck in honey, and I was stuck with it. I threw my head back and looked at the ceiling, waiting for the doors to open. Beast was staring at my neck, which I displayed unintentionally. He was breathing heavily like a real predator, his eyes flashing with danger, and it seemed like he would take a step and hit the "STOP" button any second...

A loud ring finally came about, and I dashed out of the trap past him, ran around the corner, and started banging on the door as if I was chased by a monster.

"Thea!"

Bunny opened the door, and I slammed into him, looking back down the hallway. It was empty, and I shut the door behind me.

***

Cave was painful to look at. It seemed like he hadn't slept for three days straight. His beautiful tan skin went pale, leaving dark circles under his eyes and a web of wrinkles around them. His metallic grey suit made him look even sicker. His office smelled of expensive cigarettes. My agent was not at his best.

"Come in," he shouted and gave me a sign to sit on the couch. "I got the money, I'll transfer it to you in the evening..."

That was some good news. Without a thought, I looked out of the window, automatically calculating how much a trip to Sutan, a city on the coast, would cost. I then swallowed.

"Can I have some coffee?"

Cave nodded and lit his cigarette.

"You know, it's so scary, all of it. My reputation skyrocketed in the last two days. No matter how hard I'd work, I'd never got an offer from the most famous fashion house..."

My eyes widened and I exclaimed, "*Teyvalle*?!" He nodded, and my breathing sped up as I spoke, "Wow! What do they want?"

"They saw some pictures from Dewman's presentation," Cave explained and sat on the edge of his table, "and they want you."

I dropped my cup of coffee. The secretary started running around, but I just sat there, unable to apologize. Cave took a deep drag and nodded.

"When did they tell you?" I asked, my voice quiet.

"This morning," he told me as he looked at his watch. "Maybe two hours ago. We should be drinking champagne."

I wasn't planning to drink ever again after yesterday's wine, even if now there was a great reason to do so. I spent all night having anxiety and nightmares. I dreamed about Aaron next to me, and I shook in his arms, and he was licking my neck. I woke up no less than five times, screaming, my heart pounding fast. Bunny got so nervous that he went to the kitchen at around four to try and make us some breakfast.

I didn't feel very happy. "Shocked" would be a better word.

"Wonder who'd killed him..." Cave muttered and shook his head. I snapped out of my heavy thoughts.

"Who knows. The shoot could be a good cover-up," I suggested and shrugged.

"He was really into you," my agent said as he glanced at me. "I found out later that he stopped his security from doing full checks just so we could start the shoot that day. The first checks took almost a month..."

"What was stolen?"

"The brooch that Bunny wore. It was right on Dewman's table, probably was taken because of that..."

"That's rough," I noted and put my arms around myself.

"This shoot will get a lot of publicity," Cave told me and took a drag again, "as the last act of the artist. And you're going to be praised as his last muse."

I rolled my eyes.

"There will be no doubt when we get the video montage ready. He stares at you in every shot. You are going to be a headliner. *Teyvalle* knows who to put their bets on."

I was suddenly a lead act in the business Cave was trying to run.

"I wouldn't put all the bets on me..." I countered. I was slowly realizing that my situation with Beast wasn't the only one I got myself into. "Bunny was there too..."

"Bunny was great, but Dewman wasn't after him. So the jackpot is yours."

Yes, jackpot, sure.

"What's wrong, babe?"

"I'm not used to being happy about the success that came through someone's death, Cave," I told him and looked at my hands as the secretary handed me another cup of coffee.

"I get it," he said and stood up. "You have a day to get yourself together and get over it..."

Sure, and it will be a day spent with the police interviewing me. I was expecting a call constantly. Bunny had already been called at seven that morning. I didn't understand why no one phoned me yet.

"...and tomorrow we have a meeting with *Teyvalle*'s head designer..."

Why now? Why did my wildest dream start to come true now, when I can feel Beast breathing down my neck?! Now, when I want to run away and hide in a hole no one could get me out of?! But no, I can't do that, because now doors open and I have no right to step back. I was a sacrificial lamb, who had no other way, but forward, and no choice, but to follow the direction someone else pointed me at.

"...that's what you've wanted, right, babe?" Cave asked and sat next to me, looking me in the eyes. "I understand it's difficult to be in the middle of all these events, but we need to overcome it and move forward. It's the end for some, but only the beginning for others, and that's normal…"

"Damn, Cave! It's not normal if a client is killed on the day of the shoot!" I cried and shook my head.

"There's a first for everything," he noted. He stood up and went back to the table, continuing, "I'm planning to live and work, and you better move along."

I was suddenly struck with an idea. I knew that Aaron was Dewman's murderer. Would I be able to get rid of him if I had some evidence? The idea took my breath away, and I widened my eyes, looking at Cave. These monsters live in our world, and our police are the ones investigating, so it's possible to try and find a way to manage all of this… Or at least scare the murderer and make him leave me alone! I don't trust the police, but I like my freedom more.

He will burn in his hell by himself. I stood up determinedly and left without saying goodbye.

***

"It was horrible!" Bunny cried. His hands were shaking so hard the olive in his martini seemed to have got into a storm. "He was murdered right where my hair was done! So terrifying! And they stole my brooch!"

"It's not yours," I stated. I was focused, closing one more webpage and leaving only one open.

I spent all night choosing a recording device. I first thought about something for sound only, but then got into researching devices with cameras too.

"It must've been some psycho, Thea, someone cold-blooded and merciless," he muttered. I couldn't agree more. "What if that was a serial killer? What if he goes after us?"

"He has no reason to go after us. You, especially…"

I clicked the "Buy now" button.

"What are you doing there?"

"Buying a recorder."

"Why?"

"Just in case."

"Thea," Bunny called. He moved closer and looked at the screen. I always hated when he did that. "What are you going to do about that other man?"

"What can I do about him?" I asked and closed the laptop, annoyed with the question.

"You haven't told me what happened yesterday," Bunny muttered and sighed drunkenly, trying to make me hug him. I didn't disappoint. I pulled him closer and held him tight.

"There's nothing to tell. I shouldn't tell you all of it anyway..."

"Did he threaten you?" my friend exclaimed. He seemed to suddenly sober up.

"No..."

Aaron threatened with elegance and with zero clarity, but it was difficult to doubt the reality of his threats.

"What happened then?"

"We had dinner..."

"What does he want?"

"I'm not sure yet, Bunny. He's weird. He apologized for whatever happened in the hospital."

"Apologized?" my friend repeated and sat straight.

"When beasts lose a lot of blood, they lose control," I explained and shrugged. "I was just unfortunate enough to end up near him that night. He wasn't supposed to be there..."

"Oh great! Just great! Apologized!"

Bunny stood up and started to walk around the kitchen. He probably thought that he looked dangerous, but he looked almost comedic in his PJs. He looked at me and asked, raising his voice, "Doesn't he want to give you some kind of compensation?"

"I don't need anything from him," I said. I just wanted him out of my life! "Let's stop talking about it."

And so it was, but even laying in my bed I couldn't stop thinking about Aaron Houwer. I slipped into the kitchen, listening to Bunny's quiet drunken snores, and opened my laptop. I was soon looking at the gallery of photos of Beast and his "pet." I was watching intently, trying to catch every emotion.

Not like he had any. He was always serious, cold, emotionally unavailable, even near his fiancee. She was always next to him, but they never seemed like they were together. No weekend picnics or whatever rich people do. Only official gatherings. No kisses and cuddles. Aaron Houwer was nice and fluffy even in the yellow press, or, should I say, dark and unattainable.

I felt sorry for his fiancee. Grace Dolly was a daughter of a bank chain owner, and she was a good match. She was a pretty blond, so pure, well-bred, and stylish. And although she looked like an angel, photos of her started to make me mad. I was looking at her and remembering Beast and the bite mark on my neck. I wondered if he bit her like that too; if he brought her over the edge with a single touch of his tongue.

She didn't cover her neck in any pictures; I scrolled through many of them. She had no mark. I wondered if she knew who her fiancé was.

What really didn't sit well with all of this was his demand to not take emergency pills. I had no idea what sponsored my courage this time — my anger after seeing Grace or my own stupidity — but I picked up my phone.

*You asked me to not take emergency pills... was it also a short-term madness?*

I didn't care about an unwanted pregnancy. I couldn't have one even if I wanted to. I was, however, interested to get behind his motivation. Aaron replied quickly.

*Did you take any?*

He somehow managed to get on my nerves even being far away. I felt like telling him off and letting him know it was none of his business, but spending my energy on small arguments didn't seem like a good choice. While I was touching the screen, thinking, the phone started ringing, and I got paralyzed. I named him "Beast," but wasn't too happy with my own wit now. This nickname pulsating on the screen terrified me even before I answered.

A message came in with an elegant threat.

*Do you want to speak in person?*

I lost the battle before I started it.

"No," I said, taking the call.

"What no?" he growled quietly.

"I don't want to speak in person. Is it hard for you to write more than one message a day?"

"You deserve better than that," he said, mocking me. "Answer the question."

"Did you have enough time to get away from your fiancee?" I blurted out suddenly.

Aaron took some time to answer. I heard him sigh tensely.

"I don't spend nights with my fiancee," he replied. His voice sounded calm, and that wasn't good because it definitely turned off my self-preservation mechanisms.

"Oh, wouldn't she understand your night-time rendezvous?"

I couldn't help myself.

"Thea," he started gently, "you were running away so fast yesterday I thought I had terrified you to death..."

"You did."

"Doesn't sound like it," he sneered. Something inside of me loosened up, just a little bit, but it felt like a boulder just fell off my shoulders. "Answer my question, please."

"No, I didn't take anything."

He was silent again for a couple of heartbeats.

"Good," he said. His voice went husky. "Don't do that."

"Why shouldn't I?"

"It's not going to work. There's no point."

I was sure he lied. But he was right that there was no point.

"And that's why you're calling me in the middle of the night?"

I didn't even try to cover sarcasm in my voice.

"Good night, Thea," he said, but didn't hang up until I did so myself.

I was spinning my phone, looking at another picture. "Lamb" Dolly was standing next to "Mr. Iceberg," her fingers outstretched to him. Maybe just a second ago she wanted to hold his hand, but he didn't take it, or she just showed the whole essence of their relationship with one small gesture...

What did he mean by this "We'll see" business? There was practically nothing about these mutants online, only rare news about fights here and there. It was impossible to find anything about matches and couples and mates. Dewman could probably answer my questions, but he was dead and I doubt I'd like the price he'd make me pay. Maybe Aaron wasn't too happy with the price either? I wondered whether he tried to negotiate to buy me out or just sliced Dewman's throat with little thought.

It all made me think about something else. I started researching criminal records of that night that everything in the hospital went to hell. The closest was gunfire in the center on one of the underground parking lots. The record said that the epicenter was right next to the central street, and that's where people were brought from. It was the weekend, so there were a lot of people off on the streets. There was no information about the gunmen. Who, why, what for... This made me seriously doubt that I could prove Beast guilty in the murder, but I knew I had to try.

***

Cave prepared me for the meeting at *Teyvalle* for two straight hours. It was quite hard to believe that this girl with nude makeup took so long to get ready. My hair was styled to look effortlessly gorgeous and as if I always wake up like this. He chose a knee-length dress and covered my scar with a light blush pink scarf.

"How did you even get it?" he grumbled, fixing the scarf.

"I can teach you," I sneered. "You just need to get three hundred hours of community service in the hospital, take a night shift, 'cause it counts an hour for two, and wait for a wave of night psychos..."

"Why didn't you tell me earlier?" he asked and stared straight at me.

"Was too scared to do that," I responded, staring back.

Cave shook his head.

"Well, good that you didn't. I would..." he muttered and ran his fingers through his hair, taking a step back. "I don't know what I would do."

"Great then."

I was used to my agent not being able to handle emergency situations.

"Why did Dewman decide to hold this shoot with you after all? And why in such a rush?"

"Cave, I have no idea what these... crazy artists have in their heads," I exclaimed and shrugged, taking one last look at myself in the mirror. "First he was unhappy, but I then told him about everything that happened and he suddenly changed his mind..."

Cave watched me thoughtfully and then looked at his watch and ordered, "Let's go."

The streets were half-dark, although it wasn't late. Tower Set skyscrapers' tops were not visible, covered in fog, their mirror-like walls reflecting each other. Trees and green lawns seemed muted. The autumn was upon us. I took in a deep breath of urban air and got onto the back seat of Cave's crossover, wrapping the jacket around my body.

My agent turned to look at me from the driver's seat and asked, "Did you research *Teyvalle*'s history?"

"As soon as I first moved here," I responded with a grin.

*Teyvalle* fashion house was the trendsetter in Cryton and the whole country for over a hundred years. They were the best in combining traditions and new trends. Their collections were elegant, exquisite, modern, comfortable and exclusive, and were popular all over the world. The most important fashion event of the year, the World Fashion Week, was held in Cryton for the past forty-nine years. This year was the anniversary, and they were preparing some amazing shows to celebrate it. It was unbelievable to be a step away from this event that inspired and excited me. A modeling career can't last forever, and I've been planning to study fashion design for a while now. Well, I was hoping to do that if I don't die young, which, according to my own latest trend, there was a chance of.

"You will be introduced to the head of the production department and chief editor of "Pals" magazine..."

"Artelynn Duvalle," I finished, nodding.

"Good job," Cave praised. The car entered the traffic. "She is one of the "sharks," and we have to work with her."

"We'll do great, Cave," I said. I would hardly be afraid of the chief editor of one of the biggest magazines after Aaron. She wouldn't be the first one I met in my life.

Although Artelynn Duvalle was different. She was on a whole new level that was never available to me until today. It was real high fashion, not alternative authentic young designers, who brought me here.

"You need to be very patient with her," Cave said, nervously fidgeting with his fingers on the wheel, waiting for the lights to go green. "I will do the talking as always…"

Cave and I had a well worked-out system of negotiation.

"Yes, and I will be smiling and nodding as always."

*Teyvalle* took up a full building in the stylish city center. Once upon a time, those skyscrapers were the first ones in Cryton. Now, after refurbishment, they stood out amongst their mirror-like counterparts with their beautiful mosaic. Although the motives of the mosaic were simple and included nature, flowers, and birds, they still drew attention to themselves.

When we got inside, we quickly emerged in the atmosphere. Vintage crystal chandeliers were situated next to the high-tech ceiling, old-fashioned, almost steampunk, elevators went up and down glass tubes, the walls combined elements of ancient mosaic and reflexive metal.

I started to get nervous as we were walking to the reception through the hall. The sweet smell of coffee and expensive perfume always triggered panic and anticipation in my brain. I felt like documenting every step I took in this kingdom. It was similar to the moment Bunny and I walked into our first agency. We really cared about every step we took that got us higher and higher up. I indulged myself and actually took a picture of a moving elevator pretending to look at something on the screen.

I sent a message to Bunny, *Look how far we've got.*

When we were escorted to the elevator, I took a deep breath.

"It's so cool."

"No time to relax," Cave ordered and spanked me lightly, making me move to the open doors of the elevator.

This floor had no old-fashioned details we saw downstairs; it was all grey metallic.

"This is the magazine space," Cave whispered, pointing his finger down the corridor.

"Have you been here?"

"Once," he replied and frowned. "I tried to win an article competition. Even saw Artelynn Duvalle, although just briefly…"

He grinned and opened the door to the reception room.

"Mr. Malter," a pretty secretary acknowledged and stood up nervously, "Miss Melory." In a blink of an eye, she took my suede jacket. "Let me take that. Something to drink?"

"Water," I told her. I needed at least three liters now to dissolve the adrenaline in my blood.

"Coffee," Cave responded, and that very second we heard a powerful voice coming from the office.

"Where are they?"

Cave and I exchanged looks and took a step "towards the dream."

"The dream" was not pleased to see us. Artelynn Duvalle glanced at us from behind her trendy thin glasses. She didn't even move. She looked arrogant, polished, shining with mute pearl-grey, grave-cold.

"Mrs. Duvalle," Cave started. "It's such an honor for us to be here. Let me introduce," he said and opened his hand towards me, "Theana Melory, Dustin Dewman's last muse."

He was nervous.

*Pals* chief editor looked ready to personally argue this questionable statement and my unwanted title. I would certainly be ready to give it to someone else.

"Unbelievable," she hissed, standing up. "All of us are mourning, and you seem to be celebrating…"

She stepped from behind her desk and folded her arms over her chest, standing there in an accusing silence.

"Dustin Dewman was our North star in this world," she concluded bitterly. "You were very lucky to work with him…"

I was very lucky to not become his possession! I guess my jaw clenched too tightly for a moment, and Mrs. Duvalle stared at me.

"Muse? I doubt that."

I was counting to ten for the third time. This kind of humiliation wasn't unusual in this business. I grew an armor so thick this lady's words and doubts had no impact.

"It was more of a tragic coincidence," she declared, turning back to her table. "However, I'm the only one who thinks that, so… sit down."

Hiding a smirk, I sat on the offered chair, ignoring a glass of water. I didn't want to show this lioness that my throat went all dry before we had even started. Cave seemed completely alright. He dealt with worse.

"As you know, this year *Teyvalle* is celebrating anniversary fashion week. We gathered the best artists and are preparing some incredible shows both on the runaway and in the interactive space. You're going to be a part of one of the biggest ones."

She turned her laptop to show us the screen.

The doors behind us opened, and I looked back. A man entered Duvalle's office. He looked unusual. His skin was brown, and his eyes were similar to those of a cat. He grinned cheekily. He looked stylish, but there was a certain freedom in his style, which didn't show any designer affiliation. He looked at me with admiration for a couple of seconds and then turned his gaze to Cave.

"Alexander Shane," he said, shaking Cave's hand.

His voice was smooth, almost purring, cat-like... I blinked. Since then do I see animal features in men?

"Cave Malter," my agent said smiled in return. "And this is Theana Melory."

"I know," the man said as his grin widened. He turned, extending his hand to me. I stretched my hand to greet him but was suddenly pulled out of my chair and put standing in front of him. "Gorgeous," he said, walking around me.

"Alexander is the VP of *Teyvalle*," Duvalle commented. "He really wanted to see you today."

"And I don't regret it," he commented and nodded approvingly as if mocking the chief editor. "Did you tell them about the project?"

"Not yet, you wanted to be here for that if I remember," she replied and shrugged.

She didn't try to hide her hostility, but I suddenly stopped caring about that. The atmosphere in the room changed after this man entered. It felt as if he made me special and untouchable even by Duvalle. And to think there was so much nervous tension in the room before he appeared.

"Great," Shane said, returning me back to my chain and sitting down next to me. "Let's start."

"Alright," she agreed, bringing our attention back to her laptop. Well, mine and Cave's attention, to be exact, because Shane was focused on me. It was difficult to grasp. Maybe it was paranoia, although I felt something else... "One of the main events of the opening Sunday evening will be a display of jewelry, which defined eras and trends in fashion. Some of them are kept in our museum, others will be brought here from all over the world..."

I didn't think about Alexander anymore. I still wasn't very interested in the jewelry, but I couldn't deny the importance of this show. Cave seemed like he realized it too. I took one quick look at him, his eyes shining, to understand that this is the level none of us had been on before.

"Theana, you will make history as Dewman's model. The last one. You will get to work with his collection, you'll do the photoshoots, and will get to participate in developing the look for the show…"

"And the most expensive necklace from his new collection will be the most important detail," Alexander added.

"Didn't someone buy it?" I asked and blinked.

"Someone did," he replied and shrugged. "So you and I will need to charm the new owner and make him lend it to us."

"Charm him?" I repeated. My eyes widened.

Charming Aaron Houwer? And for what? Only to wear the necklace he chose for his fiancee?

I didn't know what made me angrier — the need to charm Beast, who brought me to orgasm with a simple movement of his tongue, or the humiliation of begging him to make me borrow his fiancee's necklace. How will it look? What does "charming" even mean?! And can this all really be a coincidence?

"Why me?"

"You have a right to it," Shane said, his eyes always smiling, but his mouth curling in a grin. "You're the only one who wore it publicly."

"That's a strange basis," I noted with a smirk.

"Oh, not at all. If I'm not mistaking," he paused pointedly before continuing, "Aaron Houwer bought the necklace after seeing you wear it." Shane waited for me to look him in the eyes. "He will agree to it if you ask."

I didn't see any shine in his eyes, but my nerves got better of me as I thought that he might be a beast too. Seemed that I was either going mad or suddenly starting to distinguish men of this race.

Another one. I wondered how many of them I'd met before; how many of them are there among us?

"Theana?" Shane called, bringing me back from my thoughts.

I blinked.

"When?"

He looked at his watch and spoke, "I have a meeting with him in his office in an hour and a half."

I almost swore out loud, but Alexander seemed to hear my thoughts and grinned in a predatory manner.

"Let's get lunch, and I'll tell you more about the fashion week and some of our projects."

Cave sprang out of his chair, I stood up feeling my legs go heavy.

I will see Beast in an hour and a half.

"Mr. Shane," I addressed the man, while Cave apologized and fell behind, answering his calls, "are you sure we should distract such a busy man from work? He even came to get the necklace at night..."

We were walking down the hallway towards the elevators but suddenly turned right.

"Are you scared of him, Theana?" he murmured. His catlike grin was there again as he spoke.

"I didn't like him," I blurted out. I decided to be truthful.

"A lot of people don't," Alexander replied, his voice unexpectedly harsh. He then smiled at a girl, who was passing by. She blushed visibly and looked at me with anger. Yes, there was certainly something catlike in Mr. Shane. "It would be stupid to just send him an official inquiry. Things like this are determined in negotiation."

"Not sure I'm good at that," I mumbled, but he still heard me.

Around the corner, there was a glass wall and a nice café full of light behind it. It was full of muted music, a calm atmosphere, a slight fleur of exquisite perfume, and fashion house employees at the tables. Cave and I were also there now.

"You underestimate yourself," Alex argued. He pushed the door in front of me. "Your dress will be designed by Lawrence Cafarelli himself. The best production and stage managers of our house will be planning your entrance. People are going to cry watching the video Cave sent us. Cryton and the whole country is going to talk about you. You'll become the second Greta Valieri, babe."

That was convincing.

"I suppose in that case we can steal it if anything," I joked and smirked, sitting down on the chair next to the window.

"I hope we won't have to do that," he replied and walked to his chair.

It was good that Cave had already finished his calls because I didn't feel like having lunch with this man one on one. Although I doubted he cared about me... While they discussed the contract, I was curiously watching people in the café. All of them were gods to me. I thought that you can get that far only if you're a genius or someone very persistent, or both. Our trio didn't go unnoticed. A couple of times people came by and asked Shane to introduce us.

I started to realize that through this tragic coincidence I became famous.

*I think we are famous*, I texted Bunny.

*I'd like to be a part of that, but you were the one Dewman danced around all evening.*

*Ugh.*

When I looked up from my mobile, I realized Alexander was looking at me with his catlike smile. I didn't like him. I was searching for the familiar flashes in his eyes and feeling nervous from his strange energy.

I mentally asked him to roar or give me another sign and raised an eyebrow. He probably misunderstood the expression and went full-on on his seduction: his smile grew wider, his eyes changed... I stopped smiling. Does he think I'm stupid like that?

Shane sneered and spoke, "I think I know what Dustin Dewman liked about you. Let's go?"

My mood was completely spoiled.

***

Cave left, making some excuse about unfinished business. I didn't expect him to stay, I was old enough to deal with everything myself. Although it was kind of reckless of him to leave me with two beasts. I was still pretty sure about Shane's catlike nature. Alexander welcomed me into his convertible and got behind the wheel.

"How did you meet Dustin?"

Although the car was open, we were not interrupted by the street noise.

"As I always meet clients. Cave brought me in for a fitting. In that case, it was jewelry fitting," I replied. I pretended to be taken by the view outside the car.

"Did you model for him before?"

"No, I first saw him on the day of the shoot," I said, and Alexander went silent for a while. Did he believe me? Did he care? "Was he your friend?" I tried to keep the conversation going.

If he was offering me such close collaboration, I felt like I had a right to ask some questions myself, even if I had to think carefully about them.

"Yes," he responded, and the car went faster.

"In that case, I offer you my condolences."

He didn't say anything, but his grip on the wheel got tighter.

I had no idea where *Black&Gold Industries* was located as I never thought I would have to meet the owner of my mark there. For now,

I was distracted by the strange behavior of my new acquaintance, but the further away we moved from the center, the more I shivered.

Cryton suddenly seemed strange and hostile. A long bridge over an elite district with small houses brought us to the kingdom of concrete and metal. There was little green there, but stone and marble were in abundance. Fountains, squares and statues, even sidewalks were made of them.

*Black&Gold Industries* looked like a black obelisk in the middle of a black square. I felt dizzy, looking up, my breath shortening from this indifferent greatness.

Shane and I easily passed the security at the entrance. I only truly believed I was entering Aaron Houwer's universe when I saw a familiar man on the other side. Claud Knife, who brought me to my meeting with Beast, was there to meet us.

"Hello, I'm Mr. Knife. Follow me, Mr. Houwer is expecting you."

Shane glanced at us with predatory arrogance. I was wondering what he thought would happen now. Maybe his plan was to just put me in the middle of the office as a distraction while he tries to talk to Houwer about some fine arts or something. No, that's crazy. Why doesn't he just offer his price? Or are we here to bargain?

"How much was the necklace?" I asked quietly as we exited the elevator.

I needed a distraction because even now I felt like Aaron Houwer was looking at me from every detail in his office: sharply cut walls and ceiling and their cold metallic shine, strange silence, which made my heartbeat audible. No chandeliers or any other décor, no flowers. It seemed like even cockroaches wouldn't be able to survive here.

"So much one could buy *Teyvalle*. Black diamonds from this collection are the most expensive stones in the history of jewelry."

"Welcome," Mr. Knife said and pushed the door, and I was the first to enter.

I managed to figure out how many steps to take and how many breaths to make before I came in because it was not easy to pretend that I was not familiar with the man sitting at the desk in the far corner of the spacious office.

This office seemed like it never saw even the smallest speck of dust. And even if the dust was once here, it would certainly be burnt under the gaze he threw at me this first second. When Shane appeared near me, the fiery glances stopped, and Beast's emotions went ice-cold.

"Mr. Houwer," Alexander said. He didn't even nod nor did he make a step closer to shake his counterpart's hand. "Thank you for making time for us."

"Mr. Shane," Aaron replied and nodded, "I was surprised…"

My throat went dry when I heard his voice. I drew a sharp breath as Beast's eyes slowly came back to me and he frowned. I felt like I was hit all of a sudden, and I made no further attempts to fill my lungs with air.

"This is Miss Theana Melory, you might remember her," Alexander introduced and gestured at me, but his voice showed a slight sign of mockery in it. "She was the one to wear the necklace we are here to talk about. She wore it the night Mr. Dewman tragically died."

Aaron blinked slowly, his face showing nothing.

"I've heard about that. So, what is it you want to talk about?"

That moment Shane, being a smart "harsh" negotiator, looked at me, suggesting that I say something. I turned my head and raised an eyebrow. Me?! He nodded encouragingly and made a step back. It was just me and Beast on the field now. I was a pawn, and he was the queen.

He frowned even more and his eyes went dark.

"Can you give me your fiancee's necklace?" I blurted out. I didn't quite realize what I was saying.

I had a feeling that even if I threw a cake in his face it wouldn't be as stupid as whatever I just did.

"You?" he asked and his eyes narrowed.

"Me," I repeated. I felt like he was challenging my self-esteem.

So, it was okay to mark me, but I didn't deserve to wear this extremely expensive thing?

Beast suddenly grinned.

"Is this your only argument, Mr. Shane?"

"What makes me not good enough?" I questioned. I didn't even allow Alexander to open his mouth. I folded my arms on my chest and frowned. "I'm not some upper-class aristocrat, just a simple model, who dag herself out from poverty by working twenty-four-seven for five straight years while living in a shithole with seven other people. So what makes your fiancee more deserving?"

Beast's eyes flashed with familiar fireworks.

"You felt sorry for her if I remember."

"You have a good memory."

"My answer is no," he said sharply. It felt like a slap in the face, and then like a sudden caress, when he said, "This necklace is for a special woman." His voice went hoarse, and I couldn't help but draw another sharp breath. "She will be the only one to wear it now."

It was now easy to hold his gaze because I felt like killing him with mine. He showed me my place in all of this. So, his lamb is "special," and I can simply go to hell...

I turned and went straight to the doors. Shane didn't say anything and followed me, catching up near the elevator.

"Well, negotiations are not your strong suit," he muttered and he shook his head in displease. "I thought that you'd do better with Houwer after Duvalle..."

"It's not the same," I replied. I threw my head back, my cheeks burning. I felt so powerless I wanted to cry. "I really don't know what you were counting on..."

"Me neither," he said and stepped into the elevator. "Let's get out of here."

***

I got a text from Beast at six. I closed the apartment door behind me and walked to the couch. I had spent all day meeting people I will get to work with. Shane seemed to not be upset about Aaron's rejection. He was still planning my participation in the jewelry show.

According to the script, I was meant to be the center of the runway. It was much more than simply a runway, it was a whole animated production. I haven't seen anything like it before.

I spent the rest of the day watching the demo-model of the show, and it looked incredible even in this pre-production version. Bunny was rushing home with some Chinese food, ready to listen to my story and see photos that I had taken on my phone.

But our plans got canceled. I tried to tell Beast to fuck off when he requested me to go downstairs in half an hour and join Mr.

Knife in a car. He replied that in that case, Mr. Knife will carry me out on his shoulder.

"Bastard!" I swore, slamming the door behind me.

Anger rose somewhere inside, and my complete inability to do anything made it even worse. I didn't reply to the guard's greeting and got onto the backseat.

"Bad day?"

"Is interviewing me a part of your job?" I snapped. "Yes, it was a bad day. And the evening is too."

"Alright," he said and shrugged his wide shoulders. "Well, you could at least try to fix the evening…"

"Mr. Knife, what are the chances that the man who messed up your day isn't going to mess up your night too? Mr. Houwer seems to have no desire to make any changes."

"Depends on what you would like to change."

"I would like to be left alone."

"Alright, Miss."

I was furious, and the driver's melancholic way of moving the car and classical music electrified the atmosphere inside the vehicle. Those fucking aristocrats! Listening to classical music and being so polite all the time! Full of dignity and class…

"Are you a beast too?" I asked and turned my head to look at him, but he pretended to not hear my question.

He only spoke when I ignored his outstretched hand while exiting the car.

"You know nothing about the world you became a part of," he murmured, getting close to my face, "so be careful."

I looked back at him angrily and pursed my lips.

This time we came to *Golden Palace* hotel, an extremely expensive place, too expensive for me to feel like a cheap prostitute, but that was exactly how I felt. I was wearing jeans and a loose T-shirt, which brilliantly showed my attitude towards the person who invited me. However, I felt naked walking through the luxurious hall.

"Mr. Houwer is running late," Knife informed me in the elevator.

I rolled my eyes and muttered, "Amazing."

He didn't follow me into the room. He waited for me to enter and close the door behind my back. I took a breath and looked around. The first thing I noticed was the smell. It was duplicating this thin aroma that followed me everywhere. I suddenly felt tones of this bitterness pierce my sternum with strange desperation and unfamiliar desire for protection. I shook my head and walked to the living room, separated from the entrance with a transparent panel. The table near the window was set, a reflection of candles visible in the window. It reminded me of the monster's eyes, watching me from the other side.

The smell of food made me realize I left before Bunny came in with dinner, so I decided to eat. I found a remote control and turned on a flat-screen TV, sitting on the couch with a full plate of food in front of me. Everything inside was burning with adrenaline as I waited for Beast, but I was trying to calm down and enjoy shrimp pasta and warm salad.

I didn't hear him arrive, but suddenly felt desire inside become stronger, and my heart made an extra beat. I turned around. Aaron was standing behind me, his hands in his pockets, and was looking at me, considering whether or not he should get closer.

"How's dinner?"

He sounded tired.

"It's nice, thanks," I responded and shrugged, turning my attention back to the TV.

"Turn it off."

My body shivered as his demand hit my nerves like a light breeze. I took the remote control and clicked the red button.

"What's wrong now?"

He walked around the couch and went into the depths of the room. I soon heard the sound of water. I moved towards the table where I last saw a bottle of wine.

Aaron came back a couple of minutes later. He wasn't wearing a jacket, his shirt's collar was loose, and his hair seemed wet, although it was hard to see in the half-dark room. I was sitting on the chair and splashing the wine around my glass.

"I couldn't say 'yes' to you today," he blurted out, slowly walking towards me. The lights of the city moved inside my wineglass reminding me of flashes in his eyes. I didn't reply and took a sip. "Thea…"

"What are you planning for tonight? Why am I here?" I asked bluntly and stared at him. He sat on the opposite side of the table in silence, and it made me angry. "Are we only talking about things that you find convenient?"

I didn't know where the courage came from, but I was sure he would be quick to shut it down.

"We're not talking," he commented coldly.

"You're right," I agreed and nodded. "It is quite difficult to chat with a man who bought me like a thing and regularly puts me in my place…"

"Your place?" he repeated as he narrowed his eyes.

"I can't even call myself a whore because you don't fuck me… anymore," I spoke and shrugged, shivering and taking another big sip.

"Do you want me to?" he asked, taunting.

"I want to get out of here!" I shouted and threw my half-full glass at him. I didn't notice him getting out of the way but saw that he didn't even flinch when the glass shattered.

“Never do this again.”

Something inside of me trembled as his voice went into this strange guttural growl.

“Do you understand?” he said through clenched teeth. “I don’t like to repeat myself.”

“Yes, I understand.”

My intuition told me I need to keep silent as a lamb. No wonder his fiancee reminded me of one so much.

“My world, Theana, is different from what you’re used to. Things that are crazy to you are my reality,” he explained and took a deep breath, calming himself down. “Our women are taught to be men’s partners from birth.”

“Dewman told me your women are infertile,” I declared and put my head up.

He burned me with his angry gaze for a couple of minutes.

“It’s true,” he finally replied.

“What about children?”

There was another long pause.

“Children aren’t a problem.”

I wished I didn’t look at him.

“Is that why you buy women like me?”

“We don’t BUY women like you for that,” he replied, and his voice got its hoarse tone back.

“Do you keep them somewhere?” I asked. My voice was shaking. He didn’t respond. “Why do you need me?” I cried as my breathing got faster. He didn’t respond again. “What did I do to you?” I shouted and shrank, shivering.

I felt my throat squeeze with despair. I was like a fly in a spider web, but it only caught me tighter, giving me no chance to break free, no chance to ask for help.

His gaze changed.

“Thea...”

Something warm and soft touched my chest, calmed me down... I blinked, and the feeling disappeared and left some unexpected confidence behind.

"Is Shane a beast too?" I asked. I then took a deep breath and sat straight.

"A beast?" he echoed, smirking.

I shrugged and explained, "That's what they call you on TV."

"Alright," he accepted and switched his attention away from me, averting his gaze. "Yes, Shane is very much a beastie."

I frowned. That meant that my new workplace was another ball of lies and intrigues, not a fashion house.

"What does he need?"

"Me. Stop shaking."

I wondered how they raise their brides. What were the things they needed to learn all their lives?

"So why do you go through this torture with people like me?" I asked.

"Torture is not a strong enough word."

"Why don't you teach us when we're young like you do with your own women?"

The flare of candles reflected in his eyes collapsed into small sparks every time the air around us moved.

"Your government doesn't allow us to interfere with lots' lives before the auction."

"So, our government sells us?"

"Well, two worlds need to co-exist somehow, so it's a small price to pay for that. More wine?"

"Yes, please," I agreed and handed my glass to him. I was tired, and I felt that Beast was tired too. "Your office is very impressive..."

He smiled.

"I wasn't ready for your visit. Shane didn't let me know."

"So you didn't have time to prepare to humiliate me even more?" I questioned and rolled my eyes as I remembered his words.

Our conversation went south again. I celebrated another diplomatic failure with a big sip.

"How did I humiliate you?" he asked, watching me drink.

"You really don't get it, do you?"

The wine had a completely different taste. It was sweet and relaxing. This first glass energized me and burned my throat.

"I think you're the one who doesn't get it."

"Great," I said and grinned.

"I'm not really explaining it."

"I think you're explaining more than you were planning to," I noted sarcastically.

I was his pet. He decided to get a pet and now was watching my reactions closely. I saw interest in his eyes watching my every move, every emotion. Well, isn't that entertaining! Lost, scared, untrained…

"I didn't plan anything, Thea," he protested.

Another big sip of wine made me think I could have dinners with him every night.

"Then why would you need to prepare for my arrival?" I asked and licked my lips still sweet from the wine.

I saw him watch me especially closely at that moment. He turned his head a little bit. I was hardly aware that I was watching him back, drowning in his eyes.

"You make me lose balance."

I wanted to drown.

"You don't make it obvious."

"I can't allow him to figure it out," he explained, blinked, and glanced down at the candles.

"Why?"

"Alexander Shane is the head of his clan. He brought you in to check if you're mine."

I suddenly realized I was ready to listen to him forever because I liked the way he talked, the way he tried to talk. We spoke different languages and hardly understood each other, but it only made it more interesting… more sensual. I was slowly floating into a trance, my breathing became quick and light. I wanted to shake away this strange anticipation and I used our conversation as my focus, my way out.

"Why would he do that?"

"Dewman."

Something clicked in my mind, and my heart skipped a beat. I wanted to bring him to this topic, and we were finally here. He started it himself. Beast's eyes narrowed, but I didn't notice. My pulse quickened and the last bits of common sense and caution disappeared.

"Because… Because you killed him?"

I never saw eyes like that. I knew I needed to be terrified because that's how predators look at their prey on animal channels on TV. I didn't scream, but only because my throat went numb from horror. Aaron slowly stood up and took a step towards me as I tried to blend in with the chair. When he got closer, I was already shaking. I felt my skin burning as his fingers touched my chest right next to a small camera pendant. A sudden pull left an unpleasant feeling in my neck. Beast was staring at his trophy intently. The pull had probably left a red mark, but at this point, I didn't care anymore. His hand grabbed me by the neck and pulled up. I clang onto his wrist, shaking in panic, as he pressed my head against the glass.

"Are you trying to find some dirt on me?" he growled in my face.

"I…" I wheezed and punched him in the chest. He obviously didn't even feel it.

"Listen and remember," he snarled again, "I own you, all of you. If we don't survive this 'happy little accident,' no one will care to try and find you except maybe your gay friend. Now you live, work, walk, and breathe only because I allow you to! Do you understand?!"

His hand stopped pressing against my throat, and I finally took a breath.

"Bastard," I hissed.

He brought his face closer, almost touching my lips with his.

"Beast," he corrected and let go. "And don't tell gay as much as you do," he added. "Get out."

When the doors closed behind me, something inside the room shattered with a loud bang. I dashed across the hallway. Barefoot.

***

I tried my best to look calm and babble about *Teyvalle*, but Bunny didn't buy it. When I jumped up for the fifth time to get him something, he grabbed me by the arm and pulled me closer.

"What did he do?" he questioned, scowling.

"Noth…"

"Don't lie."

"He just scared me!" I exclaimed and pulled my hand from his grip, turning to the table. "Nothing new."

The truth was that when Knife let me out of the car, I almost ran back home. I first thought that I'm not going to stay here for a second longer, but then decided to wait for Bunny to fall asleep, pack up and leave at night. For a little while, I felt numb, I stopped caring about my career, money, everything. Later, after a long hot bath, I calmed down and realized I had nowhere to run. I could be on the run for a couple of days, maybe even a week, but there was no doubt that eventually, he would find me. I had no idea how to be on the run. I knew how to destroy obstacles on my career path, knew how to walk the runway, knew how to pose, but I had no idea how to run away from men like this. I never had to learn that. I could possibly trick Bunny, but no one else… And where would I go anyway? Back to poverty? Back at the hotel, having his huge hand on my neck, I was sure that I would prefer anything to being around him, but I wasn't so sure anymore. I don't want to go back to filth. I was there before, and it wasn't a pleasant life. I decided that running wasn't a choice. He allows me to live and breathe? Good, at least I have that. The camera was totally my fault; it was a stupid idea from the get-go.

"Thea…"

I felt the pressure of despair multiplied by uncertainty. I could only wait for his calls and those strange dinners, which only seemed to lead to total trainwrecks. I was messing up Beast's life, he said so himself. It was only a matter of time he gets fed up with this "luxurious pleasure."

My lips formed into an angry grin.

"Thea…" Bunny called again.

"Hm?" I muttered and opened the fridge to get a box with a beautiful bow on it. "I have some cannoli for you."

Bunny sighed and pursed his lips, but he couldn't be silent for long.

"Thea, do you think there is a way to… negotiate with him?"

"Do you think I'm not trying?" I questioned, put the box in the center of the table, and pulled the bow.

"Well, I know you, so I would think that you're not," he stated and stared straight at me.

"I bought a necklace recorder," I told him as I opened the box. "He caught me."

"Was it that new necklace?!" Bunny cried and pulled his hair. "Are you out of your mind? You're lucky you're back here!"

Maybe I was. I calmly took cannoli out and sunk my teeth into it. I had a feeling that when I'd left he took his anger out on a table or on his flat-screen TV. When I'd finally got into the car, I felt like something special was ripped out from my chest. Beast didn't only take my time, but something else. This mark was changing both of us, and it terrified me much more than his threats.

"Shane brought me to his office to make me ask for the diamond necklace."

"The Dewman necklace?"

"He didn't give it to me. Told me it was for a special woman."

Bunny closed his eyes and shook his head.

"What a jerk."

"Take some cannoli," I said and smiled.

"And spend next three weeks on a treadmill," he continued and rolled his eyes. "Bitch, you're the one who can eat whatever you want."

"Eat," I ordered and pushed the sweet into his hand. "You also can eat whatever you want, you just like being dramatic."

"Not me. Cave always makes a scene when I don't fit into the clothes," he complained but took an obedient bite.

I ruffled his hair and hugged him.

"Love you."

"Love you too," he whispered and pecked me with his filling-covered lips. As soon as we finished laughing, he suddenly looked very serious. "I will do everything you say. I'll leave if you tell me to, and I'll stay if you want me to stay."

I watched him for a little while, smiling, but went sad in a mere second.

"I'm sorry I got you into this."

"Thea," he started, but I shook my head.

"You told me you'd do anything."

"I won't leave you alone in this," he proclaimed and pursed his lips, showing that the conversation was over. "If you try to run, I will never forgive you."

I felt the last bits of energy leave me, and my head just hung down. I wondered why life taught me to always overcome things by myself without any help or support and then put me in front of an obstacle I might never be able to overcome. Should I try and negotiate? Forget all the humiliation, my freedom being taken, make a step, and… negotiate.

When Bunny went to sleep, I walked out to the balcony and took a deep breath. I loved my life too much, I sacrificed so much to have it, worked so hard. I have this night, this balcony, and this park with small bits of light coming from behind the trees… I used to have a feeling of being complete, being full and confident in tomorrow. All of this was mine. All of this is mine. I felt strange emptiness pulsate inside my chest, and I took my phone out.

*Promise me to not harm Bunny. He doesn't know anything.*

Beast told me he knows everything about me. Should I trust him to make a promise and keep it? I stretched my arm and took a pack of cigarettes from behind a flowerpot.

*Promise me to quit smoking.*

I almost dropped my phone, bit my lip, and felt my breathing get faster. I turned around, wondering if he can see me.

*I can only see the balcony*, the message said.

It was easy to imagine him standing here. I sat down and curled up in the armchair.

*Don't you think there should be a limit?*

*Don't you think you passed all limits with your little camera?*

My chest started hurting, and I felt bitterness in my throat. I slowly inhaled and let out a small cloud of smoke.

*So you want to exchange my stupid habit for Bunny? Really?*

He told me I'd have to bargain.

*I won't harm your friend. I promise.*

I was yet to promise anything in return.

*Why do you care if I smoke?*

*I hate the smell, especially from my special woman.*

***

"We will take it up a little bit here…" Wesmir Tucci, Lawrence Cafarelli's designer, was walking around me for a good hour, while I just stood there in a heavy wedding dress, which was supposed to complement the necklace. "Bella…"

It was an unusual warm grey color and shone brightly in the morning light, reminiscent of diamond dust scattered across glass. Corset made my bust look great and was so tight that it took my breath away both literally and figuratively.

Mr. Tucci and I were the only ones in Cafarelli's office. It was too early for employees to arrive, and nothing could stop me from slowly realizing that all of this was really happening to me… One of the legends was making an expensive outfit exclusively for me…

I was ready to worship every centimeter of this office. One corner was taken by the next spring-summer collection. I heard that they rented a whole ski resort to present it. In another corner, there was a table covered in sketches for the fashion week.

"Mr. Shane," Tucci said, "we're done here."

I turned to look at myself in the mirror. My hair was pulled back into a bun, and it was clear that was the best option for this look. I was happy the bite mark wasn't visible anymore. I woke up this morning, and it just wasn't there. My reflection inspired, made me want to forget everything and just be happy. It was so nice to trick myself for a second, to believe that in front of me there were only things that I've dreamed of. Even if I had another horrible evening waiting for me around the corner, I didn't care, because this day was mine!

"Can I send a picture to a friend?" I asked Tucci.

"Sorry, no," he replied and shrugged, apologizing. "It's a trade secret."

"Okay," I said and smiled back. Bunny would have to wait for the fashion week.

"Do you like it?"

"Are you kidding?" I exclaimed as my smile widened. "I'm so happy I could faint."

"We wouldn't want that," he chuckled. "Be careful, you'll wrinkle it."

I nodded, biting my lips, as Tucci continued to shower me with compliments, telling me that this dress and I are both pieces of art.

When the door was shut behind me, I was prepared to see Shane. I knew I should be cautious around *Teyvalle*'s VP, and so I was planning to be. However, when I turned around, I fell silent. My eyes widened and my smile disappeared.

It was Grace Dolly, "the lamb," Aaron Houwer's fiancee. My Beast's fiancee.

"Wesmir!" she exclaimed with a breath and run into the designer's arms. She then turned and introduced herself, "It's so beautiful! I'm Grace Dolly..."

She took her white glove off and stretched her hand out to me. She was wearing an awfully cute sky-blue dress and a pink jacket. They were trendy, thanks to *Teyvalle*, but never in my life would I wear something like that. This season they tried to soften the aggressive image of a modern woman, and it looked so appropriate on Grace Dolly. It was sugar coating to her vanilla cake. So sweet it made me sick.

"Theana Melory," I said, squeezing her fingers lightly.

"Oh my god, it's you," "vision in pink and blue" exclaimed and raised her eyebrows. "What a dress! Wesmir, it's magical!"

Grace walked around me, blinking with her blue eyes. "Maestro is the god amongst men!"

I watched this bubbling admiration and tried to imagine her around Aaron. Why is he marrying her anyway? Didn't he say that their women can't have children? Well, maybe she is a good cook or plays her role well.

I was staring at her, studying her closely, but she was only looking at the dress. She was hardly twenty. She was posh, even the hairclip in her blonde hair was worth twice the amount I got for the Dewman shoot. She was upper-class.

The door opened again, and Shane came in, followed by two guys with another dress in their hands.

"Alexander!" Grace babbled and took a step towards him. "Hi!"

"Hi, gorgeous," "the cat" murmured. He was the most innocent I've ever seen him, leaving a chaste kiss on her cheek. "I knew how to make you come see me more often," he said, pointing to the dress. "Try it on!"

"Oh my god!" Grace squeaked. It was hard not to laugh, watching her be so delightful about practically anything. Although, I would probably squeak myself if I had a Cafarelli wedding gown.

While she looked at hers, Alexander walked towards me.

"Theana…"

He slowly looked me up and down, and his eyes were full of admiration. It only made me feel better.

"Good morning, Mr. Shane."

"Oh, don't pretend this isn't the best morning of your life," he teased and grinned, and I smiled back.

"It is!" I agreed, nodding.

"Beautiful neck," he commented as he came closer, and my smile disappeared. "It's like it was made to wear that diamond necklace…"

His eyes narrowed, staring at the spot the bandage was last time. "Cave said you'd had an injury after the hospital attack."

It seemed he was holding back from touching me.

I wanted to pull away, but let a reply out, "Just a couple of scratches."

"Got lucky then," he replied thoughtfully and smirked. "No scars or anything."

"Yes, very lucky…"

I felt dizzy from his sudden attention. He seemed to be looking for a connection between Aaron and me, but why? Maybe he wanted to prove that he was guilty of murdering Dewman. If Shane knew that Dewman had bought me, then knowing I bore someone else's mark would give him a hint on who the killer is. Aaron visited Dewman that night, and it all seemed to be a mistake. He came. He saw me. He bought the diamond and then said that it would only be worn by a special woman. Yesterday he made it clear that I was that special woman.

"Alexander!"

I twitched, and Shane grimaced and then grinned, looking me straight in the eyes. He then turned to Grace. What a jester! She stepped from behind the curtain in her wedding gown, so sweet, so soft. I pursed my lips and turned away. My life seemed like a real madhouse. The best morning of my life was spoiled by the sudden appearance of Aaron Houwer's fiancee. Aaron Houwer himself was basically keeping me as a pet for whatever strange plans he had.

"What do you think of 'the special woman?'" Shane whispered, pretending that it was the best spot to admire Grace.

"I think you might be a better expert to answer that question," I said and grinned, watching "the lamb" in the mirror.

Shane smiled approvingly, turning his glance back at me. I started to feel tense near him just as I did with Aaron. The latter was dangerous and made it clear, while the former was certainly the master of intrigues. I was afraid that if I ever understood his actions, it would be too late.

"So, Grace, how's Aaron?" Shane asked loudly.

I went tense as Grace turned to us.

"He's great, thanks. Looking forward to the wedding!"

I felt like I was hit with something heavy. I blinked, my legs went wobbly. Corset suddenly felt too tight, the gown became too heavy.

"Thea?"

I heard Alexander's voice as if I was underwater.

"Corset is too tight," I muttered, shook my head, and fell down, clinging onto man's shoulders. He picked me up with unexpected ease.

"Wes, we need a doctor!"

"No, please, don't," I whispered and shook my head again, trying to pull myself together. "I just didn't have breakfast…"

***

I saw colors come back to the surroundings as I sat in the café with pastry in one hand and a cup of latte in another.

"Do you faint often?" Shane asked and raised his brow.

It seemed that he had no other work but to babysit me.

"Only when I'm out of my mind from happiness wearing a dress from Cafarelli and hadn't had a proper breakfast," I replied and smirked.

I would like to believe that I was getting out of the trap he set for me, but I had a feeling he was just leading me into one.

"Well, then now I will always make sure you have breakfast before trying the gowns on," he told me and smiled with an unusual expression as if he actually cared. "So, what do you think about his 'special woman?'"

"I'll be drinking sugar-free latte for weeks," I blurted out and winced, and he laughed. "Although I think she's easy to charm…"

He narrowed his eyes and argued, "Grace Dolly is not as simple as she looks."

"Of course she isn't," I agreed and shrugged, "if she was chosen by such a man."

He is looking forward to the wedding! My cheeks started to burn as soon as I remembered the sponsor of my fainting. This fucking hypocrite! I didn't feel sorry for "the lamb" anymore, she chose him herself. I was however sorry for myself because I had no choice. Now I was feeling as if I was walking on the shattered glass blindfolded, and this "cat" was grinning with pleasure!

"Well, a marriage of convenience can be very strong," Alexander said.

And that's how the best morning of my life was completely spoiled.

"What will you do if you don't have the necklace by the time I need to wear it?" I didn't really care but was desperate to change the subject. It's not like everything in this world was about it.

Shane didn't quite agree.

"It's not an option, Theana," he told me and winked. "This is *Teyvalle.*"

***

The day got better, but I was still bitter after meeting future Mrs. Houwer. I was irritated by everything: the fuss, the same questions people asked me over and over again, monotonous repetition as *Teyvalle* got the event plan ready. I was exhausted from all of it. Lingerie fitting for one of the runways was the last straw. Artelynn and her assistants spent two hours choosing between a lavender set and an exact same set, but with different panties, which covered my hips tiny two centimeters more! I had to change at least twenty times, running back and forth behind the curtain.

It could seem like they were mocking me, but it was a normal working day for a professional. However, I didn't feel like a professional anymore, but much more like a victim of circumstances in the middle of zoopolitical intrigues. I was expecting Aaron to text me and ask me to come just so I could tell him everything I thought about him, but he was silent. Shane stepped into the room as I was standing in front of Artelynn for the twentieth time, and he wasn't alone. Apparently, Grace spent all day at *Teyvalle*.

"Oh, it's lovely!"

I drew a short breath. Standing in front of Beast's fiancee in my underwear was the biggest humiliation. It was a marvelous illustration of our roles in all this: I was almost naked, as a prostitute should be, and she had already got rid of whatever monstrosity she was wearing in the morning and was now gorgeous in a long black evening gown. It was probably another Cafarelli work, expensive and covered with dark stones.

"This is Wayne Amolli's last collection," Shane commented, walking Grace closer as if I was a piece at a museum exhibition. "It will be presented at the show; no one can buy it yet."

"Alexander," Grace murmured and smiled, biting her lip flirtatiously.

"The cat" grinned.

"I'll leave a set for you," he assured her, nodding.

That was certainly the last straw.

"Alright, I have to go. Aaron and I have a dinner tonight, we need to discuss the guest list," she said and pecked Alexander on the cheek. "Thea, it was lovely to meet you!"

I didn't bother to reply or even react at all. I just stood there, biting my lips until they hurt. Artelynn and her team left without giving me any sign that I was free to go. Shane and I were left alone.

I was unable to cover up my emotions. I was so fed up with all of it I could kill someone. If Aaron was here at that moment, I would probably throw couple more glasses at him. He should definitely get used to that.

"Thea," Alexander called. He slowly looked me up and down, and I turned my head to see him. My lips curled into a seductive smile, and he narrowed his eyes attentively. "You're shivering... Are you cold?"

"Do you have any plans for tonight?"

His grin became dangerous, predatory.

"I don't think I should ask, but..." he continued, watching me closely.

"Would you like to have dinner with me?" I spoke quietly, almost whispering, but we were close enough for him to hear me.

The air went tense in a small second.

"Thea," Alexander said and made a step closer. "Are you sure?" he asked, putting a hand on my neck and pulling me closer as I put my hands forward. It didn't take him much strength to break my resistance. "I don't think I could look and not touch," he muttered as his face got closer. His eyes looked devilish. I clearly saw familiar red flashes in them. "And if I touch you, I'm afraid I will be in the same position Dustin Dewman is in..."

I didn't even try to cover up the smirk. He knew. He knew everything. He knew who I was and who killed Dewman. He was not there to make my life easier or show sympathy. I was just another clothes hanger and just another victim of his manipulations.

I broke free from his hands, took a wobbly step behind the curtain, and spoke, "I'll see you on Monday, Mr. Shane."

***

Bunny was calling me nonstop, but I couldn't pick up the phone until I got home. He was expecting descriptions of incredible dresses and an amazing day, but I was feeling angry and humiliated.

"Tell me, do you still have access to that party's website? The expensive one?" I demanded. I didn't even look him in the eyes when he opened the door. He was cooking and wore a funny checked apron.

"CTS?" he asked, surprised.

"Yes," I confirmed and threw my shoes into the corner of the hallway, walking straight to the bathroom.

"Thea, what happened?" Bunny interrogated, running after me.

"I fucking hate all of this," I snapped. I unbuttoned my blouse, almost ripping the buttons away. One of them finally broke, falling straight into the sink.

"Thea," he called and tried to hug me, but I took a step to the side.

"Don't come closer," I ordered and put my hand forward. "You will calm me down for a moment, but I will be crying into my pillow late. I don't want that!"

"What happened?!" he cried. "I was certain it would be the best day of your career! I bought you wine and cooked dinner…"

"I had one of the worst days of my life, Bunny… So I will be a bitch now! I'm sorry, but I'm planning to argue with you and hurt you, take a shower and leave into the night and get drunk!"

"I'll go with you!" he said and clenched to the bow on the apron.

"No! I don't want to babysit you like a younger brother. Leave me alone!"

Hurt Bunny – done. Two more left.

I chose a short sleeveless dress and a dark jacket with high-heeled shoes. I wanted to feel avenged.

He could choose who to spend evenings with, and I was supposed to wait for his phone call? No, doesn't work that way. Even his threats didn't matter anymore. I wasn't planning to sleep with anyone, just relieve some stress, get a confirmation that I still had my freedom. CTS party was exactly what I needed. It was crazy expensive, but it felt right.

I found an invitation in the drawer. It was a pretty velvet envelope with an empty black paper inside.

"Bunny…" I called, confused.

"It's the invitation, now leave," I heard coming from the kitchen.

"Thank you…"

***

On my way, I got into some heavy traffic, but it didn't take away my anticipation. The end of the working week was close and everyone was going out. The taxi brought me into a parking lot, full of exquisite cars, and stopped in front of the guard post. When I first saw these scary men I wanted to get back into the car, but it was too late — they'd already seen me.

"Come here," one of them ordered, smirking.

I stuck the envelope out, afraid they would shoot me straight at the entrance, but the man only grinned wider.

"First time?"

"Yeah," I confirmed, nodding.

He took the black card out of the envelope and lit it with a lighter. The card showed the club's logo and a number and quickly burned down.

"Impressive," I said.

"Welcome," the guard said as he looked me up and down. "It's free. Come in…"

They brought me to one of the cars, and it moved along a narrow badly-lit alley surrounded by trees. The three-story building looked old-fashioned almost like a castle. As soon as I was escorted out of the car, I noticed that all the windows were black-shut.

"Good night, Miss," another guard said and smiled. "Welcome."

I stepped to the front door that was immediately opened for me and walked to the reception desk.

"Take a bracelet," a girl on the reception instructed, giving me a narrow metallic band. "There are three zones inside. The blue zone is for meeting people, chatting, watching the show. You can spend all night there. The red zone is for kissing, petting, no nudity, only underwear."

"What does that mean?" I decided to clarify.

"You can leave your partner or partners nearly naked, in their underwear, and they can do the same to you," she replied eagerly. "The bracelet shows your preferences, so no one makes a mistake and bothers you for no reason," she explained and touched it, and the bracelet lit up. "Yellow is for 'open for new acquaintances', white – 'not available for conversation,' red – 'ready for sex with one partner', blue…"

"Thanks, that's enough for me," I interrupted and nodded.

"Sure," she said, shrugging. "The last zone is crimson. It's the only sex zone. We have protection everywhere, in every room of the crimson zone. Can I have your phone?"

I knew it was serious in places like this one, but the whole instruction process really got my courage down. I wasn't the one to back away, so I tried to get it all back.

The blue zone was impressive. The light was dim, but the bar, soft couches, armchairs, and tables, - everything, really – was visible. In the center, there was a dance floor. I walked straight to the bar, trying not to look around.

"Miss, turn your bracelet on," the bartender reminded and
smiled softly before I started speaking.

I quickly put it on white, the safest one.

"Thank you…"

"Your first time?"

"Yes," I confirmed and sat down. "Can I have some
champagne?"

"Of course."

I just wanted to hang out, have fun, get crazy. I needed to
not want break glasses and throw them into Beast's head. The more
I drank, the braver I got. Fifteen minutes later I was looking around
the zone, noticing that most of the people were single, only five or
six couples sitting together. Sensual lounge music changed the
mood, and I finally started to relax… almost.

When the lights got dimmer, I took my glass of champagne
and moved into a comfortable armchair. A couple of seconds later
the show started, and it made me blush so hard I was glad it was so
dark here. The only visible lights were the bracelets changing their
colors from white to something more adventurous. Women in
leather clothes were moving in the center. Their costumes didn't
cover much, showing off their beautiful bodies and faces. It only
became more interesting when half-naked men joined them. I
wanted to make myself invisible in the armchair.

I'd never been to parties like this, only heard of them. Now it
was clear I got myself into something strange, but it was definitely a
great way to distract myself.

The action on stage was beautiful and more intimate than
sex, although they didn't actually have it. Their moves were well-
rehearsed; they were all very graceful. They were flowing around
each other in a kaleidoscope of movement. When I was ready to
finally breathe out, the action changed and I hold the breath in. One
of the couples took their clothes off in their dance, while others

went to the background. The guy grabbed the girl by the neck pressing his stomach against her back, and I started to hyperventilate, feeling a drop of sweat run down my back. It looked so similar to what had happened to me. The girl was struggling against her partner, she was trying to break free and stood on her toes just like I did in that broom closet trying to match Beast's height so his hand on my neck lost some pressure. That's one of the things I'd thought back then — that I don't want to be choked to death.

When he slowly slipped inside her, there was no music left, but the heavy breathing of the woman and deep drum beat. The light pulsated on their bodies, leaving their faces covered with darkness. I wanted to stand up and run away, but my feet were glued to the ground and my eyes were locked on the couple. The man was moving faster, and the girl was clinging to his neck, submitting to him. They looked as if they forgot they were performers. The man's hand was flying between her legs, and then he bit her neck as he started coming. I instinctively put my hand on my own neck, blinking for the first time in minutes.

The light went completely dark, leaving pulsating shapes and contours jumping around on the back of the eyelids. I was sitting there, my eyes shut, and tried to calm down. No one applauded, and we all kept silent until the music was turned back on. People started to slowly move around the room, waiters walked up to the tables as many couples made their way into another zone.

"Can I have more champagne?" I muttered. I had to cough to bring my voice back.

"Something to eat, maybe?" the waiter suggested. "We have canapé…"

"Sure," I agreed. Three glasses and no food would definitely make me fall asleep in this exact chair.

There were more and more guests around, and soon two men were sitting next to me on both sides. One of them was meaningfully looking at my bracelet, my legs, and the glass in my hands. He was definitely waiting for the bracelet to switch to the color he needed. I smirked.

"You can always jump behind the bar, I'll cover you up," the bartender offered and smiled, taking an empty plate from me. "You have at least three of those trying to hunt you down…"

I swallowed. Was that really what I wanted? I had all my doubts disappear as soon as I remembered where my "owner" was. My lips curled into an angry snarl. I stood up, took my glass, and walked into the next zone before another show started.

It was very different here. The room was half-dark, darker than the previous zone. The music was louder, but it wasn't overpowering.

"Good evening," another guard said as he approached. "The rule is that you can't stop and watch someone for more than 5 seconds. And… Miss…" he whispered and leaned closer. "White bracelets are not in favor here…"

"Okay, thanks. It's my first time…"

He nodded understandingly, while I tried to remember what color was next. My bracelet went yellow, and I slowly moved into the depths of the zone, into darkness.

"Can I get you a drink?" the voice behind said, but I didn't turn.

"I have one, thank you."

"Are you always so independent?" he chuckled. I liked this voice.

"Unfortunately, not anymore."

This weird night finally let me in, and I felt like a part of this party. I felt relaxed and as if I left all my anger on my situation in the first room.

"You were watching the show… And I was watching you."

I turned around. He was a young man, very aristocratic, tall, good-looking. I smiled weakly and turned back to the couch. I sat down.

"Can I join you?" the man took a step closer.

I nodded, bringing my glass back to my lips and taking a sip. I had enough alcohol already but I needed to fill in the silence. I wasn't planning to fuck him, but I needed an alibi to stay in that zone. I remembered that I shouldn't be watching anyone for too long, but even quick glances around allowed me to drown in the atmosphere. On the couch next to us, a girl in her bra straddled a man and was licking his ear while he was biting her nipple through the lace. The picture was arousing, and I took another big sip of my champagne.

"It's your first time here," the man commented.

"Yes," I said, turning to see the stranger.

"Why are you here?" he asked and grinned.

"Wanted to run away," I replied, shrugging.

"You're not going to the crimson room…" he said. His voice bore no anger or resentment. He was simply stating the fact.

"No," I confirmed and shook my head. "You don't have to waste your time."

"Don't make this decision for me," he told me, smiling. "Would you like some tea?"

My smile widened.

"Coffee would be great."

"Good choice. It means I have more time if you don't get tired of me."

He stood up and walked to the bar, showing other "hunters" that at least for now I was taken and out of their reach.

At this exact moment, another person entered the zone and dashed straight to me…

I recognized him from his inhumanly fast movement. When my eyes met his gaze, I felt an immediate desire to disappear into the darkness of my corner. I knew I'm not getting away with this. His angry eyes with red flashes in them told me I'm not getting away at all.

"Out," Aaron barked. My previous conversation partner took a step back, but I didn't pay attention anymore. When Aaron approached me, his hands smashed on the couch on both sides. "Good evening, Theana."

I felt my face burn as if Beast was a demon from hell. On my periphery, I saw the guards walk another man out. The new guest seemed to put a new set of rules into place, and protecting me was not one of them.

"Did you pick all the guests for the wedding?" I questioned and folded my arms on my chest.

"Didn't have enough time," he snarled. His nostrils widened.

"Such a pity!" I exclaimed. I felt that I was going too far, and his red eyes just a couple of centimeters away from mine confirmed it... "Grace will be so upset."

"I don't care," he growled.

"She is so sure you're looking forward to the wedding," I whispered and moved my shoulders.

I didn't even notice the moment he sat me on his lap. His rough fingers grabbed my hips, my world span, and I fell on his chest. Aaron ran his fingers into my hair and secured my head so I had to look him in the eyes.

"Let me go!" I squeaked and tried to punch him. "I don't want to live your and your Grace's lives! I don't want to stand in front of her in lingerie while she decides to buy it! I don't want to and I won't!" I tried to punch him harder.

A loud female moan reminded me of where we were.

"I see," he hissed into my lips, "how you live your own life..."

"Fuck y…" I hissed back, but he didn't let me finish.

It wasn't a kiss because people don't kiss like that. They just don't have it in them. Beast burned my lip with a sharp bite and then covered my mouth with his hot lips. I cried from the contrast and moaned, not even trying to fight. I suddenly was all out of strength to fight. This deep desire that followed me through this evening jumped forward to his owner as he seemed to only be getting started. He left my lips and switched his attention to my tongue. He sucked it into his mouth and bit it. His sharp teeth touched the sensitive surface, and my body felt like I was drenched in boiling water. It ran from my tongue into my throat, my stomach, and further down. He disarmed me in short minutes and could now do whatever he wanted with me.

And he did. He picked me up and carried me somewhere. All I saw were dim lights, but even they were too bright. The door opened and I felt cold sheets under me. I arched my back but was immediately pinned down to the bed. The beast took the dress off, and how he kept it all in one piece was a mystery for another time. He then tore my panties to shreds, and I was sure I got couple more scars for my collection. He didn't take his t-shirt off and I clang to it when his fingers slid down my stomach and finally reached my personal switch. His first movement sent an electric shock through my body, I screamed and squeezed my legs together, throwing my hips forward. I felt the bite awaken, and I trembled. It was not an orgasm just yet, but something more soothing, something that left me conscious.

It was hunger. I was hungry for intimacy, and it made me fall into particles. I became a beast, hungry and out of my mind… I was scratching his stomach under his t-shirt, squeezing his hips with my legs, and rocking my hips as if he was already fucking me. And he did, but with his hands, and I wasn't sure if he was teasing me or punishing me.

I bit him through the agony adding a strong metallic taste to the kiss. His ice-cold belt buckle touched my stomach, sobering me up. Everything inside fought against him, and I even managed to push him away and turn to my stomach.

"No!"

His claws on my hips made it clear that "no" wasn't an option. He pulled me to the edge of the bed and then shoved his dick inside, hitting my hips with his and pressing me into the mattress. He sighed loudly into my neck, and I couldn't hold a moan when he moved back. My hands were shaking and holding me up, the lower part of my belly burning and pulsating, not giving a single fuck that I didn't agree to this. My body welcomed his with admiration. It twisted my mind.

"I hate you," I whispered, my lips trembling with hurt. His fingers squeezed my neck with familiarity.

His heavy breathing brought back the memories of our first night, but his soft clawless hands broke the sensation. His fingers were rough and sent shivers down my skin. They pressed me further onto him, setting the rhythm, and I followed it and let go. I started moving with him, allowing him to push deeper, harder. I wasn't scared of his desire to go wild, and even when the claws dag into my hips I only felt more fire burning somewhere deep. I shut my eyes and bit my lips trying to hold the cry inside. I heard other couples go through their own agony, and it only sharpened my own. Heavy female breathing and moans ricocheted against my nerves, and sweat ran down my spine as I felt a tight knot of a close orgasm form down my stomach. I froze, but Aaron didn't even notice it. There was no way back for any of us...

I didn't scream when it washed over me, I couldn't even draw a breath. The world narrowed to just the two of us, and I thought I'm not going to make it. An incredible relief overtook me with the first spasm, and I trembled in his arms. Beast breathed heavily into my neck, growling, and then suddenly... bit it.

***

I felt him licking the wound, covering my jaw with open-mouth kisses, tracing my stomach with his fingers, and breathing heavily. I couldn't move. It was as if all of my muscles, bones, nerves were removed and replaced by pasta. Nerves were the first ones to come back to life. Beast was getting me back into the dress. I moaned when he picked me up and carried me to the exit. I preferred to close my eyes and hide my face in his neck because looking at the lights was physically painful.

Soon I breathed in the cool night air and shivered in his arms. A low male voice asked something. A door of a car opened, and Aaron sat on the back seat with me in his hands. I heard another sound.

"Go," he demanded, and the car moved. "I need a medical kit."

The smell of antiseptics almost overpowered the familiar smell of musk. It long stopped being flowery and faint and was now heavy and expensive.

"This... All over again," I cried, barely lifting my head up. The neck didn't hurt as much as the last time, but it didn't make it much better. "You're making it so difficult, Mr. Houwer."

"You're not the one to talk," he whispered. He carefully lifted my head and settled it comfortably on his shoulder. He ripped a pack of bandages and stuck one onto my neck. As he was looking at it I was looking at him. Although he was a bastard, he was a handsome one. He was warm and cozy... The lower part of my stomach tensed, and Aaron suddenly looked me in the eyes and clenched his teeth.

"The flight is in an hour and a half," Mr. Knife declared from the front seat.

"Great, thank you," Aaron replied.

"Let me go," I asked and started moving, feeling my strength return to me.

"No," he replied. The strength was gone with his single word.

"You have a flight soon anyway," I argued and winced.

"We have a flight," he corrected.

It took me a couple of seconds to get it, and then I straightened up.

"I can't fly anywhere with you… I'm not wearing underwear…" I whispered.

His face sharpened in a very attractive manner, and his eyes flashed. He sighed and licked his lips. I obviously threw him off-balance.

"We'll buy you some," he promised hoarsely.

"In the airport?"

It felt right to speak about things that didn't matter because I was terrified of asking where he was bringing me and for what reason.

"No, we're not going there. Trust me…"

"It's not like you leave me a choice."

"Right."

"My ass hurts," I informed him and raised an eyebrow.

"Wait a little bit," he said, steady and cool again, "or, if you prefer, I could lick all your wounds here."

Now he was the one to catch me off guard.

Getting out of the car was a show on its own because I tried to keep the dress down. It was quite cold on the runway and the wind was blowing. Aaron walked me to a private jet.

I realized I needed to call Bunny but forgot about it straight away. I had bigger problems, and one of them was the unusual task of going up the stairs in a short dress with no underwear.

"Come on," Beast held me close and almost carried me inside. "Make yourself at home," he said, put me down in a room, which looked like a hallway, and went back down the stairs.

I immediately went further in, further away from the cold wind. A flight attendant stepped out to greet me.

"Miss Melory," he called, made way for me, and showed me the "room". "Make yourself comfortable. In the far corner of the cabin you can see a door to the bedroom and the restroom. Would you like something to drink?"

"Tea, please," I said as I wrapped my arms around my body. "Where is Mr. Houwer going?"

"Apollynis," he replied with confusion.

It was a high-class ski resort on the other side of the country.

"Alright, thanks," I muttered. I was hoping to just walk around this private jet and go home. I didn't expect a carpet under my feet and a full-on luxurious hotel room in front of my eyes. And it would all be great if not for the stinging sensation between my legs. "Can I go to the bathroom?"

"Of course. Are you going to take your tea in the bedroom?"

I laughed throwing my head back, but it didn't bother the flight attendant.

"Excuse me, I... drank too much," I said and touched my lips.

He smiled politely and replied, "That's okay. I'll show you where the bathroom is."

The bedroom was out of this world. It wasn't narrow or small, it was huge and cozy and it had a king bed and a wardrobe, and a desk. It was light beige with a lot of wood detailing.

"Incredible," I commented.

"You can find towels here," he instructed and demonstrated. "Here is your tea. Should I tell Mr. Houwer you're taking a shower?"

What for? So he doesn't bother me or so he can join in?

"Yes."

"Have a great rest."

The bathroom was just as big. There were a shower and a sink made of natural stone, so I quite liked it.

Hot water made it painfully obvious that I was left with lots of small reminders from our last sex. The owner of these autographs soon came in himself. He was silent, but I thought that I didn't hear him because of the water. I slipped out of the shower as he washed his hands standing with his back to me. I almost managed to grab the towel, but Beast, who, apparently, was not taught any manners, turned and stared at me.

I froze with my arm stretched, stopped by his gaze, unable to move. I saw his breathing quicken and his eyes go dark. When they flashed red, I shut my eyes, grabbed the towel, and jumped back into the shower.

"Thea," he called, coming closer. "Am I that scary?"

"Your eyes are," I replied breathing heavily and shaking.

"It doesn't mean anything..."

"What doesn't?"

"The eyes don't mean anything..."

"Haven't you seen yourself in the mirror for a while?" I asked. I needed another towel, but I didn't want to get out of where I was. "Your eyes are flashing, shining, flaming..."

"Come out," he ordered coldly after a small pause. "We're taking off soon."

He left the bathroom, and I finished drying myself. I covered my hair with another towel and carefully stepped into the bedroom. Aaron was there with his t-shirt off, only in his jeans.

"Not a lot of people see the eyes. They change from emotions," he stated with slight displeasure. I noticed him holding a medical kit in his hands. "Come here."

"You're scaring me again," I said and slowly walked to the bed.

"Lay down," he demanded, and I almost choked on adrenaline that was set free into my veins with his order.

"Let's not," I said and took a step back to the door.

"No," he countered and looked at me. "No options."

I clenched the towel knot on my chest and put my hand forward.

"I don't want to... like this..."

"You will have marks on your skin," he stated matter-of-factly. "And you have a job that doesn't allow it..."

I swallowed loudly.

"So, the bite mark on the neck disappeared because you..."

"Oh yeah. I wasn't kidding when I said it needs to be licked..."

"Oh my god," I exclaimed, rolling my eyes.

"He isn't going to help us here," he joked and grinned. "Lay down."

"Just..." I mumbled, breathing hard. "Can we... not have sex..."

He closed his eyes and frowned.

"No, and I know you want it, too. Your reaction today..."

"I don't understand what you're doing to me!" I cried.

"I can't control myself!" he replied. "I haven't touched you for all that time! Do you want me to rip you with the claws?! I already have your blood on my hands, Thea!"

I jumped back and hit my back on the bathroom door. Beast threw the medical kit into the drawer and left the room, shutting the door behind him.

*** 

Never in my life have I watched the takeoff from a bedroom. I just got slightly pressed into the bedframe, but that was it. Soon I could see the beautiful lights of night Cryton, and that's when it hit me. I didn't call Bunny.

"Fuck," I muttered and grimaced. It certainly would be a long flight, and he's going to go mad from worry if I don't come back home. "Fuck, fuck, fuck…"

When everything outside the aircraft went dark I finally turned to look at the door. Staying alone in the bedroom scared me more than being next to Beast. The last time he broke something heavy in the hotel, what are the chances he's going to do the same shit here? I was getting on his nerves, and nervous beasts, no doubt, are uncontrollable. I put the dress back on and walked into the living room. I really tried to forget the fact that I was not wearing anything underneath.

Aaron was sitting at an empty table wearing only jeans and looking out of the window. I walked to the chair on the opposite side and sat down.

"Hi," I said, folding my hands on the table and looking up. He didn't reply but frowned. "Let's talk."

"I just calmed down, Thea… We are in the air, I can't really break anything here."

"I was thinking about that. It's a good reason for us to try and be civil and talk…"

Aaron looked unfamiliar: he was desperate, so on edge, he could explode any moment. His attractive muscles were tense and sharply defined by light.

"Nothing I say helps…"

"You can start with an explanation of what's going on with us," I asked calmly.

He finally brought his gaze back to me.

"After the hospital and after the first bite we are bonded, and this connection, this bond is only getting stronger, it demands attention..."

"You told me that women of my kind are a luxurious treat."

"Whoever said that obviously had no idea."

I smiled.

"Well, you're no picnic either."

Our eyes met, and I saw a weak smile in the corner of his mouth.

"They buy you lot as if you're an extravagant drug," he started sharply; his eyes flashed red. "It twists the brain inside out, makes you feel everything differently, and then there's passion, so strong it makes you lose your mind..."

His tone made it clear this was not exactly what he'd dreamed of. I regretted deciding to try and negotiate on the plane. From the sound of it, it would be easier for him to just put a collar on my neck and leave me in some basement so he can fuck me whenever he wants and then simply break another TV and go out into the world wearing his usual Mr. Iceberg demeanor until the bond calls for him again. I was sure that my freedom was not the only important thing in question. Would it only be a matter of time before he actually did all of it?

I curled in the armchair.

"Where are we going?" I asked. I didn't look at him.

"Mountains..."

"Why?"

I wanted to just leave and hide in the bedroom again.

"To spend time together."

"In that case, we can turn back," I chuckled.

"Thea, there's no way back," he said, and I lifted my glare at him. "I'm not going to give you up."

"Aaron," I replied, taking a deep breath and sitting straight, "I don't know what to expect of you, do you understand that?"

"I do."

"There are different ways to 'not give me up,' and one of them is locking me up in some basement…"

He closed his eyes and frowned.

"Let's do it a different way," he started as he straightened in his chair and looked at me. "I'll prepare a contract…"

That sounded like a good business approach.

"How do I know you can't break it?" I said. Contracts were my favorite part of work.

"I can't," he replied. He smirked. His eyes were shining.

"Alright."

I licked my lips.

"Are you sure?" he asked and grinned. "I could put anything in there."

"Do you suggest I run away into the shower again?" I snarled. "Why are you trying to scare me?"

"Because you somehow are still under the impression that everything can be as it was," he said, moving slightly forward. "At least during the day."

I swallowed when he stood up.

"Does your ass still hurt?" he asked.

"Not as much, you know how to distract," I said and curled deeper into the armchair.

"Come here."

"Nope."

Beast grinned.

"Oh, don't you play tag with me…"

"Aaron!" I screamed, fear overtaking me.

"I think you need to take a closer look on the subject of the contract," he said and took a step towards me, picking me up from the armchair. I bumped into his chest and was suddenly in his arms. He pushed the bedroom door with his shoulder and put me down onto the bed. "Don't move."

"Aaron," I sighed, but he was already on top of me.

"Calm down," he said and looked me in the eyes, "and feel."

So far I'd felt my heart beating hysterically and fear overtaking me and making me want to beg him not to touch me. However, I knew well enough it wouldn't stop him.

"Close your eyes," he said and pulled the dress up leaving my legs and ass bare. I squeezed my legs together. "Shhhh…" His hot palms stroke my hips, and I felt him kissing right next to where his hand was and then licking it.

My back arched from a strong spasm down my belly, and I moaned, clenching the bedcover.

"Aaron… Don't…"

He did it again, moving onto the next scratch. His hand slid between my thighs, right to the hot center, warm and wet. His other hand moved the dress out of the way and squeezed my breast. It was as if I hadn't just had sex a couple of hours ago, as if I hadn't had sex for years even. Strong wild desire spilled into my veins. He turned me to face him and took the dress off.

"Do you get it?" he asked, looking me in the eyes.

I didn't understand anything anymore. My eyes were closing and everything around looked as if I was watching it through thick white fog.

"Not really," I whispered. "Explain again…"

I was tired of jumping and screaming and being terrified, and this was such a perfect way to switch my brain off. It was better than any antidepressants.

Beast leaned to my neck and tore the bandage off. I felt obedient vibration between my legs. When he touched the mark with his lips I cried and clenched onto his shoulders.

"Please…"

"What, leave?" he asked and bit the skin, sending a wave of burning warmth down my body. "Should I leave you alone?"

"No…"

"No? Or yes?"

"Beast… Jerk…"

His satisfied smirk hit my nerves. He wasn't in a hurry. He left my neck and moved on to my breasts. I should've already been into my right mind, out of the trance he drove me into, but I had no desire to break free anymore. He felt that and relaxed, became more confident and rougher. He let his own desire go.

When he backed off to get rid of his jeans, I opened my eyes and shivered from the cold air he left behind. I was struck with a sudden thought that it would always be like this, but it was forgotten as soon as I saw his glare. It promised me a challenge, and I was ready for one. Beast leaned closer, and I could feel his breathing on my lips.

"Brave girl," he whispered with a smirk. "Come here." He pulled me up and flipped me to face him. "Look at me." His hot hands grabbed my hips and lifted me, pulling me closer. I squeezed his shoulders, my sweaty palms sliding down them, and made an unsuccessful attempt to get away. I didn't want to be face to face with him and wished I had my head pressed into a pillow. "Sh…" he whispered disapprovingly and caught my hair in his fist.

"Aaron," I said, shaking and blinking fast in confusion.

"I like it when you say my name," he replied and smiled. He then frowned, pressed me into his chest, and filled me with one long movement. My knees pushed into the mattress and my back arched. I closed my eyes, but he returned his hand to the back of my head.

"Look at me," he demanded and rocked his hips up. "You're mine." Another rough movement got a scream out of me, and I was silenced with a tender kiss.

He was impossible to let go with: he was harsh and tender, his fingers were soft and sensitive, but he burned my skin with his bites only to cool it down with kisses. It drove me mad. Aaron didn't let me take a breath, he caught every emotion, he demanded me to open up, he explored me. It seemed like our first time as if the man who took me against my will was a different man. This one almost seemed careful. I trembled from his movement, wrapping myself around him, and he was tender. He accepted the hell we were in and he took me there with him. He was hungrily thrusting inside me. His husky breaths hit my neck, and the moment we both were about to fall over the edge, he pushed me to my back and clashed our hips together in one strong motion. He left a path of small stingy bites on my neck, and I shook in his arms with my eyes wide open. He didn't let me go and didn't stop, and I trembled on him like a butterfly on a needle. It was a moment of despair, a moment I had no mind of my own, no power, no free will...

The first thing that came back was the monotonous hum of the airplane. Next, I finally started to feel my body again and realized it didn't belong to me. I was pressed against Aaron's chest. He was breathing hard, and his heart was pounding right next to my ear.

"You have a heart," I mumbled.

He smirked.

"I had no idea."

"Oh, is it that bad? Do you also eat virgins on Saturdays?"

He chuckled.

"Almost."

"Why don't you try and give me some hope that you're better than you are?"

"Yes, I do eat virgins on Saturdays."

Now I was smiling, although it was still incredibly difficult to move.

"What are you doing to me?" I asked as I tried to move in his grip.

"I'm fucking you, Thea. That's what it's called."

"I know what it's called," I snapped. I tried to break free of his arms, but he only tightened them more around my ribs. "I feel like I've taken a pack of sleeping pills!"

He went silent for a short while.

"Intense emotions, your body reactions, orgasm… It's normal."

"Does Grace have the same reaction?" I asked innocently. I almost sounded like I was in a business meeting, but then I felt a tight lump in my throat I could hardly swallow.

"I don't know…" he replied. His fingers on the back of my head tangled in my hair, his body tensed and his breathing was hard again.

"What do you mean?" I asked and frowned.

"She's a virgin," he hissed and grabbed my neck with his hand. "Shut up, Thea," he growled into my ear.

"Why?" I asked and swallowed loudly.

"Because I'm going to fuck you now… Again…"

"How lucky for you to have me around!"

His angry animalistic growl and vibration it sent through my body were strange, but not new. It was like a horror film, where a predator was about to take a leap to his prey. He did. One second later I was on the bed face down, my screams dry, not enough air left in my lungs. He wasn't hurting me, but whatever he did was sharp, wild, and madness-inducing. It was surprising I hadn't yet died in his arms. The bed was a mess, and it reminded me of my own soul. Throughout the night Beast torn it to pieces, and in return, I got three ecstatic orgasms which left me unable to breathe and move.

I found enough energy and whispered, "Your virgin would be so happy…"

****

"Thea, we're here."

I flinched, sat up, and frowned. Aaron didn't turn the lights on, and I only saw his silhouette in the doorframe.

"Get ready."

My head hurt as if I'd drunk myself to blackout the night before. I quickly managed to make myself as presentable as possible and walked into the living room, wrapping the short jacket around my body. If I could exchange it for a nice set of underwear, I would. When we went on to the stairs I wasn't so sure anymore. Icy morning wind pierced through the air and if not for Aaron's strong figure near me, I would probably go flying with it. Instead of a normal car, there was a tall jeep. It seemed like a mockery and another attempt to humiliate me.

"What's going on?" Aaron asked when the door shut behind us.

"Nothing," I replied and turned away.

He wasn't satisfied with the answer. I contained my scream when he grabbed me by the waist and sat me down on his lap. I guess I was getting used to it all.

"Thea, if I'm asking you, then you probably should give an answer that makes sense," he growled into my ear.

"Why are you so mad?" I replied and put my hurting head on his shoulder. "I just have a headache! Probably something I drank yesterday wasn't very good…"

He took a deep breath and sighed.

"I'll find you some painkillers when we're there."

He didn't let me go, ran his fingers into my hair, and started to massage my neck. "Tell me if it hurts."

When he pulled the hair slightly, I let out a quiet moan. My eyelids grew heavy, but I tried to stay awake, watching the landscape outside the window as the sun was rising. What's happening? What did my life come to? What had I done to be thrown into this mess?

I blinked and the fog disappeared. I returned to watching the scenery.

It was breathtaking. Apollynis was a small and cozy town in a picturesque valley surrounded by a mountain range. The first ray of sunshine was peeking between two mountain tops as if representing my silly hope that everything would be alright and the sun would come out. I licked my lips. I wanted to breathe in the cold air but instead felt my heart beating from the man's smell. I would forever remember this moment like that — the marvelous breathtaking beauty of nature and Beast's smell, his arms, his breathing, and my loud heartbeat. He carefully put his other hand on my chin. I thought that he could do whatever he put his mind to. I had no power to fight.

The car was moving down the road, but no more than fifteen minutes later we entered a small town full of "gingerbread" houses. If I was here in different circumstances, I would smile, but as of this moment, I was indifferently looking at the signs and miniature backyards, and the warm glow of windows. The snow was white and crispy under the tires of the car, and the town was covered in it.

When Apollynis was left behind, the coziness disappeared. I was frowning, looking at the endless forest of snowy trees. I felt goosebumps down my back although the heating in the car was on.

"Thea, everything is fine."

I flinched in his arms. I wasn't terrified as I'd been before, and I didn't know why. Being in his arms was different and it made it incredibly hard to remember the despair and sadness I felt yesterday. I was, however, determined to dig them back out.

"What's the plan?" I asked.

"Whatever you want…"

"I want to go home."

"No," he replied. Well, good chat. "There are limitations."

"See?" I asked and took an opportunity to get away from his lap.

"If you don't want anything, I'm going to start making my wishes true…"

Beast really widened the range of my reactions. A small electric charge went through my spine and I felt cold after being in the warmth of his arms.

"I want coffee, some painkillers, food, and sleep!" I snarled, getting as far away from him as I could.

"See," he said with a satisfied smirk, "that wasn't that difficult."

With all the arguments I didn't notice the car pulling into the driveway in front of a magical castle lit by the rising sun.

"Quick," Aaron ordered, opened my door, and dragged me inside.

The hall was not what I'd expected. My high-heels were painfully loud against the stone floor. It really looked like a medieval castle. The light was dim, the ceiling — dark and covered with wooden beams, and the reception desk was right in the middle of the room. The air in the building was slightly damp, but it smelled of pine. I wasn't sure if it was a perfume or a freshly gathered bouquet on the desk. It also smelled of food and fire, and it made my stomach turn.

"Mr. Houwer," the man behind the reception desk said, smiling. "Welcome!"

"Mr. Rosenberg," Aaron replied, shaking the other man's hand.

"Miss Theana," the man acknowledged and gave me a polite nod.

I didn't have enough energy to be as polite, so I just said, "Hi."

I really wanted, however, to be sarcastic and ask for the keys to my cell.

"It's ready," the man declared and pointed to the side. "Would you like breakfast?"

"Yes, something substantial. I need to put some meat on her," Aaron commented with a smirk and walked me through the hall.

"Yeah, not going to happen," I snarled with little enthusiasm as I looked around. "I have a contract with an agent."

"So, you should always stay the same size?" he asked with sudden interest.

"Yes," I replied as we walked from an arch at the end of the hall.

"Not smaller, not bigger?"

"Yeah, something like that. It's a job."

"It's always so difficult with you, Theana," he confessed as we walked to the elevator. Its black shiny doors reflected our dark duet.

"You too, Aaron. And you always damage the subject of my contract with my agent."

Standing next to him in the elevator, I knew with unexpected clarity that this man made me feel two drastically different things — he made me want to run when he was close, and made me want to stay with him when there was no more chance to run, and not only because I knew he wouldn't let go.

"The mark will heal," he said and let me out of the elevator. "Do you want a separate room?"

"No," I replied and froze in the middle of a light corridor so different from the one downstairs. The carpet was grey as well as the walls. There were chandeliers, paintings, soft shapes. It actually looked like a five-star hotel.

I didn't quite realize he wasn't following me. As I turned, I saw him standing two steps behind.

"I thought you'd choose a separate room," he noted with an admiring smile.

"I don't want to stay in my room and shake in fear waiting for you to arrive," I said and shrugged. "I'm tired of being scared for today. I know you'll come anyway and you'll do whatever you want to do, so what's the point of running away?"

Beast slowly approached me, looking me straight in the eyes.

"It's like you only have one day to live, Theana. It's all or nothing for you. You are afraid, but you still move forward. My brain hurts from trying to understand you."

"Well, that's how I live. And I didn't ask you to..."

"You can't live like that with me," he interrupted. He didn't even question that I would live with him. "I'm not going to allow it."

"Aaron, why do you care how I live outside of our meeting? Or are you controlling that too now?"

I suddenly staggered, but he caught me before I stumbled to the floor.

"Let's make a deal. We both shut up until tomorrow," he said, picking me up and carrying me down the corridor. "I don't work for a modeling agency, but I also have a job I get tired of, Thea..."

I chuckled and replied, "That's nice, Mr. Houwer. So, we don't talk? At all?"

"Yes," he said and pushed the door.

I love attic rooms, and that room took my breath away. It was light and spacious, the floor was nice wood that made me want to kick my shoes off and walk barefoot. It had a soft couch and a clean fireplace, and it was fresh and airy.

Aaron lowered me to the couch and walked to the landline phone near the entrance.

"Can you please bring everything from the lady's room to mine? Thank you."

I put my legs down and turned to him.

"You told me we're not talking," I reminded him.

He walked to me and sat on the floor near me.

"Starting this moment, we are not," he said and looked me in the eyes. "We are obviously bad at talking to each other."

"I…"

"Shut up, Thea," he interrupted. "This place is for listening and being silent, but not for talking."

"Who should I listen to if we're not talking?"

"Well, words are not the only way to talk. Now close your mouth."

What the fuck?! I felt lighting coming out of my eyes, and his flashed with familiar satisfied flame. He was looking me in the eyes for a couple more seconds and then started taking my shoes off. That's when it finally hit me that I got myself into a rather interesting situation! I hadn't even asked him what would happen if I didn't agree to this stupid experiment. Seemed like he just wanted a silent body to fuck and not annoy him on this marvelous snowy day. He also seemed very pleased with himself, and I saw a smirk in the corner of his mouth. When he touched my feet with his hot hands, I flinched. Aaron frowned, stood up, and went into the depths of the room. I soon heard the sound of water.

Someone knocked on the door.

"Good afternoon," a room service man said and smiled. "Your breakfast and your purchases..."

I had no idea if I could talk to anyone else, so I just gestured for him to come in. Aaron had already come back and was standing behind me, watching the breakfast being set up. The water was still pouring in the background. Was he making a bath? Did he think I was going to get into it? He should've asked me first! I wanted food and no bath!

When his hands appeared on my waist, I slapped them but was immediately reminded I shouldn't be cheeky. Aaron grabbed me and turned me, pressing my back against the wall. He was right when he said that words weren't the only way to talk. His glare told me that if I didn't do what he wanted I would become another virgin on his Saturday morning breakfast table, even though I wasn't one. He undressed me and carried me to the bathroom. I sighed.

The bathroom was only slightly smaller than the living room. The panoramic window opened to a snowy forest and mountain range behind it lit by the bright sunshine. The floor was warm, I realized when Aaron put me down to test the water. Maybe he had hoped I'd get in by myself. When he turned and looked at me, I felt silly. Maybe it was silly, trying to cover up from the gaze of a man I had sex with, but I wanted to feel a little less naked, so I got into the tub.

When I saw his smirk, I frowned, realizing he was training me like a dog! Without much thought, I made a loud splash that left Beast soaking wet. His eyes were speaking volumes. I even moved into the furthest corner of the tub, but Aaron just shook his head, got a towel, and left. I didn't stay there long myself. As soon as I got warm, I wrapped a robe around my body and walked into the room. It was warmer too, and it smelled like smoke. I then saw the wood slowly burning in the fireplace. Beast was on the couch with a wine glass in his hand... absolutely naked. He raised his eyebrow at my frozen form and silently ordered me to sit down.

Our little silence treaty opened up new horizons. At this exact moment, I would have hissed at him and he would have stopped me, but all I could do is stare at him and go through a weird withdrawal. His perfect body excited me, his careful and attentive eyes didn't let me breathe. My glare was going back and forth from him to the table, and then I finally settled on looking at the fireplace, a sandwich and a cup of coffee in my hands. I hadn't yet finished eating when I was struck by a painful thought that I hadn't called Bunny.

Aaron watched my dash to the clutch and continued drinking his wine. I had no messages and no calls, and it was strange. I first thought that there was no connection here, but then I texted him, and the text was immediately sent.

*Bunny, I'm fine, I'm with Aaron.*

I didn't make it back to the armchair when the phone rang, but I declined.

*Can't speak rn. Everything is fine.*

*I know you're with Aaron. He called yesterday.*

I froze halfway to the chair and stared at Beast. He really looked like a predator. He was full and satisfied. He lay down on the couch, keeping himself up on one elbow, absolutely shameless about his naked body. I blinked fast to make myself stop looking at the tight muscles on his stomach and dark hair leading its way down... I swore silently, rolled my eyes, and looked back at the screen.

*Did he? What did he say?*

*That you're going to Apollynis for the weekend, and that he'll return you tomorrow evening.*

My lips curled into a smile.

*I asked him to give you the phone, but he said you weren't sober enough. He threatened to punch me if I ever let you go to an event like that again.*

It was good that I wasn't allowed to talk, because I don't think I could at that moment. I sat back down and continued having breakfast, making sure to not look at the concentration of testosterone laying down on the couch. It didn't sit well in my head that Aaron actually worried enough about me to call Bunny. The man, who obviously didn't care about my world and my life, had suddenly done something that made me doubt that. He hadn't told me anything, but had called my friend and let him know I was fine. Even promised to return me!

I took the last sip and turned to catch his gaze. As soon as our glares crossed, his eyes flashed with familiar sparks.

I thought that he was impossible and shook my head, pursing my lips.

He smirked, stood up, and walked to the bags in the corner. I watched him go there and back and when he gestured me to come closer, I had to reluctantly stand up. Seemed like whatever was in the bags was meant for me, and he was now suggesting I should take a look. He lay back down ready to observe my next action. He wasn't looking for approval but wanted to spark interest in me. He certainly succeeded. There was black lace lingerie with three small black stones between the cups. It could be trivial without them, but it was incredible and reminded me of our shared trigger. It was from Wayne Amolli, the exact brand I wore standing in front of his fiancee, humiliated. I felt satisfied.

I stared at Beast, but couldn't out-stare him, and lost again. I let a tense sigh out and started to go through another bag. There was nothing else that was as meaningful, but I now had a tracksuit, a coat, and a pair of shoes. I needed a break. I felt like too much Aaron Houwer was even more dangerous than not enough of him.

He was too much even in the smallest details, and I was only getting used to that. I felt like being by myself for at least some time, and I was wondering if he would understand.

I took the lingerie and walked into the bedroom, closing the door behind me. It was the middle of the day, but I wanted to sleep, to turn my mind off, to give it time to digest all of this. The phone buzzed in my clutch, but I didn't want to reply. I fell onto the bed and was asleep as soon as the blanket fell over me.

***

I was not destined to get enough sleep.

As soon as I fell asleep I was falling into the abyss, unable to get out, unable to find something to hook onto. I tried to scream, but the scream turned into a broken sob. I tried to get out of the dream, but I couldn't. Then someone caught me. Strong arms cuddled me, harsh fingers pressed into the back of my head, and someone's hot breathing hit my lips, giving me warmth.

"Thea," a hoarse voice said. "Thea, wake up."

I mumbled inaudibly and fell forward, pressing my forehead into someone's chest. My own chest was hurting with warmth as if I just came into the house after being outside for too long.

"Fuck…"

"Everything is okay," Aaron said, his voice confident and calm. I clung to his wrists, desperate not to slip back into the nightmare. "Talk to me."

"I had a nightmare," I replied through clenched teeth. "Wake me up, distract me, slap me, do something!"

He threw the blanket away and picked me up. I realized we were walking somewhere, and hoped he would bring me into the shower. Although I wasn't falling anymore, I still felt as if I was in midair. The shower I'd hoped for didn't happen, because Beast brought me into the living room, sat down, and placed me on his chest.

"Aaron…" I whispered.

"Everything is okay…"

"Everything is bad… I feel bad…"

"That's normal."

Was it normal that I wasn't feeling well?! Great! I snorted and felt better. It was similar to coming back from anesthesia. I could now hear more than just his voice and his heartbeat. His fingers were pushing the muscles on my back, restoring the blood flow. His other hand was massaging the back of my head, and I soon was able to open my eyes.

"Are we talking now?" I asked.

He smiled and I smiled back. It was suddenly warm, calm, comfortable… It was a perfect illusion to fall for. I pressed my hands against his chest and finally was able to see his face without blur.

"I'm not very good with acclimatization…"

"You're not very good with our bond," he objected calmly and tiredly. He didn't seem scared but was now shaking slightly. I stroke his shoulder with my hand trying to catch that feeling. "It's not something you can touch, Thea…"

"You're not happy."

"I've never planned anything like that," he said and shrugged.

"What happened to me?"

"You can't fall asleep without me now."

I swore and straightened up.

"Is there an injection to reverse that? Any pills? Surgery?"

"There is the first couple days…"

"What?!" I shouted. "You knew and didn't do anything?!"

I tried to jump up, but he held me in place.

"I didn't. I couldn't bring someone else's woman in after I bit her. Dewman could! And he was planning on doing that. You could be in bed with him now."

"I'd prefer that!" I replied and twitched in his arms. "At least he didn't have a fiancee and I wouldn't be in between…"

Aaron grabbed my hair and pulled me closer.

"The longer you try and fight, the worse it will be," he growled. "Would you, now?"

"You made a whore out of me!" I shouted and punched him trying to break free. "Why should I care who to sleep with?!"

Talking was a bad idea. Beast's eyes were flaming with red.

"I want to get out of here!" I hissed. "I don't want to be here with you! I hate you!"

I would never forget what happened next. Aaron's face became sharp and his upper lip tightened, showing his fangs. He exhaled and I felt his claws go down my hips. My terrified heartbeat quickened, and an icy gale went through my chest. I jumped up from his lap and leaped to the bedroom door. I tried to lock it behind, but couldn't. My palms were sweaty, and I was shaking from an adrenaline rush. I scanned the room, trying to find something I could use to defend myself, but there was nothing but a heavy candlestick.

No one tried to get inside. Beast didn't come then or an hour later, and the suit was silent. I put the candlestick back and looked outside, hoping there was a way to get out. As soon as I opened the balcony door, the door into the bedroom opened.

"Thea…"

Aaron took a step in, shoving me down with his glare, and I pressed my back to the glass. He didn't come closer and froze in the middle of the bedroom. I could jump out of the balcony any second, but then everything changed. I felt as if I just drank a glass of wine, and it warmed me up from the inside. My legs buckled, my breathing slowed, and all the panic went away. I took a slow breath, hardly managing to stand on shaky legs.

"What are you doing?"

It was sinister. I knew I needed to be terrified because he obviously controlled me, but I couldn't.

"I'm calming you down," he said, his voice emotionless.

"Trying to fix my brain?" I snarled and grimaced.

"Have you stopped hating me yet?" he asked.

I swallowed and tried to get my thoughts straight. I still felt all the same feelings towards him, but I didn't want to run anymore.

"First safety rule, Thea," he started, slowly moving in my direction, "don't run away and don't hide."

The warmth disappeared and I started shaking.

"The second rule, don't tell you'd prefer someone else," he continued, coming so close he could touch me. "Dustin Dewman wouldn't know who you belong to. Would you really prefer to be on his leash?"

"Should I prefer being on yours?" I whispered.

"Does it look like a leash?" he asked. I looked around the room. "You have nothing to compare it to."

"You said Dewman wouldn't know?" I asked and licked my lips.

"I was drawn to you..." he said and leaned forwards. "I made up a stupid excuse to come to Dewman after losing a hell load of blood... He wouldn't let you go," he whispered in my lips. "I'm not planning to either."

I was sure Aaron killed Dewman because Dewman knew that I was marked by someone who was in the fight. He couldn't just demand me back, because it would then be obvious. Turns out that Dustin Dewman would be the best solution for Aaron if he wanted to get rid of me. He would just keep me, remove Aaron's mark, and everyone would be happy. Except me.

"I thought you were planning to kill me... I think you confirmed..."

"I answered your question truthfully then, but it didn't mean I was planning to do that at all..." he replied and put his hand on the glass window close to me.

"You could save me from being your whore," I whispered. I felt a tear go down my cheek. "You apologized for that, but you didn't regret it..."

"I don't regret it now," he said, but his voice wasn't indifferent. He was looking at my face, tearing my soul apart. He even seemed concerned. "I don't want to try and cover it all up. I don't want to hide you, Thea, because it is impossible."

"Are you going to tell everyone?" I asked and smirked skeptically.

He was silent for a little while and then said, "Thea, your life will drastically change the day after tomorrow. Mine will too. Us fighting will only make it worse."

"Fighting? With you?" I repeated, trying to cover up how worried I was. "When was the last time you looked in the mirror?"

"I don't need to look in the mirror to see what you do to me."

"Great, now I'm the one to blame!"

"Just so you know, even Saturday's virgin-eating-session doesn't make the fangs come out."

I chuckled. The tension washed away in a heavy wave, and I almost slid down the glass, but was caught by Aaron and pressed against it.

"People would buy tickets to see you," I whispered and looked him straight in the eyes.

"Well, then we'll always have something to make money with."

I was staring at him and realized how different he looked. He was not the same I had seen him at Dewman's. He still made me shake inside, but he didn't have this lively fire in his eyes. None of his pictures had it, and I was sure I watched over a good hundred of those.

"You want all of it at once."

I still had my brain and my stubbornness, so I felt like I was still myself.

"I know, but the mark doesn't give us much time. It shouldn't be like this…"

"How should it be?" I asked.

"Let's have dinner and I'll tell you."

"Any flying glasses available?" I chuckled.

He smiled and took my hand.

"Have you ever heard of Beauty and the Beast, Thea? I'm your beast. And if you throw glasses and break them, I will turn into a dangerous one."

The fireplace still made the room lighter. Aaron sat me down on the couch and got on his knees.

"If I stay human or turn into the beast depends on you."

"Sounds like a scary fairytale, Mr. Houwer," I said and swallowed.

"Nobody said it was easy, Thea," he replied and grinned.

"Oh, sure no, you said it would be hell," I said and watched him lift the tracksuit from the floor.

"We both are in our own versions of it," he explained and looked at me, stretching the leggings out for me to take. "Yours is trying to keep control over your life, trying to be free and not submit."

He watched me get dressed.

"And yours?"

"Mine," he said and zipped my hoodie up, "is that I can't control myself, and it's not something that's allowed for people like me."

I never thought that it's possible to dress someone so sensually. The zipper in his fingers was gliding up, connecting the parts of the jacket and tensing my trembling nerves.

"Why? Would you completely lose your temper?"

"Yes, and I wouldn't come back," he said and looked me in the eyes.

"The fairytale just gets scarier," I declared.

"I'm a Prime, Thea. It means I'm the head of our hierarchy. People don't only obey me because of my status, although it's important too."

"You are a little bit like animals..."

"We are," he replied and nodded. "Prime's power is an important part of how our families survive. The families are bigger than the human ones, the connection is stronger. If I am weak, it will change everyone's lives."

"Why shouldn't you bond with someone like me?"

"Because the instinct of making a complete and perfect match is more powerful than those lower in the hierarchy have. I wouldn't go for it, but the circumstances changed it," he said. "That night the blood loss left thirst, hunger, and the instinct of trying to find a genetically perfect woman overtook, was left uncontrollable. Then I saw you..."

I closed my eyes and lifted my head. He grabbed my neck, pulled me closer, and touched the mark with his nose, inhaling.

"I thought I could ignore you, then I hoped I could make you submit, but it's not the way to go," he whispered and his fingers squeezed my neck slightly. I wasn't moving. I knew he wasn't dangerous. "It's not the way to go with you. Your emotions hit me, and your fear burns anything human I have inside, and it's almost impossible to control the monster when it wants to do everything only to be near you.”

“What happens to those who don’t manage to control the monster?”

“They’re sentenced to death.”

“Aaron… Stop, I can’t…” I said and blinked.

He hugged me.

“See, I can’t even explain it without terrifying you.”

“Because this is all horrible and difficult to comprehend…” I replied. I started to get used to my reactions. “Let’s do the silence thing again?”

***

The dinner went surprisingly well, and all the glasses were left intact. It could’ve been because we kept silent or simply because we were both tired. I felt as if I was run over by a truck.

Inevitability… It wasn’t the first time I felt it. Never before, however, was I bonded with a man whom I could never run away from. I didn’t quite think that I wouldn’t be able to live without him, because one nightmare was really not that big of a deal, considering how many of them I had in my time. What was surprising was the way he could control how I felt.

I already had regrets about suggesting we kept silent again because after a nice dinner the reality seemed more digestible. It was nice to think I wouldn’t need to struggle financially again. Lots of people would probably do lots of things to be at a luxurious resort with an attractive billionaire. They also probably wouldn’t care he sometimes growled and scratched.

All of those calming thoughts shattered as soon as I looked at Aaron. His gaze was a deadly trap in the light of the candles. A deadly trap lined with sparkling stars. One step, and there it was, the abyss I fell into in my dream. I wasn’t stupid to think that it would be easy. He wasn't just an attractive billionaire. He was the beast. I knew I sensed him better and better, although I tried not to notice it. The smell of spices and citrus, vanilla, and pine, all mashed together, replaced the air I was breathing. It changed and became stronger and more complex. It was more powerful when we fought and more delicate in the rare peace. It gave no false impression that this would ever be over. It was like a death sentence. It wouldn't be a direct one if I managed to tame the beast. He wanted me to. He was wild but so fragile at this moment.

I remembered his words. Those who can't keep the monster inside are sentenced to death.

His words were carved into the back of my mind, and I wasn't sure whether it was a terrifying warning... or a hope for freedom.

***

The evening ended on the plane. Someone called Aaron and, judging from his face when he picked up, he didn't like it. It wasn't a work call either. No one has a face like that unless it's about someone important. Beasts were quite like humans in that regard.

Had something happened to Grace?

Aaron didn't speak for long, just a couple of phrases, but then he took my hand and walked me to the room. Fifteen minutes later we were in the car. He continued our little game of silence, but right then I was happy with it. The weekend was over, and my tender Beast was gone with it. This weekend he tried his best, and it was over now. The man I entered the jet with was a more familiar, strong, put-together "steel" Aaron Houwer.

Prime. It was obvious. Someone like him could only be superior, the best, with no weaknesses and addictions, with a well-thought-out strategy and total control. I had a feeling I had no idea what I got myself into. Mr. Knife was right about that...

As soon as we got onto the aircraft I went into the bedroom and walked back and forth waiting for a plane to take off. I lay down, but sleep didn't come. I was thinking about what would happen next. I had no idea what tomorrow would bring, and it really shook me. My whole life I had been trying to avoid that, to stay down to earth and be steady, but right now it wasn't working.

I didn't know how long I was napping, but I then suddenly felt the bed sag under another person's weight. Aaron carefully crawled under the blanket and pulled me closer. I tried to flinch, but the time when my wishes counted was over. He squeezed me in his arms and froze. His breathing became heavier and faster, it burned my neck, excited me, bringing something unknown up from the depths of my soul. Technically, I had a choice. I could stand up and leave, but I felt free in his arms. It was as if my jail was far away from him, outside, and he was what gave me real life.

I arched pressing my body into his, and he broke. It was the first time it hadn't scared me. It was like drinking a glass of a strong cocktail in one sitting. I had no more thoughts, and his rough fingers on my hips and his teeth on my neck were the most appropriate thing ever. As soon as I obeyed him, his claws turned into tender fingers, and instead of his teeth, I felt his lips kissing me, driving me crazy. I could as well be the one to let the claws out from his touch. My fingers grabbed the covers, hoarse moans came out of my throat, changing into screams when Beast plunged inside me.

He made me an animal. I'd never felt this much hunger for intimacy. Our bodies clashed, but it didn't feel like enough. I was twisting and writhing in his arms, pushing back and forcing more of his cock into me. I then bit his neck, and melted away in sweet revenge and a breathtaking orgasm...

***

It seemed as if I spent an eternity on that plane. The quiet humming of the engine became as familiar as silence. So did Aaron's lips on my neck, his fingers in my hair, and his body next to mine.

"Good morning," he said hoarsely into my ear. "We're back."

I took a deep breath, torn apart by emotions. Part of me wished I could stay next to his warmth forever and at the moment it was winning over the part which was supposed to be happy about finally being free.

"Get ready," he ordered. That put a stop to my inner dialogue and took all the warmth away, leaving me blinking at the dim light coming out of the window.

My body hurt, but the pain was pleasant and reminded me of the sex marathon we had last night. I'd never thought I had so much hunger in me.

"Damn," I swore, shook my hair, and got out of the bed.

When the water stopped in the bathroom, I came in and suddenly realized that none of my desires had disappeared. Aaron was standing in front of the mirror and drying his face with a towel, and I swallowed hard at the sight of his body.

"That's fucking ridiculous," I muttered and pressed my lips together.

"Are you always like this in the mornings?" he replied turning to look at me.

"I'd think about my next words if I were you," I threatened and took a step to the mirror, not looking forward to seeing my reflection.

Strangely, the sight was rather pleasant. Fresh air certainly was good for me. No bags under the glowing eyes. I could do a shoot right there and then.

"Why?" he asked and closed the gap between us, but I jumped away.

"Please, don't touch me, I don't feel well," I said and took a deep breath.

"Would you like some coffee?" he offered, frowning.

"Yeah, that'd be lovely…"

I suddenly became aware of bright bruises on his neck, and my nerves gave up.

"Oh, God…" I whispered and started slowly sinking onto the floor when Aaron picked me up.

"Calm down, Thea," he said, sat down on the floor, and looked me in the eyes. "It's okay."

"I bit you!"

"And that's fine," he repeated. "I'm yours, and you marked me."

"I don't usually mark my men!" I squealed.

"I'm special then," he commented and let out a satisfied grin. He then touched my forehead with his own. "Everything is perfectly fine, so don't worry."

I was trying not to, but it was hardly working.

"Am I contagious?"

"I would punish you for saying this, but we have no time for that," he commented with a smirk. "So I'll have to leave it for later. Come on, I'll see you out there…"

I calmed down surprisingly quickly, considering everything. I suppose, my nervous system got better at dealing with all of this. It wasn't even a big deal that I'd bit him. People also leave marks on their partners. Aaron would now have the pleasure of explaining this to his fiancee. I walked into the living room in full tranquility. He was waiting for me at the table. The armchair where I sat last time we tried to negotiate was now assigned to me, and there was a cup of coffee expecting me there.

"You should pack tonight; you're moving into my place."

I clenched my teeth and squeezed the cup in my fingers.

"I don't want to move in with you."

"Thea, stop that," he said. He wasn't in his full-on beast mode, but there was a warning in his voice. "I asked you to not fight with me."

"I can not fight with you the evenings, Aaron," I replied and took a sip of my coffee. "You're working during the day anyway."

I'd noticed a long time ago that whenever I drank coffee the smell, our smell, tended to fade away.

"You're going to sleep with me anyway, so what's the point?"

"There's a point for me. And you promised me a contract."

Aaron's eyes flashed red, but he didn't say anything. He didn't say anything all the way back from the airport. He only spoke when he helped me to get out of the car.

"I'll pick you up at eight, be ready," he said and suddenly pulled me closer. "Please, don't fight with me, Thea..."

"It can be dangerous, I remember," I replied and shook my head, but he didn't let go.

"I need you," he whispered and made me look him in the eyes.

"Aaron, it's just chemistry and physical addiction..."

"You'd be surprised how much easier it is to live with an addiction than with whatever we have," he said and let me go. "See you in the evening."

***

The flat greeted me with grumpy silence, but a second later I heard a loud snore. I found two empty vermouth bottles and some leftovers in the kitchen. I looked around and sat down, exhausted. I knew there was no point in putting up a fight. Aaron would get me out of here anyway. Even now he started to wipe my life out because I didn't feel at home anymore. It was as if I came here only to pack up, just as he told me to...

"Back already?" a hoarse voice said in an accusing tone.

"As you see."

I then heard a loud sigh.

"I'll make breakfast."

"Let me do it," I said and threw my clutch on the floor.

"Okay," my friend replied and hiccupped. "Sorry, I need a shower."

While Bunny was cleaning himself up after his protest against my Friday rendezvous, I managed to tidy the room and fix us some eggs and bacon. He came back shortly, still sleepy and hangover.

"How did it go?" he asked.

I put a cup of coffee in front of him.

"Ambiguously."

"Well, let's look at facts," he muttered. "Where did he take you?"

"Apollynis."

"Wow," my friend said, finally waking up. "It's like a ten-hour flight."

"Nine and a half."

"How was it?"

I sat down opposite him. I didn't want to eat at all.

"I don't know what to say to you. He wants me to pack, and he told me he'll pick me up in the evening..."

"Is he taking you away?" he asked, and now I was certain he was fully awake.

"He's planning to."

"You aren't going with him, are you?" Bunny asked and frowned. "He has a fiancee, Thea! How can you move in with him?! He's getting married in two weeks!"

I had no sound reply to that. I still wasn't sure what Aaron's plan was in regards to Grace. Would he ask me to just accept that?

Marry Grace and sleep with me? Would Grace not resent that? Would I?

I couldn't ask him either, because right that moment I wouldn't accept any of it.

"Do you have any vermouth left?"

"One more bottle… I can't even look at it anymore."

I sat back and pulled the plate closer.

"Did you try to reach an agreement with him?" Bunny asked.

"I suppose," I replied, dragging the fork through the food. "He promised me a contract."

"What's that?" Bunny exclaimed as he pulled my collar down. "Again?"

"I gave as good as I got."

I shouldn't have said it. Bunny would probably not be able to sleep for some time now.

I soon found that I underestimated my friend.

"Well, he deserved that!" he declared.

"He wasn't too upset about it…"

"Let's go for a smoke."

I followed him to the balcony. The city was waking up. It was a lazy Sunday morning, and the treetops were covered with fog, which was slowly slipping onto the alleys. The cold dim sun was slowly rising above it all. Bunny offered me a cigarette, but I shook my head and sat down.

"He asked me to quit."

"Really?! Why does he care?!"

"He told me he hates the smell," I explained and shrugged. "He also has cameras overseeing our balcony."

"So I can give him a middle finger any time I'd like?" Bunny asked and blew out some smoke.

"Well, you can do anything once," I said, breathing in the smell of coffee.

It was as if everything was still like it was before. Morning, our flat, Bunny next to me... I felt my life slip through my fingers into the early-morning fog. The day was going to be sunny and bright, but would my life be?..

"I don't like your attitude," Bunny said and sat down in front of me. "What happened? You were furious only two nights ago..."

"It's pointless, we're connected much stronger than I thought," I replied and touched the mark instinctively. The mark hurt a little be as if in need of touch. "There's no running away from it."

"Is there anything that could be done?"

I looked my friend in the eyes, too afraid to even admit that there was something that could. Aaron's words about the death sentence came back to me, but the thought scared me as if I would have to be the one to get a gun and shoot him.

"I don't know," I said and suddenly realized that maybe Aaron could not only see us but also hear. "Let's go back inside."

As soon as I stood up, I felt my phone buzzing in my pocket.

"Thea, hi," Cave said. He sounded very nervous.

"What happened?"

"Our servers were hacked last night, and all of the raw shots from the Dewman photoshoot disappeared!"

"What happened?" Bunny demanded silently, but I shook my head and frowned.

"Well, weren't some of them already transferred for retouching?"

"Of course! That's the only good thing, but it seems someone doesn't like our success."

"Good thing you managed to send them before that happened."

"Yeah, and now I'll always make copies…"

"Cave, calm down, it's fine," I told him as I walked into the room. "Do you want me to come there?"

"No, I'm okay, and you have a busy week ahead of you so have some rest."

"What is it?" Bunny asked again.

"Someone hacked Cave's server and deleted all of the Dewman photoshoot pictures."

Bunny sat down on my bed.

"Is it a coincidence? Or is it Houwer?"

I sat down next to him. It could be Aaron, but what was there in the pictures he would want to get rid of? I was struck with a realization. Of course, the mark. No one but Dewman and Bunny saw it that day, but there could still be some shots with it. So Aaron removed any signs that he had marked me then, but why?

I didn't get enough time to think about it when my phone rang again. It was Cave.

"Should I come?" I asked carefully.

"Well, if the news is right, you shouldn't even leave the house," he snapped. "Why didn't you tell me? Are you out of your mind?"

"What's going on?!" I questioned, returning his pointed tone. My patience was thin as it was.

"Turn channel thirty-two on," my agent hissed. "You don't make it easy for me. What do you think you're doing?!"

I couldn't reply, because my tongue stuck to the top of my mouth as soon as I turned the TV on. CBU was a popular entertainment channel, and they never took on paid gossip, only things that actually interested them. And it seemed like whatever they got on now was interesting. Aaron and I only parted a couple of hours ago, but the photo of us was already the biggest news.

Bunny sighed and swore.

I hung up, although Cave was still scolding me. Bunny was sitting on the floor, and I sat down next to him.

It was a great photo, and I was sure it was shot with a professional camera. Aaron was holding me by the neck and looking at my lips, and I was holding his wrists and looking him in the eyes.

I had to rewind it to actually hear the news.

"We got a sensational photo on our hands today!" the host blabbered excitedly. He was a red-hair with an unhealthy shine in his eyes. "*Black&Gold Industries* CEO Aaron Houwer, whose wedding we all anticipated for the past couple of years, was caught with a famous model Theana Melory. Theana was recently brought to stardom after taking part in the *Dew* jewelry shoot. Now she has a contract with *Teyvalle*, and she attracts the attention of many of the rich and powerful. Well, seems like one of them couldn't resist her charm..."

"Oh my god..." Bunny commented, shaking his head.

I had no words. I felt exhausted from not being able to do anything.

"Wait," Bunny said, but his voice sounded distant as if I heard it through the water. "It's weird. There was no 'infamous model,' also nothing about your career going uphill after 'a mysterious death of a famous designer?'"

The channel rolled some footage from my best runways and photoshoots. There was little Aaron, but so much me. It almost felt like they made effort to showcase me from all the best angles. The only thing left would be to say that I was brought up in a poor family and had to work hard to get where I was, both of which were true. I suppose no one would be that interested in that though.

I only had enough energy to turn the TV off and walk to my bed.

"I need sleep," I said and wrapped a blanket around my body.

"Thea," Bunny started, kneeling next to me. "I think he did it…"

"I have no idea what you're talking about."

"It wasn't your first time out together, but the photos only went public today, and it looked as if he was posing with you!"

I remembered how Aaron had pulled me closer just as I was trying to walk home. I shook my head. I didn't want to think about that. That's it. Let things be because I couldn't do anything to stop them from being.

"He chose you," Bunny declared.

"Can I please sleep?" I replied and rolled to face the wall. I just needed to run away from reality.

Reality let me go into the darkness, and there was no falling, no fear…

****

"How long was it going on for?" he whispered hoarsely. It was the first thing I heard, and I felt goosebumps down my back.

I took a deep breath and tried to move, but couldn't.

"She is coming back…"

Someone sighed loudly very close to me. I felt fingers in my hair.

"I'll call back… Thea…"

My mouth was dry as a desert, my throat hurt, and I started coughing.

"Bunny!"

It was Aaron. I was lying on top of him. I then heard a knock on the door and quick steps.

"Is she okay?" Bunny cried.

"Bring her some water," Aaron ordered and sat up. "Thea, everything is fine."

His soft fingers were carefully massaging my neck, and he was holding me close with his other hand.

I opened my eyes. The room was dark, except for the lamp on my nightstand. It was clear that it was late. How long was I asleep?

"What are you doing here?" I muttered.

"Bunny called… Here, take a sip," he replied and brought a glass of water to my lips.

I didn't think I would be that thirsty. I finished the glass, leaving drops of water on Aaron's shirt.

"What time is it?"

"Six," Bunny replied. "How are you feeling?"

"I'm fine. What's wrong with you lot?" I asked and shifted in Aaron's arms, but he pulled me closer and ran his fingers through my hair. He looked at my face anxiously.

"You weren't waking up, Thea. I told you, you can't sleep without me right now…"

"That's just nonsense," I said and shook my head. "I was just tired and exhausted with all the flights."

"Tell your friend that," Aaron told me and frowned.

"Fuck, you weren't breathing!" Bunny shouted. "I thought I'd die there with you! I'm still shaking!"

"Well, go and drink up," I asked, pointing Bunny to the room exit.

He let out a protesting snort but left the two of us alone. I looked at Aaron but lost again because his glance burned me.

"I told you, you mustn't sleep without me!" he growled.

"I'm so fucking tired of you!" I replied and tried to get out of his grip.

This time he didn't try to hold me down, but I didn't go very far and started walking back and forth across the room.

"What the hell was that?!" I demanded pointing at the TV. "Why didn't you warn me?! Don't tell me you didn't know!"

"This is the fastest way to make people react," he said and sat up straight, but I almost felt like he was hanging above me.

"Make people react?" I repeated and clenched my fists. "Did you ask me if I needed their reaction?!"

"I can hide you from everyone," he said, stood up, and took a step towards me.

"Wait, don't come near me," I replied and put my arm forward. "I'm not going to hide from anyone! My work is important for me! It's what I love! Do you want an indifferent lifeless creature?! 'Cause you're not going to like it, Aaron! Although, that's a choice! Make me one of those and throw me away, so I can start getting back to life!"

He took another step to me, and, although I was not happy about it, grabbed me and pressed me against his chest. He waited through my hysteria, my shouts, threats, and attempts to punch him, and then, when I was powerless, he looked me in the eyes.

"You don't need to hide. Take a deep breath and calm down. You're my woman."

"Grace is your woman!" I snapped.

"It's done with Grace."

I hung, clinging onto him.

"How…"

My hand went up to my lips to stop them from shaking. His words blew my mind. That's it. He was not getting married, and I probably could've guessed it if I remembered things he had said in Apollynis. Contrasting emotions mixed my thoughts up, confused me… I'm not going to be a night-time mistress. The alternative that he demonstrated to the whole world today, however, was also scary and undesirable.

"Bunny!" I called hoarsely. I guess he was standing outside the door the whole time because he suddenly opened it and looked inside. "Can I also have a drink?"

Aaron let me go and went into the kitchen to answer his phone. I sat down on the bed.

"I called the ambulance first," Bunny said, giving me a glass. "Then I called him. He told me to cancel the ambulance… Got here in seven minutes…" Vermouth didn't go in very well. I took a small sip and put the glass onto the nightstand. "He was so scared," Bunny whispered. "If he was human I would think he was head over heels for you."

"He is just trying to find a perfect mate," I replied and frowned.

"Don't we all?" my friend said.

"What do you mean?"

"Well, humans also try to find a perfect match. Someone healthy, handsome, someone who smells good… The only thing is that we can cheat, choose someone rich instead of someone genetically healthy. Kids can be screwed, but the person would be rolling in money. I mean, children can be cured if there is money around. Those ones, though," he said and pointed his head to the kitchen, "they can't cheat their nature, good for them!"

"What the fuck are you talking about?" I exclaimed. "They are not like people, at all! He had no choice…"

"That's because you're stunning. If I were him, I'd also pretend I had no choice."

As soon as I took a deep breath and was ready to reply to that, Aaron entered the room.

"You didn't pack, did you?" he asked and narrowed his eyes.

I wanted to reply but was interrupted again.

"If I understand correctly, she can't sleep without you? How long will it take to go away? It looked very scary," Bunny asked and hugged me.

"The first couple of days," Aaron answered calmly.

"You told me it wasn't well researched," I protested.

"It isn't, officially, but I know someone who had experience with that, and we can trust this experience. Get ready, please."

Bunny and I looked at each other.

"I'll help," my friend said.

It was clear we had different ideas of how long I would stay at Aaron's because Bunny was trying to pack a huge suitcase, while I was more set on a small bag.

"It's not for long!" I told him, trying to get my bag out of his hands.

"He broke off his engagement," he whispered loudly, not letting go. "Do you think it'll be a week?"

"I don't care!" I snapped and turned my head to look at the balcony. Aaron was standing there and looking over the city.

"Look at him," Bunny said, frowning. "He is suffering too! Imagine how much shit he'll get now. Media, his ex's family, everyone else. Even worse if there was a business agreement somewhere in there! He put everything at risk for you!"

"Oh, here we go," I said and rolled my eyes. "If you like him, you can keep him!"

"Are you out of your mind?" Bunny asked and rolled his eyes. "I'm not going to pack last year La Croix collection..."

"Yeah, they wouldn't like that in the elite..." I said sarcastically.

"Exactly, you don't want to give them another reason to talk about you behind your back," Bunny agreed and started to pack my stuff.

"Well, they will have a reason to do that for a while, Bunny," I replied and sat down next to the suitcase. I melancholically watched him fill it with my clothes.

We didn't talk much afterward. My friend packed everything he thought I needed and probably did a better job than I would have done myself. Aaron took a quick look and carried the suitcase out of the apartment without saying goodbye. He only spoke when we entered the elevator.

"I got Bunny a bodyguard."

I didn't understand him at first.

"Why?"

"So nothing happens to him," he replied and exited the elevator.

"Can it?" I asked, almost running to catch up with Beast. "Who?"

"Grace's family wasn't very happy that I broke our agreements."

Mr. Knife was waiting for us next to the door. He took my suitcase from Aaron and walked to the gates, but I froze in place. There was a crowd of journalists outside. As soon as we exited, they surrounded us, the crowd erupted with chatter and flashes of cameras.

"Let's go," Aaron said.

There was no chance we'd walk to the car without them getting at least one shot of us. There were many guards, so many it seemed I suddenly became a nationwide celebrity, but even they couldn't help us.

"Mr. Houwer, how long have you been together?"

My eyes were watering from all of the lights, and I even tripped a couple of times until Aaron pulled me closer.

"Are you going to end the engagement?"

"What does Grace Dolly think of it?"

"Theana, are you in a serious relationship? Are you moving in with Mr. Houwer?"

"Theana, how did you meet?"

"Why didn't you let the world know about your relationship earlier?"

The last question was asked to my back, and then the door was shut closed. We left the house in heavy silence. It's strange how life changes sometimes... When I first went out into the night streets of Cryton, they gave me hope. I wanted to live here, work here, try to make it here. Nothing changed in the outside world. The lights were the same, and people, bright and happy, running around before the beginning of the working week, were also the same. I was the only one who would never have the same life again. I thought about Bunny's idea to run away, and it didn't seem so stupid anymore. I could at least try.

"Thea, are you okay?"

I turned to Aaron so I could hiss at him, say something unpleasant, but I just couldn't. I turned back to the window.

"Can you stop patronizing me? Don't you have enough of your own problems?"

"Your problems are mine. Yours I can at least try to solve..."

"And by that you mean," I asked as I turned to face him, "you can intervene with my emotions and overpower them?

"I can only calm you down, Thea, not overpower your emotions..."

He had a lot of patience. I even was embarrassed for a second or two, but then I looked out of the window again and saw the life that was taken away from me, and all of the embarrassment disappeared.

Aaron's phone rang, and I tried to completely insulate myself from him by turning away and not listening to whatever he was saying as much as I could. It didn't quite work.

"Yes, it's okay, she's fine... We're going to my place now. No, I'm not leaving her again," he said, and then there was a pause. "Let's talk about that later, I'm not sure the time is good," he said and paused again, listening to the reply. "Thanks for the support. Love you. Bye."

Love? Does Beast love someone?

The car drove onto the Cryton-Glass bridge. When I first moved, I came here regularly to look at this incredible marvel of glass. During winter it almost resembled an ice bridge from a fairytale. Now it somehow led me into my own fairytale, which was sure to be scary and full of unknown. On the other side of the bridge, there was a new residential area, which was all expensive and full of metal and stone, just like the district *Black&Gold Industries* was located in. You wouldn't need a GPS to find the building Aaron lived in, because it was surrounded by journalists. Mr. Knife and all the other guards had to step out of the cars to allow our vehicle to drive through the gates. I could hear annoying questions even through the soundproof glass. I slowly started to get it and had my own concerns.

"How am I going to *Teyvalle* tomorrow?"

"We'll need to talk about that..."

"I'm not planning to talk with you, Aaron!" I cried. "I'm also not planning to just sit in your apartment and hide!"

It seemed that I forgot who I was dealing with. He was quick to remind me. He dashed out of the car and pulled me forcefully.

"Listen, Thea, here is the rule," he said as he kept pulling me to follow him, "and I advise you to remember it and act on it." He put his palm against a screen next to the building door. "You don't raise your voice at me around other people!" he concluded and pushed me inside. The concierge tried his best to pretend to be invisible. "Do you understand?!"

"Yes," I muttered, looking at him.

"Great. If you want to scream or express your opinion, wait until we're alone, and then let it all out," he continued with a much calmer voice. "I told you that I'm not only the head of the family by the inheritance. You mustn't challenge my authority in front of my family."

Here was "lamb" Dolly's secret. She was actually brought up to not provoke a predator and drive him into fury.

"Sorry," I sighed. "You should probably tell me all the rules beforehand and not the moment I break them..."

He gave me a tense nod, still breathing heavily.

The elevator doors opened in a small private hallway. The next room, however, took my breath away. Dim lower lights lit up and showed a small podium, which was just slightly above the floor of the room. Panoramic windows opened up to a full view of night Cryton. My eyes widened and I tried to look at all of it as if I could see all of the city in one glance.

Aaron walked somewhere behind my back, and I knew that I would soon hear the sound of pouring water. I even got distracted from the scenery, turning my head to where I expected the sound to come from. It was an interesting habit of his, and I was wondering whether it had something to do with his animalistic nature.

I surprisingly liked the living room. Every detail was to my taste. The podium zone surrounded by panoramic windows was definitely my favorite thing about it. There also was a light and soft couch which would probably be great for watching the sunrise or looking at the night city. On the right, there was a kitchen with a bar. On the left — flat-screen TV and another couch. There was a screen, which probably separated the living room from the bedroom and bathroom. The water finally stopped.

It was weird because I usually didn't like new places. I always spent a lot of time choosing hotels, and I would never be able to sleep in one I'm not comfortable in. Here, however, I felt as if I just came home after a long day at work.

"Do you have anything to eat?"

I didn't hear his steps but felt that he was near me again.

"I didn't think about that," he replied. "Are you hungry?"

"I wouldn't ask if I wasn't," I confirmed.

"Do you want anything in particular?"

Aaron was still tense and upset, and I was fed up with everything.

"How about I deal with that?" I asked and turned to face him. His glare was cold. "Your apartment is pretty cool."

"Do you like it?" he questioned and raised his eyebrow.

"Surprisingly, I do," I replied. "I'm usually not very good with new spaces, but it's very cozy. Kind of as if I chose it myself."

He hardly managed a small smile and lowered his tense shoulders.

"Good."

"What do you want to eat?"

"Meat…"

"Steak?"

"Raw, with blood."

"Where do I turn on the light?"

He let me go forward.

"There is a bright light, dim light…"

"Make it so I can still see the city. This view is amazing! We're so high up…"

Aaron touched the switch, and kitchen cabinets lit up with a backlight.

"Good enough?"

"Great. Wine?"

"Sure…"

"Be my guest," I joked and smirked, "and don't look at me as if you're going to attack me this very moment."

"Sorry. I'll get your stuff and go change."

He didn't drag me straight to the bedroom, gave me some time.

While I was ordering food, I walked around the living room, not touching anything, but exploring. There was a room divider with flowerpots inside of it. The flowers weren't the ones you'd talk to or even the ones you'd need to water regularly, but rather those which grew in deserts and could probably survive a nuclear bombing. They were still pretty though. Some of them were even blossoming, possibly from desperation.

How are you? Bunny enquired.

Ordered some dinner. Will try to feed Beast before he bites me.

Good job! Good luck!

Aaron would appear silently if it was not for the delivery.

"Mr. Houwer, you should've said the delivery is for you..." the delivery man said when he appeared at the door with Mr. Knife right next to him.

"And what would happen then?" Aaron asked, infusing fear upon the poor man.

"Sorry, it was me. I ordered it," I said, getting in between the men with a smile. "Thank you very much!"

"Sorry," the delivery man said before finally getting out of there.

"Even feeding you is complicated!" I said and rolled my eyes. "All this act, all these difficulties."

"Well, now you know that..."

I looked at the man and had to admit he looked softer, nicer, cozier in his home clothes than he did in a suit. Aaron walked to the bar, and I finally got a chance to search through the cabinets. The conclusion was, sadly, that this kitchen was not used to cooking. There were no spices, no oils, not even pasta. The coffee machine was the only appliance that had a vague smell, but it was unclear when it was last used.

"Why do you need a kitchen if you don't use it?"

I was full of anticipation. I was still afraid of him, I was afraid he would demand I give up my job and I had a feeling he wanted to start this conversation. I was hoping he would be more pleasant when drunk and fed. I was also hoping to try and get myself more rights and find out all the rules. I'm not Dolly, "the lamb", and Aaron was not the center of my universe.

"There were no available places without it," he replied and sat down at the bar.

I smirked.

"Well, then we have some hope…"

"Do you know how to cook?"

"Aren't you supposed to know everything about me?" I chuckled. "Can you open the wine?"

Steak, even still covered with foil, smelled incredible. It was still hot…

"I didn't go that far in the reports," he said and suddenly appeared behind me. He found the cabinet with the bottle-opener in a swift second.

"So, you do use the kitchen sometimes," I teased, grinning.

"I just know where things are."

"I wonder why. So you can disarm a robber if he gets in?" I suggested, having fun with it.

"I organized it myself," he replied coldly. "It is our nature to make a home for ourselves. People can leave it to a designer, but we can't. No one really comes here…"

He unscrewed the bottle.

"What do you mean?"

I smelled the wine. I always judged wine by smell, and, to be honest, I did so with many other things. Bunny found it funny.

"This apartment is my personal space," he said and got two glasses out. "Foreign smells are not welcomed here…"

I probably should have started believing him. It was still hard though

"What about me?"

"You're my mate, Thea," he declared indifferently, probably expecting another hysterical act from me. "I chose you and brought you home. We don't live with our matches before the wedding, but we have already gone through everything that would be unacceptable in normal circumstances. So…"

I felt as if I got tipsy from the sole smell of the wine.

"Can you pour me a glass, please?"

We sat down at the table, and Aaron held a full glass out for me.

"What does your… family think of all this?"

"They don't know you're my real mate. I told you it's prohibited for those of my kind to have one of your kind."

"You told me you're not going to hide me…"

"You, but not the connection we have. Everyone will think…" he started and looked straight at me, "that I just fell in love and was so crazy about you that I put my reputation at risk." The wine tasted bitter. "Now I should give no reason to doubt me as a Prime."

I left the glass on the table.

"Did you remove the photos from my agent's server?"

"Yes," he admitted. "Some of them have the mark, and no one needs to know I marked you… earlier. It would only mean you're my mate, my perfect match."

"Do you want me to stop at *Teyvalle*?" I asked because it was the question that bothered me the most. I hoped to get the answer before we moved on to our usual stuff, breaking and shouting.

"When did I say that?" he asked, frowning.

"You told me in the car that we need to discuss my visit tomorrow. I was sure that with all the journalists you're not going to let me…"

"Thea, I usually understand things the first time," he interrupted harshly. "You told me it's important to you and that you don't want to hide. I wanted to discuss your guards. Claud is going to go everywhere with you, and it's not a discussion I'd like to have."

I blinked, surprised by his words. It took me a minute to come back to my senses.

"Okay," I said and shrugged. Not being locked up was good enough, and a personal bodyguard wasn't that much of a problem. "Thanks."

Aaron sneered.

"You thought I'd lock you up here, didn't you?" he said and shook his head. He finally seemed relaxed and even I felt that it was easier to breathe now.

We took a small break from talking to eat and think each about our own. Bunny sent me pictures of his lone dinner and a big half-empty bottle of vermouth, and I was chuckling at his funny faces. Aaron looked curious.

"Bunny already misses me," I told him and put my phone aside. "Would you like some coffee?"

"Yes. I'll make it."

He also didn't let me do the dishes and then suggested we move to the couch.

"Why do you live with him?" he asked suddenly when he came back with two cups of coffee.

"I don't know, it just happened. Do you have anything sweet?" I asked and looked at him. His face was guilty as if I just caught him doing something illegal. I almost felt bad for him. "Well,

Mr. Houwer, that's not a way to do that. This home is officially incomplete."

I could only hold the laugh for a couple of seconds while his face went through all of the emotions of a total fiasco.

"You can complete it tomorrow," he said and smiled. "I'm not the only one responsible for that part of the agreement."

"And what exactly is my part?"

He sat down next to me.

"If you were here willingly, you could settle down, do anything you want to the place, paint the walls, do some crazy redecoration..."

"Are you saying that I don't have the right to do that in our circumstances? Well, good for you," I said, chuckling.

"You can do whatever you want," he replied, still smiling. He wasn't relaxed, still expecting me to throw a cup at his head. "If you want to, of course."

"You don't say!.." I said and looked at him doubtfully.

"You can do anything as long as it's not dangerous."

I closed my eyes and felt goosebumps go down my arms. It was so different from normal human life. Settling down at home, even restrictions were all normal to human experience, but inside there was an unusual filling. Beast's world was dark, unclear, and unavailable, it scared me. I also wasn't sure whether Aaron would be willing to open it up for me. He answered my questions, but only while the answers were not terrifying enough.

"You don't want to show me your world, do you?" I asked. He looked at me but didn't reply in silent agreement. "Is it that bad?"

"It's unusual."

"Are you afraid of pushing me away?"

"I'm afraid of scaring you away."

"Is it even possible? I mean, to live with you, but outside of your world?"

"I don't want to scare you even more, Thea. It's important to leave your own view of the world the same."

"For your sake?"

"For your own sake. You're a part of me. If something happens to you, I'm not going to make it."

I swallowed loudly, staring straight at him. I wasn't sure if it was due to his attractiveness or his words, but I suddenly decided to come closer… I stood up, putting my cup on the floor, and walked up to him. I froze for a second, silently asking him if I could touch him. I wasn't expecting him to grab me and sit me down on his lap, wrapping his arms around me, running his fingers through my hair, and tracing my neck. His hungry gaze made it clear that he was holding back all this time, trying not to yield to temptation. When I walked up to him myself, he could not hold it any longer.

When I had first seen the amazing view from the window, I had no idea that the first thing I'd do in front of it was having sex. Nor did I think I would be the one to initiate it. I let him take what he wanted, and he did. I barely managed to save the lingerie he gave me. Aaron turned me to face the window and spread my legs, submitting me to his desire.

There was something special about it, something on edge… He could do it any way he wanted, he could be powerful, furious, hungry, but he was careful. He was breathing heavily, and he was tense, letting me know how hard it is for him to be tender, to not hurt me. He slowly lowered me onto him, filling me with his desire, and growled when I arched my back, letting him inside and putting my neck on display. He even let me lead, moving just the way I needed to, supporting me and not letting me fall into madness. It didn't take me long. The thrusts were fast, the breaths short, and my heart was pounding in my chest as if competing with our rhythm. When I had no more strength, Aaron turned me to face the couch and pressed me against it, allowing me a second to come back to myself.

Not for long. He knew me too well, and knew how to deal with me... One slight bite to where the mark was, and I was already squeezing my legs and twisting my body, choking on air, feeling his every movement. He was killing me with his passion, pushing deeper, harder, leaving me powerless and exhausted.

I was happy to exchange my thoughts, fears, and doubts for a momentary bliss.

***

I didn't quite remember how I appeared in the bedroom. It looked unfamiliar in the dim morning light, and I almost panicked. I sat up and blinked, trying to see the room. It was big and very obviously belonged to a man. There were no decorations, only a wardrobe, and a bed. Not even a nightstand. The windows were covered with dark blinds. What time was it?

I jumped up, wrapped myself in a blanket, and peeked outside. It was right behind the screen I saw yesterday. The door to the bathroom was right next to it. Aaron was in the kitchen, watching something on his tablet. He saw me and was about to say something.

"Why didn't you wake me up?" I interrupted. "I'm going to be late!"

His eyebrow rose.

"It's six."

"Really?" I said, losing all the fury in a second. "It's so light in here."

"I thought I put the blinds down."

"Well, it's light here..." I said and gave up completely. "Okay, can I stop making a fool of myself and go to the bathroom?"

"Go," he chuckled, "but leave the blanket behind…"

"Yeah," I quickly muttered and left.

I was in a great mood as if I spent the night with a normal, no, with an amazing man! My reflection in the mirror quite agreed with that. My cheeks were rosy, my eyes – shiny, and my face looked nice and smooth. I frowned and washed it with ice-cold water.

I found my clothes on the side of the bed, and the suitcase was in the corner of the room. I got dressed and walked to the kitchen.

"Good morning," he said. "Do you want an omelet?"

"Is there any meat?"

"Bacon."

"Then yes."

"Our contract," he said and nodded to the table.

My good mood and my appetite both disappeared. I sat down at the table and looked at the stack of paper. I quickly looked over all of the points but didn't find anything about early termination, or any termination, really. There were only the responsibilities of both sides.

"It's strange," I said, frowning. "What about termination?"

"We don't have that option, Thea," he declared grimly.

"Then what's the point of the contract?"

"It will give you an idea of things you can and can't do, and it also outlines fines and fees for me."

"Money? Are you for real?" I exclaimed. Somehow I seemed to forget I should not criticize his decisions. Beast with claws and fangs quickly reminded me of that. "You're really good at spoiling my morning…" I sighed.

"We discussed it and I promised…" he said and put a plate on the table in front of me.

"Can we do all this without a contract?"

"We can," he told me. "But I would like you to do a full medical check." I snorted, but Aaron was serious. "I want to make sure you don't have any health problems, Thea. It's as important for me as it would be for any normal partner."

"Are we partners now?" I asked, narrowing my eyes to copy his look.

"Would you like that?" he asked back and turned to the coffee machine. "It can be partner, lover, your man…"

"Beast," I blurted out, but then bit my lip.

He was silently taking the cups of the cabinet.

"I can be that only when we're alone," he said but didn't turn back to face me. "I'll remember it. So, are you going to do the medical check?"

"Do I have a choice?" I looked at the plate and took to walk to the couch next to the window.

Morning Cryton view was more than I'd ever expected. However, it didn't make the breakfast taste better. I was grimly chewing my bacon.

"Thea," Aaron said and sat down next to me. "Responsibilities in the contract are things you need to know, they're the answer to your question about things you shouldn't do."

"I got it. Thanks for the coffee and breakfast."

He looked at me intently.

"Thank you for being with me and for trying…"

***

On my way to *Teyvalle*, I was looking through the contract, searching for things I shouldn't do. I had to be faithful and give no reason to be jealous, I couldn't live on my own or spend my nights anywhere but with Aaron without his consent. So I couldn't just leave and sleep in the hotel after a fight. I wasn't allowed to smoke or otherwise harm myself. Well, he didn't think that he is the reason

I would need a cigarette once in a while, did he now? I wasn't allowed to do business, make connections or decisions that concerned both of us. Everything I read had a small detail I couldn't do it "without his consent." So, if we were a normal couple who trusted each other, all of those would be okay as long as he knew.

The only problem was that we weren't a normal couple.

The only thing that made me doubtful was the point about "not provoking other men." As if I wasn't the one walking down the runway in my underwear. All of this was only a quick glance at the restrictions because I saw *Teyvalle* and couldn't think about anything else. Somehow I forgot that I wouldn't be left alone if I wasn't with Aaron. The area in front of the building was occupied by journalists, and as soon as the car pulled over, all of them sprang into action.

"Be here," Knife ordered and got out of the car. Even from the inside, I could hear all the questions, which were the exact opposite of delicate.

"Is this a PR campaign for your career, Theana? Are you planning to break it off?"

"How are you connected with the murder of Dustin Dewman? Did the police have any questions for you?"

"Are you planning the enter Aaron Houwer's family, or is it an opportunity to become famous?"

"Fuck you!" I snapped at one of the journalists who got in my face.

"Thea, calm down," my bodyguard told me and opened the building door for me.

I walked to the elevator, trying not to look at people. It was clear it was just the beginning. Grace Dolly was waiting for me in the hallway. Well, it was more of what was left of her, because she really didn't look well. Her eyes were dim, her face went grey, and her lips were a narrow line. She clenched the handle of her dark blue designer bag and was wearing a dark suit of an almost identical color. When she saw me, the bag nearly fell from her grasp.

"Can we talk?" she hissed as soon as we were near.

"I'm sorry, Miss," Knife intercepted and caught me by the arm. "You're not allowed to…"

"Is she untouchable now?!" the "lamb" cried, her exterior breaking. I felt bad for her.

"I'll talk to her," I declared, turning to my bodyguard.

"Only if I'm there," he protested.

"I'm not going to do anything to her," Dolly said. "Does Aaron think I'd scratch her face off?"

I was suddenly interested in whether Grace could turn into a beast. Was that what Aaron and Knife were afraid of?

"Can I call you after work?"

Grace nodded and quickly pulled her business card out of her bag. She left without saying another word, and I was sure she met all those journalists who were waiting outside. When we entered the elevator, I started shaking.

"Can she turn?"

"She can, but she wouldn't be able to turn back. Right now she is probably taking medicine to prevent that."

"Aaron knew she was so vulnerable and still let all of this happen?!" I cried, outraged.

I was supposed not to care because there was nothing I could do, but I still did. I could only be glad that compassion was one thing that made humans different from animals.

"Believe me, she got a generous compensation for this breakup, and she certainly had no emotional strings attached."

"Are you talking about love?" I asked, raising an eyebrow.

"They had nothing even remotely similar to what you have," Knife replied coldly.

I was suddenly interested in how he was related to Aaron. It was unlikely a simple bodyguard would have this conversation with me.

"Aaron told me Grace was promised to him since she was born! She basically lost the purpose of her life!"

"No one banned her from finding other purposes, Miss Melory," Claud reasoned, trying to distance himself with the official titles. "She could find other things. It's only the girl's fault that she planned to spend all her life first under her parents' eye, and then – under her husband's. Mr. Houwer can't be the one to blame, and you have nothing to talk to her about."

I was looking at Knife with rising interest.

"It almost seems like you approve of whatever happened with Aaron and me."

Claud paused for a long time, ignoring opened elevator doors.

"I approve of whatever makes Aaron happy. And I make sure no one interferes with his happiness."

"Does it look like happiness?" I asked.

"It's only temporary difficulties," he said and smiled. It was the first time I saw him do that, so I just stared at him.

It was even weirder that I wasn't quite against it. I was expecting fury and rebellion, but I only felt a strange longing. I wanted to hide, just like Aaron suggested. I was only walking to Shane's office but already felt as if I pushed through a couple of shoots and a runway.

The atmosphere in his office only made my desire to run away stronger. He met me fully armed with his predatory grin and sharp gaze, and he was enjoying my hesitant walk.

"Sit down," he ordered and then turned to my bodyguard. "Mr. Knife, I'll ask you to leave my office." Claud didn't move. "You know I'm not going to do anything."

"You don't need to touch her to destroy everything," he replied. I was again surprised by how much he could do.

"She is not stupid, she'll be fine," "the cat" grinned.

Claud let one loud sigh out, but then turned on his heels and left.

"I'm glad I didn't agree to that dinner..." Alexander said, switching his attention back to me.

"Well, you'll never know now," I countered, raising an eyebrow.

"It's a pity," he said with a sneer and made all of my confidence disappear.

"Really? Don't they say everything happens for the best?"

"Well, how is it for you? Is it the best?" he asked, narrowing his eyes as he leaned forward.

"It's alright," I muttered and shrugged.

"Don't lie to me," he told me, and his smile went away, leaving a dark shine in his eyes. "I can help you."

"Excuse me?"

"You and Houwer... It's not supposed to be like that, is it?" he said. He was certainly well-prepared for a full-on attack. He obviously thought I was stupid after all. "Did he catch you in the hospital?" he sneered. "I couldn't find anything wrong with your little circus act in his office. He didn't give you the diamond, while it was obviously yours. And it always had been, right, Thea?"

"I have no idea what you're talking about."

"Do you want to be free again?"

He hit too close to home. My breathing fastened. It was enough to make him understand everything, but it also gave me a chance to think. I couldn't trust this man. Let's be honest, I also wouldn't. I wouldn't look Aaron in the eyes and hold a knife behind my back. Whatever Shane offered would be exactly that. Aaron felt me, got under my skin, and could manipulate my emotions. I never was the one to break my principles, to be in the middle of intrigues. It was harder and slower, but it allowed me to still be me. I wasn't planning on doing that now.

"I am free, Alexander," I said and took a deep breath.

He was surprised. His eyes froze, his neck tensed.

"Well, I suppose I made a mistake. I thought you were different," he said and grinned unpleasantly. "Money talks."

"I thought you were more perceptive, Mr. Shane," I replied, and it was incredibly easy to smile after his initial confusion.

"Really?" he said and smiled back. "You thought about me?"

His shallow flirting brought back the illusion of having control over this situation.

"I don't need his money," I said, ignoring his words. "To be clear, no one offered me any, and I'm fine with whatever I have."

"No one would say you don't get enough from this."

"You should know that money is the last thing I can think about in this situation."

His face suddenly became human again. He was the master of illusion!

"You have no idea what you're getting yourself into, Thea. Our world has a reason to not let people like you in without a contract."

"And you apparently want to help me just out of kindness," I said, rolling my eyes.

"No," he replied sharply and sat back. "One of my family members died. I want to know whether he was killed like an animal or like a man. Was he murdered because he was a random victim, or did he die in a fair fight for you? If it's the first option, I'm going to destroy Houwer."

"Why don't you just go to the police with this?"

"I have no evidence. I was actually surprised you came in today."

"Why? Have I been fired?"

"No," he replied and sneered. "But someone like me wouldn't care for your job…" His grin was wicked, devilish. "And if he does, it means that you and Aaron have something more than just a simple impulsive crush on a pretty girl with black diamond. Primes are not emotional, and their only emotions are driven by addiction. You are his obsession," he concluded. "I suppose it runs in Houwer's family…"

***

That day was nerve-wracking. I was thinking about Alexander's words… If Primes didn't have emotions, what is Aaron doing, trying to make everyone believe we're in love? Is Shane lying to me? And if yes, why?

I must say, that this puzzle really helped me get through the day at *Teyvalle*. It was buzzing with yesterday's news, and everyone was looking at me, even guards, even waiters. People whispered behind my back, froze, and watched me with widened eyes. "It is that girl, who…" I heard from every corner.

I was slightly distracted by the viewing of the hall where the show would take place. Although it wasn't fully decorated yet, it was still very impressive. There were amazing metal flowers on the ceiling; walls had panels with shapes changing from graceful women to flowers to birds. Every element here was a piece of art, and I would have to be a part of it. I was looking forward to that before I was taken aback by one special someone.

Duvalle had an even sharper gaze and was even more critical, using every chance she got to criticize. She didn't like the lighting, the music, how fast I walked, the emotions I had. All I heard was her "no-no-no," and when I was brought some coffee I almost said no just because of how much this word imprinted in my brain. My final walk became the last straw. While I walked down the runway, Alexander stepped into the room, and I tripped under his gaze and fell down.

*Can we be humans today and go out?* I texted while Knife was dealing with the bruise on my knee. Shane was looking at me as if I drove his expensive car into a tree. I wanted to see Aaron like I never before. Only he could make me forget about those mundane problems by creating even larger ones.

"Thea," Alexander called. "That's it for today, but you'll have to stay late tomorrow. Duvalle is not happy, she says you don't understand the composition."

Knife made a show of opening the bandages.

"Are you going to be helping?" I asked, sneering, but then I flinched when the bodyguard pressed the bandage to my knee.

"Yep, I'm keeping an eye on you," Alexander said, grinning. "You only have two weeks until the wedding, so you won't have much time for rehearsals…"

I wasn't really sure what he was saying. My thinking was too slow.

"I won't?" I asked, looking up at him, and realized I just stepped into another one of his traps. My coffee cup fell from my hands right to the bodyguard's feet.

"Get out," Knife growled, leaving me in no doubt that he was a beast too. He was certainly a special one.

Shane grinned wider and left. I was sure he was very pleased with himself.

"Was he joking?" I asked, trying to catch Knife's gaze, but he was focused on cleaning everything up.

"How do I know?"

"I'm not getting married! Nobody proposed to me!" I snapped.

"Well, then there is no reason to panic," he said, standing back up. "You're a smart grown woman, and if no one proposed, then there is no proposal. Right?"

"No, not right!" I muttered, feeling my heartbeat fasten, and my breathing grew heavier. "Aaron can make me do that in a second…"

"He is just as much of a victim here as you are, Thea," Knife interrupted. "Let's go and talk outside." We had to leave through one of the back doors. My bodyguard spent his time wisely, exploring the building and getting us the passes. "You have no idea what he's going through!" he said, coming back to the topic of the day. "You're only worried about yourself!"

"He told me he could reverse it the first couple of days!" I shouted. The echo scared some birds from the building, and they tried to get out of the narrow passage. Knife stopped, grabbed my hand, and turned me to face him.

"Reverse it and lose this chance?! He knows how good it can be if you take this responsibility and walk this path to the end," he spoke passionately, looking me straight in the eyes. "You need to grow up and take the responsibility too. He has enough people to bother him, don't be another one. You won't regret standing by his side. You will have everything you can dream of, you'll have care, protection, freedom."

"How do you know?" I said, trying to break free, but he didn't let go. It seemed he almost felt embarrassed by his own impulse.

"I saw that before," he replied tiredly, averting his gaze. "My parents are like you and Aaron. I know that even a situation like this can turn into a good future not just for the two of you… So why care what you get in exchange?" he asked and turned back to face me. "Are you really going to be mad if he proposes? He? Really? He is trying his best, Thea… Tell me it doesn't touch you even a little bit."

"It's all too fast… I don't know…" I suddenly leaned against the wall and looked up. It was a freaky day, and I somehow felt that Knife's words had some sense to them.

"You just have no time to find out because you spend all of it rebelling and feeling bad for yourself," he said sharply.

"How would you know Aaron and I could make it work?"

"I wouldn't," he explained and shrugged. "You need to put some work in to make it possible. We can be as strong and powerful as we can, but people like you are our only chance to feel happy and complete. Nature made it clear."

I narrowed my eyes.

"Okay. I won't call Grace," I said, and Knife snorted in approval. "I want to talk to you instead. Is it prohibited?"

The bodyguard didn't expect me to say that.

"What do you want to know?"

"What am I allowed to know?" I asked and took a step from the wall. "Aaron and I never have time to talk, but you could at least tell me about the life he lives and the life I will have to live. Is that okay?"

Knife froze in thought, but then his phone rang. He took it out of his pocket and then looked at me, frowning.

"Where is your phone?"

"In the clutch, it's on silent," I replied and took my own phone out only to find two missed calls from Aaron.

"Yes, everything is fine, she's okay," Knife reported, still staring at me. "Sure, I have a couple of hours, we wanted to grab dinner." I smiled at him, but he wasn't very happy. "Aaron will be late," he muttered and put his phone away. "Let's go."

As soon as we left the narrow space between two buildings I read Aaron's text.

*I can't be human, Thea. I can be better than that.*

Knife brought me to the restaurant where our first meeting with Aaron took place. The open terrace looked friendlier in the daylight than it did last time I was there. So many things had changed since then.

We sat at the table near the balcony and watched the peaceful life of the elite residential area. The sounds of fountain and birdsong reminded me of the vacation me and Bunny took at the seaside last year.

"Is he in trouble?" I asked and looked at the bodyguard.

I didn't want to eat, so I just ordered coffee. Knife surprised me by choosing a vegan option and now was busy with his salad.

"I don't know, but there are some complications."

I was closely watching him, and I liked him more and more. He was confident, calm, and very protective. It was impossible to imagine him as a beast, especially one who can fall into fury as fast as Aaron did. Even Shane was somewhat afraid of Claud, judging by the way he left when he was told to.

"Is there a chance the latest news about me can hurt his career somehow?"

"No. Marriage to Grace was political, but it would bring no changes to *Black&Gold Industries*. Grace's father needed it much more. His bank's reputation would grow quickly. He is certainly angry now," Claud said and touched his chin thoughtfully. "Aaron paid a huge amount in fines, but it was barely enough…"

It was weird. I didn't know much about politics and business deals, but I knew that playing with people's feelings was not something I would get on board with. Knife felt me getting tense, but was pleased with it and started his coffee.

"It's quite difficult between us and normal people, Thea," he said, put his cup down and looked at me. "Is that what you wanted to find out?"

Possibly. I kind of knew that already. Their world looked as human as ours, there were calculation and disappointment, and loss. For me it seemed like building my new life on the broken dreams of another woman was too much. It was wrong.

"Where do people like you come from?"

"Our species is called homo predatum – a predator. Our race had to survive in very harsh surroundings, and evolution went a slightly different route for us. There weren't many of us, and we were separated from civilization, but close to nature… Our people lived with predators of north woods, where Northerbridge and Dwaynecloud are now…"

I was listening to him, afraid to make a sound.

"We don't have much information about that time, but it's clear we always had tensions with you people. For a couple of centuries, they tried to destroy us, because there was certainly more of them… It was even worse because of how we procreate. We needed ordinary human women, who were suitable for that…"

"How do they register us? How do we get into the database and then on the market?"

"Well, there is no war now, Thea, only because we proved our survival skills and our cunning. Databases of good matches are essential for our survival."

"Do you rule the world or something?" I asked.

"Kind of," he confirmed. "Not many people know, but nearly seventy percent of the ruling elite are of my race. It's not too difficult to push laws when we need them. Don't worry, humans are not under any threat. We need you."

"Aaron told me that it's not even necessary to be bound to someone like me to have a child…"

"Thea, there are things you don't need to know," Claud said. "Our journey here wasn't easy, and there are still things that are dark and unpleasant. Aaron will do everything to protect you from the life many of the women have to live. He's already chosen the path of trust, however more difficult it is. There are things you shouldn't know…"

"So, couples like Aaron and I or your parents… Are they sort of rare?"

"Now they are," he agreed.

We kept silent for a little while, and I thought about things I had heard.

"Aaron told me I make him unstable, and he can… lose control," I started carefully. I was surprised that my companion was aware, and I had nothing to hide from him. "How do I prevent it from happening?" His face softened, and all of the tension went away. He sighed and sat back, looking at me. "What? Did I ask something wrong?"

"No," he said and smiled. "It's all good because you asked something right. Good job."

"I have no idea what you mean," I said, feeling angry.

"We can feel when someone lies to us, Thea," he declared suddenly. "You wouldn't be able to lie to me, to Aaron, to any other one of us."

"I can't lie?" I asked and sat straight.

I tried to remember all of my conversations with Aaron and whether I had ever tried to lie to him.

"You have a lot of power over him, I suppose he mentioned that. It can be difficult to hand this power to a stranger, even if this stranger is such a special woman. You're not the only one who has things to lose here… I would even say that he is in bigger danger because he has his responsibilities with the family…"

I was happy Aaron got me a calm and relatively normal beast as a bodyguard because he was finally someone I could talk to. I appreciated it more than anything he had ever done before.

"Most of the men who get a woman like that find a way to avoid any extreme situations..."

"What do you mean?" I asked. It became clear that Dewman hadn't told me everything. The honeymoon phase probably ended much earlier than expected, and with much worse consequences. "What happens to them?"

"Thea," Knife said, frowning. "Don't."

"Don't 'don't' me. I want to know."

"No, you don't," he repeated. "The most important thing is that YOU are going to have a normal ordinary life. Sometimes things need to be compared, but that's not the case. So, don't."

"Why do they do this? Is there no other way?" I asked as my breathing quickened. Things I imagined were all quite unpleasant. As if the jeweler would really date me or whatever! I was now sure that wasn't his plan!

"I told you, not everyone is willing to give power like that to a human woman," he noted. "Centuries of wars leave their mark, and there is still no trust."

Twilight fell on the city, and the first star rose high in the sky. The air was fresh and cool. There were more voices downstairs, more people. Cars slowly moved through the traffic. People downstairs drank coffee, and its smell filled the air. I suddenly felt lonely. It was the first time I didn't feel welcomed by the night, by the crowd, by life. Everything around seemed fake like fun after a cocktail, which only left a hangover behind. I was drawn to warmth, quiet and dim lights; to slow breaths and heartbeat. I knew they wouldn't leave bitterness behind, they wouldn't lie and make promises. Those breaths and heartbeat lived in the moment, here and now...

"Let's get out of here," I concluded, stood up, and walked to the exit.

***

He was out for a long time... I even started feeling a little worried. I couldn't even call and find out where he was, I had no right to it. I first rehearsed my catwalk going back and forth along the table, and then just walked from corner to corner, getting even more nervous. When I finally heard him unlock the door and saw him in the doorway, I felt my body relax. We froze opposite each other. I licked my lips in sudden shyness, and he was looking at me so intensely as if scanning me.

"What happened?"

His voice was hoarse, and he was barely standing. I quickly decided that making a scene wasn't worth it and walked up to him.

"I was worried. Do you want anything?" I asked and stopped in front of him. He was staring at me with his piercing eyes. Beast's gaze was full of hunger, and his breathing grew heavier.

"I'm tired..." he muttered.

"What can I do?" I asked. I didn't like what I was seeing. He looked as if he was at war, and the only thing missing were puddles of blood. "Dinner? Bath?"

"I'll take a shower," he said and put his hand on my neck, looking me in the eyes. "Thank you..."

He seemed as though he didn't care about my attempt to be there for him. Did he feel me lying? Well, I wasn't because I really was worried about him. While he was in the shower, I made some coffee, but suddenly felt hungry and decided to make a salad. When Aaron came into the kitchen in his pajama pants, I had already finished half a bowl.

"Can I?.." he asked and took a step towards me.

"It's your house," I replied and licked my lips.

"I was asking about food."

He looked better, even his eyes were as shiny as always, as dangerous and as attractive.

"I asked you if you wanted dinner," I said and moved the bowl to him.

"I didn't before now," he told me and shrugged, pulling the bowl closer.

I chuckled in disbelief. I was so surprised with myself. I cooked for a man and was now silently "awing" at how cute he looked when he ate my culinary masterpiece. Poor him…

"Do you want anything more substantial?"

"Yeah," he replied with his mouth full.

Damn, I wasn't expecting him to agree. I slowly stood up from the chair and made my wait to the fridge.

"Do you eat eggs? Virgins shouldn't be the only thing in your diet…"

"Yes."

"Okay…"

While he continued to chew his salad, I mixed eggs and cream together and chopped some bacon in there. After throwing some more bacon on the pan, I cut one piece for myself, but before I could eat it, I heard his voice from behind.

"Can you cut one for me too?"

I turned and met his gaze. Seemed like both of us had nothing to eat all day and it suddenly became the thing that brought us closer together. He was struggling with his problems, and I was struggling with mine, but now we were healing together. I smiled. I took couple more pieces and put them on a piece of bread.

"I can't become human, Thea," he suddenly said with a smile.

I realized it was about my text.

"Sorry, I didn't think about that…"

"I'm trying to be normal for you, but it doesn't mean I'm going to change who I am," he said, and his words were harsh. "I'm not going to be a convenient pet…"

I first felt like leaving and closing the door behind, not trying any further, but I was not the one to give up.

"Did you have a bad day?"

"One of the worst ones," he replied and closed his eyes.

"Me too," I said and turned to the stove.

Bacon left an amazing smell around the room. My stomach tightened, and I realized there was no point in talking to Beast before we both got something to eat. It was an easy truth to remember, but I was too used to Aaron trying to make me comfortable all the time and establish contact between us.

"I'm sorry about forgetting that you are a beast."

It seemed that we finally started to talk successfully, but it was still actions that spoke louder than words. At least that's how I felt. I saw some movement and then Beast put his arms around me and hugged me tightly. Waves of goosebumps traveled down my body when he exhaled into my neck. His hoarse voice made me freeze in his arms.

"Don't lie to me, you remember who I am all too well. You wouldn't ask me to try and be human otherwise..."

I swallowed and turned the stove off.

"I said I was sorry," I noted. I didn't want to eat anymore. I was waiting patiently for him to let me go, but he wasn't moving. His breaths were hot against the back of my head. "Let me g..."

"No," he interrupted. His breaths grew heavier, his hands ran down my shoulders as if he was blind and tried to "see" me. "I'm sorry. I need you... Right now."

His nose touched the back of my neck, his hands crawled under my shirt.

"What's going on with you?"

"I hate that you're my addiction," he muttered.

"You wanted it, didn't you?" I asked as my palms pushed against the tabletop.

"I did and I still do," he said, pushing me to the table. I broke free and turned to face him.

"No," I said, meeting his angry gaze. "I don't want to do it like that."

Aaron sneered in fury.

"I'm not made of stone, Thea," he picked me up by the hips and sat me onto the table, pressing his body against mine. His eyes were flashing bright red, and I thought I'd be done in a second if he lets the claws and the fangs out.

"I can see that," I said and touched his face. "But you can't do this to me." I hardly recognized myself. I was calm and patient as if Beast brought me to a place where I had nothing more to lose. "You don't want to break me, do you?" I looked into his wild eyes and felt adrenaline run through my veins. "It's not you…"

His body shivered, and the despair in his eyes made me hold my breath. I squeezed his face and moved on to his hair, holding him close.

"Don't move," he said through his teeth, and I felt sweat under my fingertips. His chest was going up and down, his hands were shaking, clutching to my hips as if he was fighting himself. He seemed to be winning. His breathing slowed down, and when he opened his eyes, they were not red anymore. "I'm sorry."

Aaron pulled me into a hug and touched my forehead with his, trying to catch a breath.

"Seems like you should have another shower," I whispered.

"Sorry…"

"It's always a rollercoaster with you…" I replied, my lips trembling.

We stood like that for several minutes.

"All I really do right now is trying to stay human," he told me, looking up at me, "for you." His lips curled into an angry sneer. "I could destroy all of them with one word…"

“Who?”

“Those who think that their opinion should be important to me…”

“Would you do it before?”

He was watching my face closely.

“Power is the best argument for both humans and us. I could challenge each and every one of them and rip some throats, but who would I become to you?”

At this moment something changed in me. Aaron was ready to give me something I couldn’t accept without giving something back. My hands slid to his shoulders and I pressed my body to his. It was strange and unusual because I never saw myself being bound to a man. I doubt someone else would be able to do that, and I'd had no idea what it would take. Beast found a way. It was not something he was used to, but it was what it took. He gave me everything he could without asking for anything in return.

I stepped back, looking him in the eyes. He was tired, exhausted really, but still as wild and dangerous… My lips parted, and I suddenly felt as if there wasn’t enough air in the room to fill my lungs. I got closer and kissed him. I saw him close his eyes and scowl as if afraid of scaring me away.

It was impossible to stop. My hands found their way under his shirt, and I felt his muscles tense at this first touch. I moved them up to his chest. My lips were looking for a response, and they got it in the best beast fashion. He grabbed the back of my head and pulled me into the kiss, taking the initiative. It only took him mere seconds to take my clothes off. I only left a slight bite on his neck, when he moved me onto the table, getting a hoarse growl out of my mouth. He sat me in the middle, right under bright light as if to watch every change in me. I had no patience left and I was pressing myself onto him, wrapping my legs around him and asking for everything he could give me. He didn’t make me wait for long. He pushed me to the table and pulled me to its edge. His madness was contagious. I trembled in his arms, crying and growling from his every move, making him move faster, harder. I felt an ecstatic "yes" leave my lips, and for a second I stopped breathing in the anticipation of a climax. I fell into a vacuum, leaving him, listening to the waves of the incoming orgasm…

They say people are born alone and die alone… They also live through the trembling sensation of approaching pleasure alone. It's not possible to describe the breaking point, when it spreads through you, sweeps you away, and pulls you into the darkness… and in this darkness, I was caught by the man's hands bringing me back to reality.

So, the main course was certainly hot. We both came to our senses on the floor. I was lying on top of him, exhausted.

"Is it always like this with you?" I said and smiled weakly when I finally was able to talk again.

"Like what?" he asked and chuckled.

He seemed normal — calm, confident, and balanced.

"I've never had an orgasm with a man before," I said and put my head up to look at him.

"That's flattering. It means that I feel you well."

He felt what I wanted. This time he hadn't even had to bite me in the neck.

"I also never had so much sex in such a short time."

He clenched his teeth, and his strong jaw tightened.

"You'll do the medical check tomorrow, Thea," he declared.

"I can't do it tomorrow, Shane asked me to work late," I replied, straightened my arms, and sat up.

"Fuck him," Aaron snapped, standing up. "So, eggs and bacon?"

"What do you mean, 'fuck him?'" I said, going into the attack mode. "He's my boss."

"I'll talk to him," Aaron told me and turned me in the direction of the bathroom. He grabbed me by the waist and dragged me to the door.

"Don't!"

"Your health is my priority!"

"What time?" I asked. "Maybe we could do it in the evening? What time does the medical center work?"

Our eyes met in the mirror. Aaron looked dangerous as if testing my courage, and his next words were surprising.

"I'll try to arrange it for later…"

After the shower, I was finishing the eggs and I heard him speaking on the phone, standing next to the living room window.

"They're going to come tomorrow to take the tests," he said and came back to the table. I looked at him. He was calm and relaxed. He walked to the stove and opened one of the cabinets. "Are the eggs okay?"

"It's strange, kind of two-layer omelet… " I said. The first layer got cooked before sex and the second one — after. "And the bottom is a little burned."

"Looks great, so it'll do."

I smiled, watching him.

While he was making coffee, I walked to the flat-screen and turned it on to bring some livelihood into the silence and ease the tension in the room. I even manage it at first, but the news came on, and Aaron's ex-fiancee's face appeared on the screen. Grace Dolly sat in the evening news studio, all beauty and grace, with her extremely large sad blue eyes. Such an angel!

"Tonight in our studio is Grace Dolly, the most famous woman of the week. People of Cryton sympathize with her and come out on the streets in her support," the host said, and my eyes widened in surprise. I froze with the plate and the remote control in my hands. "Aaron Houwer, the CEO of *Black&Gold Industries*, broke off their engagement two weeks before the wedding after being spotted with model Theana Melory. The couple was photographed holding each other near Theana's house. This photo could be touching if it wasn't for the tragic consequences. Houwer's PR office has not given the statement yet, and Houwer refuses to give an interview. At the same time, Theana Melory doesn't show the same patience…"

The video of me telling the reporter to "fuck off" rolled, completing the image of my indecency.

"Thea," Aaron called.

"Wait, I want to watch that."

"Well, come here when you're done. I made coffee."

"Miss Dolly," the interviewer continued. "Tell me, how long do you think your ex-fiance and his mistress have been together?"

"Aaron isn't an impulsive person," she mumbled bitterly. To be fair, Aaron isn't a person at all. I was wondering if she knew the real reason we were together. "So, I suppose, long enough."

"Why did he decide to call the engagement off now, only two weeks before the wedding?"

"I think he got carried away," she said and shrugged. "Maybe he thought it would go away. He is very hard on himself…" This was the first time I felt jealous. Yes, I noticed that he was, but when she said it, it sounded like her personal achievement, like I was just using something that belonged to someone else. "Well, I suppose passion does miracles," she concluded and grimaced as if she was about to cry.

"Tell me, if he comes back to his senses," the interviewer continued, "would you be able to forgive him?"

"No," she said and sneered as if Aaron was already down on his knees, begging for forgiveness. "Betrayals like this are not something one could forgive. If I were Theana Melory, I would think carefully about what kind of person I'm planning to marry…"

Well, here was that again.

"Aaron?" I called and turned to find him sitting on the couch with the burned omelet. "I just heard, for the second time, that I'm getting married..."

I saw him stop chewing, and take a cup of coffee in his hands.

"I need to get married before my thirty-seventh birthday. It's one of the things I have to do as a Prime."

"You're not answering my question," I noted and walked up to him. "Am I marrying you?"

I stopped in front of him and froze in anticipation.

"You are if you agree," he said and looked at me as if challenging me, and then let out a predatory grin that made me stop breathing.

"If I agree?" I repeated. My voice went hoarse. "Do I have a choice?"

"I don't remember making any orders."

"Are you serious? Are you going to ask me?" I asked and blinked in confusion.

"Thea," he started and stood up. "I'm a polite beast. I know that women need to be proposed to. At least the woman who one chooses himself."

Frankly, I was surprised by the turn of events. The main point I got from his speech was that he didn't propose to Grace.

"Is this a challenge, Mr. Houwer?" I asked, my voice shaking. I was used to not being able to choose, and now he was suddenly sharing the responsibility. "What if I decline?"

The world froze. He was looking me in the eyes, and I saw flames dancing in his pupils.

"Then I'll let you go."

I held my breath, trying to realize what he had just said.

"You will?" I repeated, unsure if it was true.

He nodded, but the fire in his eyes grew brighter.

"If you decline my proposal, you will be free."

It was impossible to understand this man. First, he told me we have no other way but to be together, that we have no way to terminate the contract, and now he was suddenly ready to let me go? There were only two weeks left to decide!

"I need a minute," I said and quickly walked to the bathroom.

I need to understand how I feel. It would be okay to smile at my reflection and clap my hands because freedom was so close I could touch it! Sadly, in the mirror, I saw someone scared and confused, someone, who wasn't happy with the arrangement. I felt almost painfully aware of my surroundings. What would happen if I do it? What would it do to our connection, to him and to his addiction? What would it do to me?

Bathroom solitude didn't help me get my thoughts straight, and when I came back I was still a mess.

"Thea, your coffee," Aaron said. He was sitting on the couch and watching the city.

"Thanks," I said, sat down next to him, and took the cup from his hands.

"For coffee?" he asked and looked up at me. His eyes were not flashing and looked human. However, I knew that Beast was far from being calm. He was tense, only playing human.

"For everything," I replied and took a sip. Hot. "What do the flashes in your eyes mean?"

"Emotional instability."

"For any reason?"

"Yes. I told you, you're the only one who sees them."

"Is it so that I know when to calm you down?"

"Kind of…"

"Can I calm you down?"

"You can if you want to."

"Well, I should practice that…"

"We did practice today," he said with a smirk.

"Sex?"

"No, before that."

"I was just scared."

"I know."

We didn't talk for a while.

"Can I sit on your lap?" I asked, surprising even myself. "Just…" He put his coffee down and watched me sit down. "You can hug me," I said and smiled, watching his confusion. I led by example, putting my hands on his shoulders.

"Can you explain what you want?" he asked, and his eyes shined.

"Trying to tame you, Mr. Houwer," I said and chuckled. "Why? Are you timid?"

"Not timid, just wild," he corrected, grinning. He put his hands on my waist. "Comfortable?"

"I haven't decided yet," I said and moved a little bit. I felt that he was still tense, although not as much as before. "How was your day?"

"I told you it was bad."

"Sure, but if you tell me more, it would feel better," I said and looked him in the eyes. It was easier now because I was the one leading.

"Well, my position is not completely independent from my personal life. You, humans, can date, cheat, get married and divorced, and your business partners wouldn't care, but in our world, everyone is wary of those situations. I'm lucky *Black&Gold Industries* is the sole provider on the oil market. Still, I spent the whole day on meetings, where everyone tried to test the waters."

"Test the waters?"

Well, so far it was very interesting.

"Yes, it's when they come to you for a business meeting, but they really want to test if you're still sane..."

I squeezed fingers on his shoulders. It was difficult to imagine how tired he really was. Now I understood why Primes shouldn't have had life companions like me. Aaron played a stone-cold leader all day, but everything inside of him was burning.

"Can I somehow help you?"

His gaze was full of confusion and gratitude, and it filled me with so many emotions.

"You can do what you did today," he said. He didn't try to pull me closer. "You helped immensely." We went silent and looked each other in the eyes, when he suddenly continued, "I have something to ask you. Don't listen to Alexander too much, he will do anything to try and spoil this..."

His gaze was full of doubt, and it was clear that he would make me quit and not risk it, but he didn't want to ask me to do something that drastic. I just had to promise to be careful.

***

In the morning medical staff came and took the tests. Then we parted and went each our way, but we could both feel that something changed after the previous night. Instead of the line of defense on my side and grim caution on his, we were both full of curiosity. It was as if we lived in separate rooms and suddenly opened the door to connect them. No one was yet ready to step through it, but either wasn't determined to close it.

"Is everything alright, Thea?" Claud asked, smiling at me in the car mirror.

"Yes," I replied and shook the stupor off. "Why?"

"You look good today," he complimented and grinned.

"Do I usually look bad?" I asked and grinned back.

"You're usually tense, but today you're not. For the first time."

I smiled.

"Yes, it's much better today. Thanks, Claud."

"Anything for you, dear."

When we pulled over to *Teyvalle*, there was a crowd waiting for us.

"Don't you think it might be time to defend Aaron?" I asked, watching the journalists stepping around the car.

"Maybe it is," he said.

When my door opened, I was immediately bombarded with questions.

"Theana, Grace Dolly gave an interview, but why are you keeping silent? Did Aaron forbid you from commenting on the situation?"

"No, he didn't," I replied and took my sunglasses off. The reporter's eyes widened as if he didn't believe his own luck.

"Have you been together for long?"

"No."

"How did you meet?"

"At Dustin Dewman's collection shoot. Aaron came there to pick up a piece."

"Was it love at first sight?"

"Not really. Our relationship went through different stages before we were sure we were ready to risk our stable and planned out lives," I corrected coldly. "Of course in our world, it's easier to believe in arrangement and calculation than in real feelings, but I'm proud of Aaron. He wasn't afraid to fight for his happiness. I will stand by his side no matter what."

Knife was standing next to me and smiling in approval.

"Did Mr. Houwer's engagement stop you?"

"Mr. Houwer wouldn't take such a risk for something that wasn't worth it. I trust he made the best choice for himself."

"Are you going to marry him?"

"I haven't received a proposal yet," I said and grinned. "Excuse me, I need to get to work."

"I hardly recognize you, dear," Knife whispered to me. He was obviously pleased with me. "Thank you. I'm sure Aaron will appreciate this."

"He deserves some support."

"I'm glad you finally got it," Knife said and opened the door for me.

The day was tense but calm. I didn't see Duvalle during the rehearsal, so that went well. The production manager praised me, the dress didn't make me stumble, and the runway was smooth. I was really getting into every moment of the show. I was smiling and heard an occasional "good job" from the manager, which made it all so much better.

Well, I knew it was too good of a day to be true, and it was soon proved, when Shane applauded me after the last walk.

"Well, I see the experiment had gone well," he said, grinning. "You look magical today…"

"Thanks. What was the experiment?" I asked, taking his outstretched hand and stepping down from the stage.

"I sent Duvalle on a business trip," he admitted, and it felt like he was about to let out a satisfied purr.

"Do you think she is partial towards me?" I questioned. I took my hand, and he let it go with resistance.

"Are you serious?" he said and watched my face closely. "Your interview was quite impressive today."

I tensed. Alexander walked me to Cafarelli, and his satisfied grin was not a good sign.

"Really?"

"Good job, Thea. If you're with Houwer, you need to grow some claws. He didn't ask you to do it though, did he?"

"No."

"We're going to an event tonight," he said suddenly, changing the topic and opening the doors of the designer's office.

"What event?"

"I have a business meeting," he told me, looking me in the eyes. "And you need to see how tough your claws are. I suppose it will be good for you to see the world you're planning to enter..."

"So, is it about work?" I said through the teeth.

"It's about you. Aaron would never show you this..." Shane said and grabbed my shoulder, not letting me go.

"What do you want from me?" I asked. "Are you trying to hurt Aaron?"

"The question is what you want," he responded and pulled me closer. "Do you want to live in a perfect illusion behind a fence? Doesn't he throw himself at you with his claws out after a long day at work? Do you think it will get better?" he asked. He tried to hit it close to home. Our distrust, my fear of not being able to deal with him and his fury. Alexander saw me give up. "You're not the one to hide, Theana. You should take a closer look at him before defending him. Think about that until the evening."

He exited right when Knife appeared at the end of the corridor. They had a silent fight, and then my bodyguard looked at me.

"What did he do?"

"Nothing," I lied.

This bastard knew where to hit. I was only happy he was nice the rest of the day, and it was easy to ask him to let Bunny come in to have lunch together.

Now my friend was sitting opposite me in the café and turning his head in all directions.

"Damn! I can't believe it! I'm in *Teyvalle*."

I smiled, happy to have an opportunity to switch to something else.

"Eat up!"

"This is just heavenly!" Bunny said as he started on his sandwich. "Tell me, how have you been? You're glowing!"

"Really?" I asked and smirked.

"Uh-huh," he confirmed. "Is our pet beast doing a good job?"

"Our?" I chuckled. "You're quick to accept him into the family."

"Well, I can see he is trying hard," he said. "The food here is amazing! I'll probably have to hop on the treadmill till midnight. Although I've been staying in the gym for hours because it's so boring at home without you..."

"Oh, I certainly brought you too much entertainment lately..." I told him and rolled my eyes.

"Tell me," he said with a serious expression, "how are you?"

"Complicated," I replied and shrugged, not sure how to explain everything that had been happening. "Aaron told me he has to get married before his thirty-seventh birthday."

Bunny stopped chewing his food and now looked kind of funny with his unfinished sandwich in his hand. I waited for him to get water, and only then continued.

"He told that, if I refuse to marry him when he proposes, he will let me go free."

So, giving him time to drink some water was a good idea, but he still choked on his food.

"Wow!" he muttered. "That's a bold move..."

"Excuse me?"

"I'm telling you, he's a real man for doing that, you can't let him go," he said and looked at me intently. "You're a smart girl, aren't you? Do you understand what this means? He loves you!"

"It's a little early for love," I mumbled, confused.

"Please! How much time do you think you need?" he asked and rolled his eyes. "I suspect it's not quite usual for them to let go of their mates… Especially considering everything you've told me… And all of his dictator habits in the beginning… Well, at least he changed quickly, kudos to him. It means he wants to be with you on your terms."

"He told me that if I'm unhappy, he won't be happy either."

"Well, maybe that," my friend concluded and shrugged. "Anyway, an impressive choice on his part."

"Aren't you going to ask what answer I will give?"

"He obviously takes his time for a reason. And you obviously have no idea what to say," Bunny said and winked at me. "I want popcorn and a first-row seat for this show!"

I snorted and smiled, knowing all too well that Bunny was right, and I felt much better with the whole arrangement. It was true that I still wasn't sure about my answer, but I was not thinking about running away like I was before, especially now, when he clearly said he would let me go. Knife was right when he said that I didn't have time to listen, too busy with fighting. Now there was no one to fight. I wasn't delusional and knew it wouldn't be easy, because I still didn't know the rules of the game I was playing.

Maybe it would be a good idea to find them out?


In the evening I threw occasional glances at Alexander during our weekly meeting with the production team, and he responded by throwing some of them back. I knew I shouldn't be led on like that. I was, however, ready to take one step forward. Aaron and I needed some solid ground to continue all this, not something vague and blurry. The fact that Knife told me to not get deeper and to not find out more only made me more eager.

I was worried that whatever Shane wanted to show me would be too much. It was a part of Beast's life, but what if I couldn't accept it? Would we be able to trust each other again? I knew it shouldn't have been Shane I joined on this discovery, but there was no one else willing to bring me into the fold.

When Alexander walked up to me after the meeting, I knew that I would go with him.

"Ready?" he asked.

I nodded.

"Let's go," he ordered, and I quickly followed him.

Knife joined us at the exit, but Shane looked at him and spoke.

"Wait here, we have an emergency fitting, and she'll be free to go straight after."

"It's okay," I confirmed to my bodyguard. I had no idea how Shane was planning to get me past Knife, but the issue was solved quickly when we used one of the secret exits.

I was standing at the parking lot, wrapping my denim jacket around my body, while Shane drove his convertible to the parking exit.

"Hop in," he said and grinned. "Good girl." I wasn't quite as confident, but there was no way back. "Relax, no one's going to eat you alive," he said, chuckling. "Do you want to put some music on?"

"I don't care," I disregarded. "Where are we going?"

Nightlife in the center created a false sense of security, but my every cell was filled with tension. I was holding my bag tight in my hands, expecting my phone to vibrate. What would I do then? I could lie that Shane and I are on a business errand, but how would I then explain lying to Knife?

"There is an engagement party in one of the restaurants... With someone like you."

"Oh, so you marry people like me?"

"Why not? Dustin would," he said.

"Without my consent," I countered.

"Houwer is no different then."

He had no idea that this time he missed, but I didn't show him that.

"Why do you think it's okay for me to come there?"

Everyone knew who I was.

"It's not, but you're already coming."

"I can change my mind," I said and felt very stupid for a second.

"You can," he told me, "but I won't make any more offers to get you out of this mess..."

"So, how are you planning to get me out of this mess?" I asked and narrowed my eyes in anger.

All these thoughts were counterproductive and made my head hurt.

"There are options, Thea," he replied, looking at me with his eyes flashing red.

"What is in it for you? You wanted to find out how Dustin died, didn't you? Why are you suddenly helping me?"

"Oh, you're not naïve enough to think I'm doing that selflessly, are you? I'll help you and you'll help me. If you forgot, maybe I should refresh your memory on how you got into this mess in the first place..."

I started shaking, but it was too late to back out because Shane's convertible drove into the parking lot.

"Come on," Alexander said and held his hand out for me. "Why are you such a little coward?" he questioned, and I saw triumphant flames burning in his eyes. "You can't be like that in our world, Thea. You start strong, but give up quickly." He walked me to the elevator. "I can say I start to understand Houwer better. Our women are shadows, fearful and bent by the circumstances. You are so different, so lively, so warm, so real..." he whispered, looking at me with hungry eyes, which made me shiver.

"Alright, I'm out," I cried and tried to make a dash across the lot, but Alexander grabbed my arm and pushed me into the elevator.

"Told you you give up too soon," he noted calmly. My breathing quickened, and I really hated myself for being stupid enough to come. My phone vibrated in the bag, but Alexander snapped it from my hands.

"What are you doing?!"

Adrenaline traveled through my veins, and my chest squeezed in burning fear.

"You can't use your phone here," he replied coldly. I couldn't get the word in before the elevator doors opened.

"Mr. Shane," the guard greeted, "good evening."

The room was filled with an atmosphere of luxury, and from where I stood I could see the entrance to the main hall very well. There were well-dressed women and respectable-looking men. I was calmed by the fact it wasn't some lab where I would die in suffering.

"Miss Theana Melory is joining me today," Alexander said and caught me by the arm. Guards nodded and let us in. "Highest society of our world is here tonight," he told me but didn't walk me into the hall. Instead, we went to the side stairs, from which I could see everything happening in the hall below. "Houwer wouldn't dare coming here after how he treated our values and traditions."

"Values?" I asked, pretending to be interested, but really watching my bag in his hands.

"Watch carefully, Thea," he said. "I'm risking, bringing you here."

"Can't say I feel bad for you," I snapped, trying to free my hand from his. He didn't let me do that and dragged me further.

"Why are you so nervous? Do you need a drink?"

"Yes, please," I agreed eagerly.

"Alright, just don't go anywhere. In case you're planning to run away, know that they won't let you out."

"You're mad," I said through the teeth and felt my body shiver.

"No," he replied calmly. "Wait here…"

I watched him go downstairs into the hall and made a couple of steps to follow him. As soon as I was near the guards, I finally noticed there was something wrong. A man, who just exited the elevator, had a leash in his hand. A jeweled chain went up to a collar on a woman's neck. He walked her like a dog. He wasn't holding her hand, he wasn't talking to her, he even yanked the chain slightly to make her stay closer. The woman was a petite blond in a marvelous red gown, and when she suddenly noticed me I saw a shadow of utter humiliation in her glare. I was struck. I watched the couple and noticed several more men with leashes in their hands. Women were wearing different designer necklaces, each of them was a masterpiece, but under each was a visible bite mark. These women were invisible to the rest of the crowd, they were deliberately ignored.

I immediately remembered my own collar with a black diamond…

"Thea, champagne?"

I twitched and looked at the glass in Alexander's hand. Then suddenly there was a commotion behind him, and Alexander's glass shattered under his feet. Aaron grabbed him by the neck and yanked him to himself. It was hard to imagine what would happen if Knife didn't rush forward to stop him…

"Calm down," he ordered and grabbed Aaron's hand. "She is okay, let's take her and go…"

I wasn't okay though. And neither was Aaron. He pushed Knife to the side and threw Alexander into a wall. Shane hit the wall with his side, but then, true to his cat nature, landed on all fours. Both of them let their claws and fangs out and clashed in the middle of the room. It wasn't a normal fight. Aaron clearly lost control and was about to kill Alexander. Although the latter was good in intrigues, he obviously wasn't made for a violent confrontation. His shirt was red and wet with blood, and his sleeves were torn apart, with one of his arms limp. All he could do is try and dodge. The crowd ran from the hall, and there were screams and cries around the room. Guards at the entrance finally came to their senses, and one of them shouted something into his radio.

"Thea, I'm grabbing him and taking him, you're following me," Knife ordered and dashed towards the men.

Alexander dodged again, and Knife grabbed Aaron from behind. Beast roared, showing his teeth, and tried to break free. It was the first time I saw Knife in action. His eyes flashed bright yellow, and his primal growl almost shook the building, but even he couldn't move Aaron from his place. I couldn't wait any longer and ran into the middle of the fight.

"Thea, no!" Knife shouted, but I jumped onto Beast and held him tight.

"Aaron," I whispered. "Aaron, please, calm down, I'm here, I'm with you…" He shook his head and growled in warning. My blood froze in horror, but I knew there was no way back. "Come back to me, please. Calm down… I'm with you, I always will be…"

I finally found the right words, and Aaron suddenly let out a loud sigh and his shoulders relaxed. I ran my fingers throw his hair and pressed my forehead to his temple. I didn't even notice when Knife let him free but felt Aaron pick me up. The room went silent.

"Call the police and ambulance," Knife said coldly. "Aaron…"

"I'm alright," he growled. "Where can I wait?"

"Hey, he's asking you," Knife snapped at someone.

The crowd came back to life, and the voices grew louder, but Aaron was already walking down the corridor with me in his arms. Someone was walking in front and showing him the way.

"Do you need a lawyer?"

"No."

"Well, when the police come, you might…"

"No. Bring some water."

"Okay, Mr. Houwer."

Doors opened, and we were in somebody's office. All of the noise was left behind, and now I realized I was shaking in his arms. Aaron sat on the couch with me and laid his head back without a word. I didn't say anything too. It was a strange situation. Shane clearly gave me a chance to run away, but I ran to Aaron instead, because he needed me. Was it Stockholm syndrome? I saw women in collars with humiliation in their eyes! How is it even possible? They're treated like pets! That was probably the life Dustin Dewman had in store for me. And Aaron, too.

I tried to get out of his grip, but he only squeezed me tighter.

"What the fuck were you doing here?" he growled into my ear. His tone was a good indication of incoming problems.

"It doesn't matter," I said. "Shane wanted to show me this, and I've seen enough. Let me go."

He did.

"Be here," he demanded. "I'll be back soon."

I felt naked and cold, both inside and out. I curled into a ball on a couch, grimacing from all the smells around. I immediately realized that there was one scent I didn't feel anymore, the one of our connection with Aaron. It was as if he took it with him, shut the door, and left nothing behind.

There were voices outside, doors opened and closed, and sirens went loud on the street. It was impossible to fall asleep to all of that, but I managed. I saw the hospital again, blue and red hallways, my boss shouting. This time he was shouting at me because I was stupid enough to go with Alexander. Next to him was a body covered in blood, just as I remembered it from that night with the mask and the hood covering its face.

"Thea."

I woke up when someone picked me up. I shook my head and blinked. The sleep was heavy and left me with a headache. I clenched onto Aaron's shoulder, cuddling in his arms.

"You're alive..."

I quickly got a glimpse of the corridor and then saw the bright light of the elevator. I moved in Aaron's arms, but he only held me tighter.

The parking lot was busy with people, cars, and red and blue lights. Aaron walked up to the nearest car, gave a nod to Knife, and soon the building was left behind. We were driving through the streets of the city. I let myself out of his grasp and moved to the opposite window, curling up and wrapping myself into the jacket. I had no idea where we were going. The center of Cryton was long gone, and then we drove through the suburbs as the car left the city, moving onto the highway. I didn't have enough courage to speak to Beast. Knife on the front seat was also silent. He dismissed a couple of calls and only took one of them, quickly handing the phone to Aaron.

"Hi," he said, his voice dry. "Yeah, we'll be there soon. About thirty minutes. See you soon."

When would this day finally end? And where? I was more and more nervous, looking out into the night. In about twenty minutes, our car drove off the highway and through narrow streets, surrounded by neat little houses. There wasn't much light. The driver stopped the engine when we got to the gates, and Aaron got out of the car to drag me out next.

"Let's go," he said and pointed to the gates.

"I got to go," Knife told us and gave Aaron his phone and my bag. "All of the calls will be redirected to me. Have some rest… Thea," he called and gave me a harsh look, "try to have some rest too. I'll be in touch…"

Aaron waited for the car to leave and then turned to face me.

"Come on."

"Where are we going?" I asked, not following his order.

"My home," he replied through clenched teeth but didn't try to drag me further.

"Your home? Why?"

"Why did you believe this bastard, Thea? I asked you…" he finally let out.

"I saw these women with the collars!" I cried, stepping away, but he caught me and held me tight. "I don't want this! I don't!" I screamed, trying to break free. "I don't want to have anything in common with someone who lets things like this happen!"

The tension of the day found its way out with tears, and I went limp in his arms, exhausted from the incident. I had no power to fight and I didn't really want to. His arms felt like the most secure place in the world, and it was hard to believe he could be one of the men with a leash in his hands.

"Come on," he repeated and walked me to the gates.

The dark garden behind them was humid and warm. There was water somewhere close, and the insects were chirping. Gravel was soughing under my feet, and the path was surrounded by soft leaves. The path led us to a well-lit opening, which had several more paths running in all different directions. I looked around. It was like a real forest out here! There were tall trees, thick shrubs, and long thin paths. The air was filled with the aroma of night violets, and large black butterflies were flying around them in the dim light.

"Aaron," someone said, and a woman in simple jeans and shirt walked towards us. She looked quite young, not a day over forty. "Thea," she said and smiled, a net of wrinkles forming in the corners of her eyes. "Happy to see you."

"Hi, mom," Aaron replied, and I was lost for a second. Being brought home to his parents was the last thing I'd expected after everything that happened tonight. I was more prepared for a basement with a chain and collar. "She is tired…"

"Sorry," I said and blinked, holding my hand out. "It's just all out of the blue. Aaron didn't tell me where we were going."

"I'm Amalia," the woman said, introducing herself. "Let's go inside, the dinner is ready."

I was expecting anything, but a small one-story house. It was straight out of a fairytale, hidden behind the trees, with yellow windows blinking through the leaves.

"Your father doesn't know I went out to welcome you," Amalia said, leading us to the house. I heard a smile in her voice. "He will be grumpy about it, so let's pretend we met at the door."

"Mom, I think he'll understand."

I gave Aaron a side-eye. He was holding my hand. He seemed like a different person. Even in the dim light, I could see he was smiling. What was going on here? Just half an hour drive away from the city, where he was a dangerous and tough beast, he was a normal human, who just came home. It was his real home, one where one's heart and soul are. How did this woman manage to make him normal in just a couple of minutes? I seemed to always do the opposite.

We entered a narrow hallway with light-brown, caramel walls. The smell of food reminded me that I didn't have lunch because it was nearly impossible to eat with Bunny and I wasn't hungry after all of Alexander's mysteries.

"Denver," Amalia called loudly. "The kids are here."

"The kids?" I muttered and looked at Aaron. He was nearly unrecognizable and smiling with an unfamiliar smile.

"Hi, dad…"

I turned and met a curious look of the family's patriarch Denver Houwer. He didn't look like a powerful man from the photos but rather like a normal man enjoying his retirement. His tough gaze reminded me of Aaron's. He wasn't about to make it softer.

"Aaron, what happened?" he asked, standing at the dining room doors.

"Can we speak alone?" Aaron returned the question and held me by the waist.

"Thea," Amalia called, following us. "Let's have some tea…"

We walked into a small and cozy kitchen with a lingering smell of food. Nothing here was out of the house's fairytale-like appearance. The furniture was the same light-brown as the walls, and turquoise table and chairs looked old-fashioned. On the table, there were flowers and fresh herbs in a vase.

"How are you?" Amalia asked, turning to face me with a cup of tea. It looked and smelled herbal. "Here you go."

"Thank you," I said, and when our eyes met, I couldn't hold my curiosity back. "Did you have to wear a collar too?"

I couldn't stop thinking about it. Everything in me was against the idea that I would have to do that too…

"No," Amalia replied, watching me. "Thea, what happened today?"

I relaxed and sat back.

"I saw men walking their companions on leashes at the event," I started. "Sorry, I thought you were also…"

"Thea, you and I, we are similar," Amalia noted carefully and sat opposite me. "I'm also my man's true mate. It was also by accident, by not as dramatic as it was for you. I can't imagine what you're going through…"

I was blinking fast in confusion. We were similar? That's what Shane meant when he said that it runs in the family…

"How did it go for you?"

"It wasn't very hard, the hard part was on Denver. You know, they can't really be with people like us," she said, and I nodded. "But he managed. He was the Prime for twenty more years, and then he gave his position to Aaron."

"Did no one find out?"

"They did later," she noted and smiled. "Primes are only born in couples like ours. No one has ever walked me on a leash. Our family doesn't do that. In fact, many families stopped doing that."

I closed my eyes. I was such a fool to fall for Shane's act.

"Thea," Amalia called, "talk to me, please…"

"Sorry," I said and shook my head. "It's all my fault. I was led on with all these mysteries and ended up making a huge mess." I held my cup in my hands and inhaled the deep smell of herbs.

"There aren't really many mysteries there. My husband's race is very connected to humans," she told me and shrugged. "One of the biggest ones is the database. The government tests all the girls when they are fifteen and registers them."

"Well, that's also kind of creepy…"

"In most of the couples, everything is consensual, Thea. Meetings, love… Even some of the women with collars consent to wear them. It's all about priorities. Some people value love more, but some are looking for money, and it makes them forget about the humiliation…"

"Are you sure those women are even asked?"

Amalia sighed.

"Of course it's different for everyone. It's important that our family long abandoned this tradition. Denver is the head of the family and he supports the equality between us and humans."

I nodded and took a big sip to calm down.

"You know, I've been asking Aaron to bring you here," Amalia said and smiled softly.

"Yeah, I guess he should've. I don't know what's going to happen now…"

Amalia frowned, but then Aaron and Denver entered the kitchen. They both wore mysterious looks on their faces. Aaron's father looked surprised, and I couldn't really understand if the surprise was pleasant. Aaron held a smile in the corners of his mouth and looked at me with his shiny eyes.

Amalia watched both of them as if trying to understand whether they had reached an agreement.

"Amalia, let's have dinner," Denver declared. "We need to celebrate the meeting!"

He then grinned at me, completely disarming me. Did Aaron not tell him what had happened? Well, it wasn't my battle to fight. Dinner went on with all the family magic I had only remembered from my childhood, and even then it was no more than illusions. The parents were running around us, and especially me, pouring me tea and putting more food on my plate than I could eat. We talked about me, and they asked me about my family and career, doing their best to avoid any sharp corners. It was as if Aaron and I met like normal people, just as I lied in the interview, and now he was just ordinarily introducing me to his parents. I was wondering whether they actually knew how we met.

It was weird, but I was once again feeling our connection. It all came back. He was so calm, I thought he could purr. I was glancing at him with confusion, not sure about things I sensed. Again and again, I was reassured that my feelings didn't lie — he was calm and satisfied as if he had just eaten Shane for lunch.

After dinner, we moved to the fireplace in the living room. Aaron sat me on his lap and started acting on the verge of indecency. He touched my hair, buried his nose in my neck. He was testing the limits.

"Excuse me," I snapped, getting out of his grip. "Can we talk for a second?"

"Of course," he said and smirked, making me think he wasn't served tea at dinner.

"What's going on?" I blurted out when we got outside.

He put his hands in his pockets.

"What do you mean?"

"I messed up!" I told him walking back and forth on the terrace. "You're acting as if nothing happened!"

He sighed and shrugged.

"It's all behind us," he concluded philosophically. He certainly was served something stronger than tea!

"What is?!" I cried. "What about Shane?! You told me there is a death sentence for what you did!"

"Thea, there won't be, but I'm happy you're so worried about me," he said, changing back to Beast. He lowered his head and his eyes flashed. "Come here."

I had no idea what was in his voice, but I couldn't disobey. When there was only a step left between us, he stretched his arms to me and hugged me tightly.

"You shouldn't worry," he whispered into my ear.

"No one should!"

"Especially you."

“Why?”

He took a long look at me.

“Beast handling rules,” he said and smiled. “Beasts don't like nervous and worried people.”

I snorted and rolled my eyes, but then remembered there was one more thing to do.

“I'm sorry I didn't listen to your advice.”

A frog let out a loud noise as if unsure of my sincerity.

“It's not your fault, I understand,” Aaron disagreed. “It's all on Shane.”

“You knew he would do something like that but still let me go to *Teyvalle* every day,” I said, looking him straight in the eyes.

“Well, I can afford that,” he noted calmly.

“I just... I couldn't believe you could do something like that. Make me wear a collar I mean...”

“I couldn't...”

“I know. Your mom told me,” I confessed. “She is nice.”

“Yes, that she is,” he agreed and grinned.

“You probably should tell me more though,” I noted, unable to believe his compliance.

“Probably,” he agreed.

“What will happen to Alexander?”

Aaron shrugged.

“I couldn't care less.”

“You're like a cat on a catnip trip,” I said. “What are you so pleased about?”

He looked behind me for some time as if listening in.

“You make me pleased,” he concluded. His face went tense for a second and then switched to wariness. There were voices and noises from the gates. Aaron moved me to the side, but I dashed forward when Bunny stepped out from behind the bushes.

“Sh,” Aaron whispered, holding me tight. “Jaden...”

Bunny was followed by... Aaron. Well, almost. The man looked like Aaron the first night I saw him, he was wearing a black hoodie and a mask. He was slightly taller but extremely similar. I even looked at both of them a couple of times to check the differences.

"Thea!" Bunny cried, and then no one could keep us apart.

"What happened?!" I cried in return, closely watching my best friend's face, while he was clutching my hands.

"He was almost run over on the gym's parking lot," Jaden said and turned to Aaron. "Where is your phone?!"

"Bunny, are you okay?" I asked, looking at him and noticing a bruise on his cheekbone.

Aaron's mother ran out of the house, followed by his father.

"Jaden!" she sighed, looking at the man intently as he took off his mask. "Are you staying?"

"Stay," Aaron ordered. The stranger wasn't sure but frowned, left with no choice. "Thea, this is my brother Jaden."

Jaden and I looked at each other. He was younger. He was looking at me as if I was an enemy. It was clear he would prefer to leave.

"Let's get inside," Amalia called, as if afraid of Jaden running into the night. "Thea, your friend needs some help."

I grabbed Bunny's arm and dragged him inside.

"I was told someone was waiting for me at the parking lot," he whispered loudly. "I came down there... I would be run over if not for the masked dude, Thea..."

"Sh, it's alright," I said and squeezed his shoulder in encouragement.

Amalia sat us all down in the kitchen and brought in a medical kit.

"I hope you have no shoots any time soon," I said, cleaning his cheekbone. "It will take a while to heal."

"I have one for Massimo," Bunny replied. "I'm sure they'll add some more bruises though..."

"Yea, Massimo will definitely appreciate that..."

"Thea," Bunny whispered, leaning closer. "Is this his parents' house?"

"Yes."

"It's cute."

"Yeah... I messed up today..."

Aaron entered the kitchen, not giving me time to share.

"How are you feeling?" he asked Bunny.

"Alright, thanks. Were you spying on me?"

"We were looking after you."

"Aaron, who did it?" I asked, switching my gaze to the man.

"I saw her," Bunny interrupted. "It was that blonde, what's her name..."

"Grace?"

"Jaden got her into handcuffs and left there," Bunny shared eagerly.

My eyes widened.

"Thea, I'll figure it out," Aaron started, but I couldn't hold the comments in.

"This freaking lamb!" I cried. "She almost killed him!"

"I'll figure it out," Aaron repeated. "Mom is calling you into the living room."

"I think I should go," Bunny said and stood up.

"You'll stay here until my security team checks everything," Aaron declared not leaving us any room for argument. "Come on."

"Wait, your security team? We know it was Grace..."

"Thea, Alexander had access to both you and her... I don't know what he said to her, but I sure know he can be convincing and he knows how to play on people's weaknesses."

I was speechless. I was the one who asked Alexander to give me an entrance pass for Bunny... What a jerk! Shane brought Aaron problems all the way around. He was probably planning to destroy him tonight by making him lose his human side. And it was all because of me.

"Just so you know, Thea," Aaron said, walking me to the living room, "Shane's family is the only one that still uses collars. Everyone else has long abandoned this tradition."

This hit me hard, and I allowed him to sit me down on his lap. I felt guilty and was silent. Bunny got a huge portion of meat and pasta and was gratefully eating his stress away. Jaden joined us after a shower and tried to say "no" to dinner, but he couldn't refuse and now the victim and the savior were both rewarded with some food.

"How old is Jaden?" I whispered to Aaron.

"Thirty," he replied. "Why?"

"He looks older. I would think you too are the same age. Does he work for you?"

"Only now," he purred in my ear, and I got goosebumps. "He usually doesn't work for me..."

"What does he do?"

"He has his own company, specializing in security technology..."

"I didn't know you have a brother. There was no info online."

I saw Amalia try to be closer to the younger Houwer as if afraid that every question could be the last one. I was wondering why he seemed to be so feral.

"We did everything to avoid that, we don't really like being in the spotlight," he said, and I snorted. "Yes, I am in the spotlight right now. Just like my father was once..."

"Your mom told me she is a human too," I noted and turned to see him. These slow minutes went by but froze in memory as if promising to stay with us forever. I would remember the sounds of the fireplace, herbal tea, and his warmth.

"Thea, I had a good example in front of me."

That was the reason he was so eager to try and be with me. Knife had told me Aaron knew how good it could be if we stayed together.

Aaron seemed to be deep in his thoughts as he touched my neck with his nose, and I felt my chest tighten with every breath. I held his hands on my stomach, and Amalia, who walked by, smiled warmly.

Jaden and Bunny started chatting. I was sure my friend dragged Aaron's grumpy brother into the conversation, but Jaden seemed to enjoy it. Now, when everything was calm, my thoughts went back into their normal order. The question was "What's next?" It was very likely I wouldn't be able to come back to the fashion week project.

I frowned at the thought. Not exactly how I imagined my dream to come true. I was sure I had been offered this job as a way to get revenge. Shane certainly calculated everything. I felt absolutely crushed, remembering the preparation process, and the dress, the music, and how my heart was beating when I walked down the runway. That wasn't even the show itself! What would I feel on the actual day? I supposed I had to get used to the thought that it was over. I wasn't even sure how it would influence my career, but I knew I wasn't about to make it worse for Aaron. It would be stupid to continue working with Shane.

Bunny and I went outside while Amalia started preparing the rooms.

"Did you like the brother?" I asked with a smile.

"He's charming," Bunny responded and leaned onto the wall covered in ivy. "It certainly runs in the family…"

I grinned.

"So, what have you done?"

"Do you remember Alexander, *Teyvalle*'s VP?"

"Yeah, I think so. He has a beard or something. Looks like a douche."

"So, apparently, he only offered me the job to get to Aaron. He knew Aaron owned me, Dewman told him before he died…"

My friend looked shocked.

"Didn't Aaron…"

"Of course he knew," I interrupted.

"Wait," Bunny said, frowning. "He knew that was risky and still allowed you to take the job?"

"I told him how important work is for me," I explained and hugged myself. I sat down and leaned against the wall. Ivy leaves were cool and filled my lungs with a fresh smell.

"God, you're both crazy. So, what happened then?"

"Today Shane brought me to their event and provoked Aaron. There was a fight," I said.

"What a jerk!"

"The worst thing is that Aaron can be punished with a death sentence…" I whispered.

"That's fucked up, T," Bunny replied and sat down next to me.

It was. Not too long ago, I wished for it to happen and for Aaron to finally disappear from my life. Now the sole thought of it left me in pain. I couldn't articulate it but I knew I didn't want it to happen. I was dreading it. Maybe it was just guilt… It probably was.

"Aaron is sure he is off the hook," I said, trying not to think about it.

"Well, it might be because of his special status…"

"I believe the law is the same for everyone, Aaron said as much. When he is with me, he loses control, and that's why they are not allowed to be with women like me. Too much emotion."

"Well, babe… Don't you have any sympathy for him?"

"I don't," I snapped. "Though I feel guilty that he has problems because of me."

"Is that really it? You were practically purring in his arms back there…"

"Purring?" I repeated.

"Well, almost," he chuckled.

"Ugh, go to hell," I growled and pushed him slightly. It was enough for him to fall into the grass. He muttered something unpleasant, tidied up, and then we walked back into the house.

Aaron and Jaden were in the kitchen. I shot them a quick glance and was surprised to see that they were both very grim. Aaron stood next to the table with his hands folded on his chest. Jaden was copying his pose. Our eyes met, and I was showered with coldness. I even got goosebumps.

Amalia showed Bunny his bedroom, and then Aaron came in to take me to our room.

"Jaden doesn't like me, does he?" I asked, sitting down next to the fireplace.

The bedroom was so nice I would stay in it forever. It wasn't big, but it was so cozy it made me want to cry. It smelled like wood and fireplace smoke, and the glares of flames were dancing on the floor covered in a soft rug.

My eyes got watery, and it really strange because I never was that sensitive before.

"He does," Aaron said. He sat down behind me and held me close. I let out a soft moan. It wasn't long before he reacted, reaching for my neck and leaving a tender kiss there. "He is just going through a lot right now. I'm very scared for him…"

I squeezed his hands. It was a familiar worry. Once I was just as terrified for my own brother. I couldn't save him: we lived in a dangerous neighborhood, and Dylan was there all alone against street gangs and criminals, and they didn't like it. The last thing he told me with his bloody lips was to get out of there.

"I understand how you feel."

"I know," he replied and squeezed my hands in return. "I'm so sorry, Thea…"

We weren't so different after all. He was so worried for Jaden I could feel his heavy emotions as if they were mine.

"I can feel you…"

"I can feel you too…"

"Is it like that for everyone?"

"No," I said and smiled. "We got a jackpot, my love. It's the third level connection."

It was obvious I heard nothing he said after the word "love" left his lips. I froze in his arms, afraid to breathe. I had just calmed down not long ago, but he sure didn't give me much time to relax. Well, it was true that I had never given him much time to relax either.

"Third level?" I repeated. My voice was hoarse.

"Do you remember our conversation about them?"

Of course, I did.

"A little bit," I lied.

"It's the rarest and not always pleasant option," he explained and touched my temple with his lips. I realized I didn't care much. He called me his love, and it made me want to cry again. What a fool I was.

"As if we can be so easily scared away by something."

"Well, you, apparently, can. It seems one word was enough…"

I squeezed my eyes shut, trying to hide. It was suddenly clear that this option was indeed unpleasant because he could read all my emotions like an open book.

"Are you a mind reader or something?" I muttered.

"Oh no," he whispered and laughed quietly. "I just know you, Thea. I already do."

I smiled.

"Then I'm sorry for you, Mr. Houwer."

I felt him smile in return, and everything melted away and into a tight ball in my lower stomach. I knew he would respond if I ask him for it...

"Thea, not today," he told me, and his voice was husky.

I frowned in confusion. Was he tired?

"I'm sorry," I said, and my cheeks flushed. It was the first time I was the one to act on our mutual desire, and it wasn't going well.

"Thea, I would love to, you know I would. You can feel it and you respond to it," he explained and turned me to face him. "Unfortunately, the medical check isn't finished yet, and I don't want to hurt..."

"Is something wrong with me?" I asked cautiously.

"No," he said and smiled.

"Aaron," I called. My breaths grew heavy, and I looked him in the eyes. "You know I... I can't have children..."

He stared at me for a while. His eyes were full of red flames and my reflection, and it was impossible to say they weren't one.

"I know everything about you," he finally let out.

"And?"

I thought I was going nuts. Why did I care what he thought?

I wanted to do it once, and there was no point in thinking about it again. That painful break up was long gone with no signs of pain in my soul, but I suppose I had this idea in my head that I had always wanted a family. I didn't have any in my childhood, and when I met that guy, I went head over heels for him. It could end in a fairytale, and he wanted it, too. When he found out it was impossible, he left. I learned to never dream of the impossible. I had other dreams to bring to life.

"What 'and?'" he repeated.

"Are you going to go out there and make babies with somebody else?" I snapped, feeling the earth crumble under my feet. "You haven't told me how you guys do that…"

I was so sick of it! All those mysteries made me choke and then brought me back to violent reality. What would I do if he said…

"I can't make babies with anyone, but you, Thea," Aaron said and smiled, which was, in my opinion, totally inappropriate for the situation.

"Is it about this third level connection?" I blurted out.

"Something like that," he told me and pulled me into a hug.

"Let's go to sleep. All of this is too much…"

He chuckled, picked me up, and brought me to bed. He didn't even leave to take a shower, because it was absolutely impossible for us to leave each other's arms, even though he decided to not get physical. I was soon happy about that because sleep was certainly in order. On the verge of falling asleep, I felt his sudden display of affection — Aaron was carefully stroking my stomach.

***

An annoying ray of sunshine was trying to get under my tight-shut eyelids, demanding my attention as if something had happened and I needed to be up… I really wasn't ready to wake up. A faint smell of wood, smoke, pine, and flowers wrapped around me, bringing me back to sleep and further from reality. It whispered to me, urging me to stay in bed. The outside world was dangerous and had many twists and turns, and my place was there, in safety with Aaron…

I jumped up, half asleep and blinking. Aaron wasn't there. Adrenaline rushed through the veins, and I got out of bed and walked quickly across the room. The first thing I saw was my cell phone with a myriad of missed calls, and next to it were some flowers. They were probably gathered in the garden just this morning and still had small drops of water on their stems.

*I'll be home late. Don't worry.*

"Take a deep breath and follow his advice, Thea!" I muttered to myself, feeling panic rise in my chest. Not going to happen. I got dressed and dashed out of the room.

Bunny and Amalia were having a lovely chat in the kitchen, but I wasn't impressed with the spirit.

"Where's Aaron?" I muttered.

Amalia stood up, and her glare answered all of the questions I didn't get to ask. I had to find my beast, and the sooner the better.

"Thea, everything is fine," she tried to persuade me. "Aaron is busy; he will be back soon..."

"Did he tell you to expect him late at night too?"

"Thea," Bunny said carefully, "do you think he is actually in danger?"

I knew I couldn't wait any longer when I saw Amalia's eyes go wide-open and her breathing quicken.

"Claud!" I shouted into the phone. "Where is Aaron?"

The bodyguard went silent for a moment with lots of voices in the background as if he took a moment to go somewhere more private.

"We are in court, Thea," he spoke quietly.

"Where?!" I growled.

"You can't come..."

"WHERE, Claud?! If he is sentenced, it would all be because of me! Why am I not there as a witness?!"

He didn't say a word for eternity.

"I'll send a car to pick you up."

I quickly took a shower and got ready, ate a sandwich, drank a cup of coffee, and left the house. Bunny refused to let me go alone, and less than fifteen minutes later we were on our way to the city. I had no clue what made Knife actually allow me to take part but I knew I shouldn't feel guilty about it. When something was forbidden, he was the first one to tell me so. Well, first except for Aaron.

Bunny was holding my hand all the way, while I was mainly trying to remember all the facts, all of the things Aaron told me in the beginning and then recently. Something wasn't adding up. It was clear that Shane set a trap for Aaron. He knew what the consequences of letting one's beast out were. It means that Aaron was either keeping me uninformed for my own good or thinking that I didn't care about him. Well, I did! I had no idea how it happened, but I was feeling withdrawn from not having Beast around in the morning and through the night. It made me go mad with fear of all of it ending. It was just as worrying as his and Jaden's faces in the kitchen yesterday. Did they talk about today's hearing? Or about the consequences? Was it why Jaden was so harsh to me?

When we finally got there, I was shaking. I jumped out of the car so fast, Bunny could hardly follow.

"Yes, we're here," I said to Knife on the phone, looking over an unmemorable grey building in the city center. Of course, the was no "Beast Court" sign. "Yes, I see the door. Coming…"

Bunny ran after me. We entered a big dark hall. Everything here was made to crush you: cold stone walls and indifferent guards. I could feel a small pulsation of familiar emotions somewhere in the depths of the building. It wasn't stable as if it wasn't working properly.

"Thea," Knife called, stepping out of a corridor. He looked at me and then at Bunny. "Get him the fuck out of here and pretend he never was here in the first place!"

"I'll wait outside," Bunny said, not afraid of the bodyguard.

"What were you thinking, bringing a human in here?" Knife hissed when we started walking back down the corridor.

"I wasn't," I replied. "I'm a human too. What's going on?"

"The hearing is happening right now," he replied and pressed a button on the wall.

"And?" I muttered. My throat was dry. I looked at him with lifeless eyes, waiting for the details. I knew if he waited for a moment longer I would either start screaming or punch him in the face.

"Shane lost, Thea. Aaron is going to be cleared. Didn't he tell you?" Knife asked in surprise.

The rest of the elevator ride went in silence.

The doors opened to a picture opposite to the one in the hall. There was a crowd, and everyone was talking at the same time. My appearance was met with lively chatter full of curiosity, but the attention definitely calmed me down.

"They're delivering judgment now," Knife whispered to me. "Aaron has," he started, trying to find something above the heads, but I wasn't sure what, "a perfect alibi."

"Damn," I whispered, holding on to him. My legs were giving out. When I took a step into the room I almost fell under a harsh gaze that pierced me through and pinned me to the wall. It was the only explanation I had for why I was still able to stand.

Aaron was talking to a man next to one of the tables. It looked like any other courtroom. When Knife walked me in, Aaron got distracted from his conversation. His companion even turned to see what got his attention.

There was me.

Something inside of me was full of fury because he didn't explain anything! He could tell me about his mysterious alibi and assure me it would be fine without making any more secrets! I couldn't believe he told me he knew me! Now he was unhappy with me when it was me who should've been unhappy!

Judge's gavel stopped our little staring contest. I was fed up with everything. I didn't care what he thought or how he looked, he could shout and fight, and do anything he wanted as long as we left this place together.

"Take you places, please," the judge ordered and started to read his statement.

I didn't see Shane right away, but when Aaron turned to face the judge, I was able to look around. He was sitting at the table next to Aaron's and looking around the room. His cheekbone was covered with a bandage, and he was wearing a back brace. Aaron did a good job in that fight, but it still left Shane full of determination. He was looking at me, and his eyes were angry and predatory and promised nothing good.

It was hard to calm down.

"Aaron Houwer, stand up," the judge demanded. "After careful consideration of evidence you presented, you are found to not be guilty. All of your actions are deemed justified."

The crowd erupted with noise, and I finally was able to breathe. Knife turned to me to say something, but Shane stood up.

"I object, Your Honor!" he shouted and turned to Aaron. "Aaron Houwer and Theana Melory are a 'triple X' couple, a combination that is forbidden for Primes! He marked her in a hospital after severe blood loss! He then killed Dustin Dewman, unable to resist his mate!" Shane concluded, looking at the judge. "I'm using my right as a Prime and accusing Aaron Houwer of killing Dustin Dewman."

The crowd hummed. It sounded as if we were on a seaside and a giant tsunami wave has just appeared on the horizon. My heart sank.

"I'm ready to give my life up for justice!" Shane ended and slowly sat back down.

"Claud, what's going on?" I asked and jumped up. He pulled me back into my sit.

"Any Prime has a right to put out an accusation," he said through the teeth, looking at Shane, "at the cost of his life. If we don't prove him wrong, Aaron will be…"

"No," I interrupted and dashed forward. "Aaron!" I shouted. I knew something would go wrong!

He turned to me, burning me with his eyes, but I didn't care. I crashed into him and held him tight, shivering. I felt all he was feeling, and it wasn't pretty. There was fear, wild and desperate, that was burning inside of him. Aaron held me like it was the last time he did that but then pulled back.

"I asked you to just wait," he growled and looked back. "Claud!"

"I can't wait!" I shouted through all the noise. "I don't want to be without you!"

When his gaze met mine, there were no more flames. He held my face in his hands and pulled me closer.

"I won't give up," he growled into my lips. "Not now…"

Someone caught me by the waist, trying to pull me away.

"Aaron," I mumbled and felt tears run down my face. It was as if they decided to take a piece of me. I was holding onto him as long as I could and almost gave up, but then there was a loud voice that made everyone go silent.

"I killed Dustin Dewman!"

The hold on my waist weakened, but I froze in Knife's arms, turning my head to where everyone was looking. Jaden was standing next to the judge. It was hard to recognize him in a suit. He was tall, dangerous, and it certainly ran in the family.

"I have evidence," he told the judge quietly, but his voice sounded loud and clear in the silent room.

"He's bluffing!" Shane screamed, standing up quickly.

"Silence!" the judge snapped and narrowed his eyes at Jaden. "Do you realize that you're pleading guilty of a murder, Mr. Houwer?"

"Aaron," the lawyer whispered, "don't do anything you would regret…"

I was hit by his despair and left with no air in my lungs.

"I do, Your Honor," Jaden declared firmly. "My brother is innocent. I have video proof of my doing."

The wave of the sound traveled through the room. The judge called silence.

"Mr. Shane," he said, towering over the crowd, "based on your right as a Prime, you told us you were ready to put one life against another — yours against Aaron Houwer's. If Mr. Jaden Houwer proves his brother's innocence, are you ready to accept the death sentence?"

My tongue stuck to the top of my mouth. My thoughts were slow and slimy, and my heart was beating fast in my chest. Prime's right is basically a "life for life" situation. One Prime against another, each putting their lives at stake.

"Mr. Shane," the judge repeated, "are you ready to hold your ground?"

"I'm not, Your Honor."

A loud exhale to my left almost swept me off my feet as much as Aaron's emotions. I grabbed the nearest chair, squeezing my eyes shut, but was then hugged from behind.

"Go," Aaron whispered. "I'll be with you soon… I promise…"

I traveled into Knife's care as he walked me out of the room. The judge was speaking, lots of voices were left behind, but I didn't care because I knew Aaron was not in danger.

Sitting in the hallway and holding a cup of tea, I was shaking from the experience. My phone was going wild in the bag, but I didn't care.

"Did he really kill Dustin?" I asked hoarsely.

Knife looked at me.

"I don't know, Thea…"

"You can feel lies," I reminded him.

"Only Primes can," he explained. "That's why they need an audio, video, or other physical evidence to prove his innocence…"

"That's wild!" I muttered. "Is it over now?"

As soon as I wasn't looking at Aaron I felt worried again.

"Shane certainly backed away."

"What about Jaden? He basically pleaded guilty in there."

"Well, not quite," Knife said, clenching his fists. "It's still possible to reverse the damage, turn it into false testimony case. Now the only important thing is that Shane backed away. If he decided to go with it, he would be dead. We don't take Prime's right lightly here, it's like the highest judgment right. It's a big cost to pay. Jaden just showed everyone what a coward Shane is…"

"Alexander must really hate Aaron to do that," I noted in surprise.

"That's not what it's about," Knife said. "He should really see a specialist with that bruised ego of his. He thought he could get out without a scratch… That bastard."

It was hard not to agree with that.

"Thea," Knife called and smiled when I looked at him. "You did great there, dear…"

"Well, I wouldn't say so," I said, "but I don't care…"

"That's exactly what I'm talking about."

He stood up when the crowd started leaving the room. I tried to jump up but felt dizzy and sat back down. I tried to look at every face, but everything was a blur.

"Claud," I called. I tried to draw his attention by waving my hand in the air and spilled the tea. Everything around was spinning and I heard someone calling for a doctor. The sound was loud, and I stretched my arms in its direction. Someone picked me up as I clang to them.

I took a breath and knew it was the right person... Now I could finally drift into unconsciousness because I was with someone I could trust.

***

I wasn't gone for long. Less than two minutes later I had the pleasure of hearing Aaron talk and feeling him.

"Why the fuck did you let her come here?!" he growled, leaving my head pulsating with pain.

"Don't shout," I mumbled.

"Where the fuck is that doctor?!" he said even louder, paying no attention to me.

"Right here, Mr. Houwer."

I felt sick.

"Give me some water," I asked, my voice barely loud enough, but Aaron repeated it so loudly everyone on the floor heard. A couple of seconds later I had water and the attention of everyone who was observing the scene. I was blinking at the doctor, who measured my blood pressure, and was afraid to breathe under Aaron's glare.

"Did you call the ambulance?!" he demanded.

"One minute, please," someone replied.

"Why do we need an ambulance?" I asked, looking at him.

In response I was showered with so much fury I had to squeeze my eyes shut.

"The blood pressure is okay, the pulse is slightly high. Did you have breakfast?" the doctor asked calmly. I didn't manage to nod before he continued: "Well, considering that you're exp…"

"Enough," Beast growled. "You're free to go. Thank you."

The confused doctor jumped out of the way when Aaron picked me up and went forward. Knife followed.

"Why are you so mad?" I asked. "I was just too worried. It happens…"

"Shut up, Thea," he interrupted. "Claud, call my father."

"What about Melvis?" Knife asked. He was calm under his boss's anger.

"He'll close the case. I asked for a restraining order against Shane."

"Great."

"Let me go," I muttered.

I bit his ear, leaving him in confusion. It was good we were in the elevator. Aaron tried to burn me with his glare, but I wasn't about to shut up.

"Is this what you want?! Do you want me to shut up and stay in the background?!" I blurted out, trying to break free. "Well, then let's stop this right here! I'm not going to do that! Why didn't you tell me?!"

"I asked you to stay home!" he hissed.

"Well, I can't stay home not knowing where you are, what you're doing, and how it's going to end! Learn to tell me the truth, and there will be no problems! Let me go!"

With my peripheral vision, I saw Knife pretending that he had something very interesting on his phone. I wished I had no frontal vision at this moment, but that was not happening.

"I told you the truth. I was in no danger," Aaron growled.

"Before Shane used his Prime's right?!" I shouted, not giving up.

"I didn't think he was that stupid! Now calm down and stop being a danger to yourself! Or I might seriously consider putting a collar on you!"

I went silent and turned away. We left the elevator in a hurry. Knife followed. As soon as we were at the entrance, Bunny joined the group.

"What's wrong?!"

"We don't know yet," Aaron noted and went to the ambulance.

"I just fainted," I explained and rolled my eyes. "I'm fine, and he is a drama queen."

Knife pulled Bunny away, and I couldn't see all of his emotions cross his face.

"To Plaza State Hospital," Aaron ordered. It was almost as if he was in a taxi, not an ambulance, but no one objected. Luckily, they laid me down, because I would certainly fell to my knees when I heard the next thing Aaron said.

"Two weeks pregnant, fainted," Aaron stated.

Doctors started to fuss around me.

"Is there bleeding?"

"Thea," Aaron roared, and I twitched. "Answer the question!"

"No," I replied mechanically, looking at him.

"Any pain in your lower stomach?"

"No."

"Did you do the lab tests? An ultrasound?"

"Yes and no," Aaron replied. "What's with the baby?"

"Don't shout, please," the doctor said. "Your nerves will only make things worse. Although I doubt there is anything to worry about. It's a little early to tell. We'll find out at the hospital, but now she needs peace and quiet."

"What else?" he continued. "If you're losing us time…"

"Mr. Houwer, hear me out, please. I can't do anything right now," the woman said, fencing me from Beast. It made me chuckle hysterically. It was better to deal with it this way than to think of whatever was going on. "She needs peace! And relaxation! I can't do things sloppily just because you're too nervous to calm down."

Aaron shot me a blaming look, and I thought of asking her to do something to him.

Is he an idiot?! What pregnancy?! We had just discussed it the day before. I can't have children! Was it some show for everyone around? And why wasn't I up to date on that?

At the hospital, it became clear there was no show. I was transported into the ultrasound room, and Beast was following me closely. I tried to catch a glimpse of his eyes, but he didn't want me to challenge him, and it made me nervous. My heart started racing, and the ultrasound machine made a note of that.

"Theana, are you feeling alright?" the doctor asked worriedly.

"Ask him," I stated, staring straight at Aaron. It was for nothing — he paid no attention to me.

My directions were carefully ignored. My stomach was touched with cold liquid and then with the machine. I watched the movement, feeling close to a nervous breakdown. I couldn't take it… All those lies, and mess, and fear… I can't do that. I don't want to…

"Mr. Houwer, everything is alright," the doctor said quietly. "The baby is okay, there is nothing wrong. It's developing nicely, the blood flow is good…"

I flicked her hand off my stomach faster than I could think about it. However, I didn't manage to put my feet down, because I was immediately pinned down by Beast. The fury and hate inside were so massive I felt I could probably handle him too.

"Fuck off," I hissed, looking him in the eyes.

"Calm down," he ordered coldly.

"For what?! For the baby to be okay?!" I said through clenched teeth. "So it never occurred in your little fucking mind that for the baby to be okay I should be aware of its existence?!"

The doctor rolled her chair in the furthest corner, giving us some space.

"We'll talk later," he continued.

"There's not going to be any 'later,'" I replied quietly. I was afraid to raise my voice. My throat was tense from incoming tears. "If you don't let me go right now…"

The world stopped existing. I was staring at Aaron, and he was staring at me. It was as if we went back to playing a game of silence again. I really wished for that because I knew I couldn't handle another part of this resistance. All I wished for was quiet. I wanted to get into a corner and wrap a blanket around myself.

Aaron stood tall, unclenching his fists and letting me go. There was so much flame in his eyes it would probably melt concrete. He was silent. When I had enough space, I jumped up and dashed out of the room.

It was quite hard to find the exit, considering the mess I had inside my head. When I finally saw the doors I flinched again, because Knife was waiting for me there.

"Thea, wait!" he shouted, getting to me in one movement.

I turned to another voice calling for me.

"Thea!" Bunny said and came to my rescue. "Thea, what happened?!"

I widened my eyes at him and held him tight, shivering.

"I want to get out of here."

"I'll drive you home," Knife said, but I heard it as if through layers of water.

Did Aaron really let me go? I turned to see the blurred hallway and was filled with Beast's emotions; they were dark and heavy fear and confusion. I thought he would explode from all the contradicting feelings, leaving me buried under the impact.

"Go," I said, shooing the feelings away. "Go, fast…"

***

I thought I would start sobbing as soon as we entered the apartment. Nothing happened. As soon as I was left alone, I felt tired and empty. Bunny sat me down on a chair and started to work something out in the kitchen. I was slowly looking over my old life or whatever was left of it. Now all of it was certainly behind, and I had no idea what the future held. How do I get rid of this painful bond? Aaron would never let me go again. He would never give the freedom he had once promised.

"Do you want a drink?" Bunny asked, looking through the fridge.

"I can't," I explained calmly. "I'm pregnant…"

I had no idea how Bunny dealt with all of this shit. When he turned to face me, he looked as if he could be in Kurt Pristley's new "Dandy's Surprise" campaign. I should probably tell Cave about that…

"Congrats," he let out.

"Thanks," I replied, continuing this ridiculous conversation.

"Why did you run away at the hospital then?"

"He knew," I said and shrugged. "He knew yesterday, and two days ago… He knew all this time and said nothing…"

"Well, excuse me," Bunny started, frowning, "but how could he tell you?"

"Ugh, don't you start defending him!" I blurted out and rolled my eyes.

"Don't start what?! Look at you! You ran away because he didn't tell you yesterday?"

"You wouldn't understand," I declared. "You're not the one who is constantly being lied to and asked to sit quietly, taking whatever comes next with gratitude!"

"Well, why don't you sit quietly, Thea?" he asked, folding his hands on his chest. The pose kind of looked like one of the Houwer brothers'. "You did it well yesterday, I saw it myself. You even liked it."

"I want to be asked!" I said, clenching my fists. "I don't want to be told and ordered to calm down, because the great and powerful Aaron Houwer said so! I want it to be… human."

"He cares about you, I saw that much. He didn't tell you because he understands all that. If he didn't care he would just tell you straight away. But no, he was waiting for all this shit with the court to end!"

I melted down in my chair, feeling exhausted. Bunny took a step towards me and sat next to me.

"Listen, you wanted to do this… And that jerk left you."

"I don't blame him," I whispered lifelessly. "Tom wanted it too… Although I would never stay with someone who only wanted one thing from me… Don't you think it's the same with Aaron? He got what he wanted…"

"Thea," my friend started, "I talked to them a little bit... Well, you know how I am." I did. He could probably make a rock talk. "Well, do you know how they make babies?" I made myself look up and pretend to be interested. "They use surrogates, just like people." I imagined locked prisons-labs with a bunch of slaves in them. "Just think about it. Wouldn't it be easier for Aaron to just make a surrogate baby with Grace than to deal with you daily with an additional risk of being electrocuted or whatever they do for letting his beast out?”

I felt like hitting his nice little face. I was so angry because the things he said actually made sense.

“Do you know why they found him innocent?” my friend asked and smiled triumphantly. “Because you are pregnant! I heard Claud speak with Aaron’s father in the car...”

I remembered Aaron asking Knife to call Denver.

“So, I think, in their laws, Aaron could protect you any way he saw suit. Shane, however, had no right to take you anywhere even if he had permission from God himself!”

It all clicked. That was why Aaron’s father had been so cold at first but then had warmed up so quickly. Aaron had probably told him! He told his father and not me! I straightened my back and widened my eyes. Well, it seemed like I was the last one to find out about my own pregnancy. By accident.

“I’m tired,” I said and stood up.

“Don’t sleep,” Bunny shouted and caught my hand.

Only then I noticed that his phone was constantly ringing with incoming texts and calls.

“Are you skipping work for me?” I asked warily.

“Oh, fuck work...”

“Bunny, get ready and go!”

“It’s not work,” he explained, taking his phone out of his pocket. “I just met this dude in a bar... Just wait a second.”

While he got busy texting back, I walked into the room. Walking back and forth, I realized I didn’t want to be there. I wanted to run somewhere, preferably to one overconfident Beast, preferably to slap his face, so he could finally learn that he needs to ask before deciding my fate for me. As much as my soul wanted to run to him, I wanted to stay calm and think about everything in detail. I was done with running. It was too much. I didn't know how Beast was feeling but I wanted to find some things out.

*Did you know I can get pregnant with you?*

I went to the balcony for some fresh air. As soon as I took the first breath, my phone rang.

"Thea, fuck, I'm not human! I can't just ask you about those things! Yes, we wear suits and we use phones, but we are not humans! When will you finally realize that?!" he shouted, and I started sobbing. "You know I had a choice..."

"You told me you didn't..."

"Well, I left us without one! I only want you. I want to have children with you, not make them in a test tube. You were terrified yesterday asking me about kids! What changed?!" Aaron growled. "I wish I could feel guilty, but I don't! Do you want to punish me for that?!"

"I..." I started heavily. "I want to figure it out... For myself..."

"Don't do anything stupid," he exhaled. "I don't know what else you want. Do you want me to beg you for forgiveness? For this?"

Something inside tensed and pulled me forward.

"Thea!" Aaron cried, and I realized he could see me. "Step back! Sit down!"

I crashed into the wall and slowly slid down to the floor, listening to his heavy breathing.

"I can't deal with your emotions anymore! It's so hard..."

"Well, I didn't promise you it would be easy, remember?" he said. My cheeks were wet with tears. He promised me hell, and he delivered. "Thea," he whispered, "come back. You're my life."

"Is it about the baby?" I muttered.

"It's about you..."

He hung up, and then the door opened and he stepped onto the balcony. Bunny obviously lied to me about this "bar dude!"

Beast kneeled in front of me and looked me in the face. His jacket and his shirt were unbuttoned, and I could almost imagine him running back and forth in the hallway, looking at me on the screen. Did he let me go? Hardly. Aaron continued to look at me intently, and it was hard to tell whether he wanted to kill me or hold me tight and never let go.

"You can feel it…" he said reproachfully.

"I have no idea what I feel! I wasn't taught to be with someone like you, Aaron…" I sobbed. "I'm terrified of your emotions! I'm not a beast! Should I apologize for that?!"

He went silent for a second, watching me closely.

"I wanted to tell you later when all of this was over. I was afraid to lose you. I never thought you would come there today," he said and smiled, "for me." Aaron looked up at me and said, "I didn't believe in you… in us… I'm sorry. I don't really know you, but I don't want to lose you."

I was sure he wouldn't be able to make me wear a collar, he wouldn't be able to go that far. Aaron let me go today. He was full of contradicting feelings and desires but still let me go. Would he fulfill his promise and free me forever?

He knew I had reservations, and he suddenly leaned closer. "Marry me."

I tried to merge with the wall. Now? He is asking now?

"Are you sure you don't want to lose me?" I asked with a smirk, looking him in the eyes. Beast looked serious.

He could wait for everything to calm down, but nothing went according to the plan, and now we were on my balcony, trying to figure out what to do with all those huge differences we had. He wasn't thinking about time anymore, because nothing was going to change. He would still be the beast and my baby's father, and I would still be human. This would never change.

I thought of asking him if he would ever let me go. It seemed unlikely with my pregnancy. I thought of it but couldn't do it. His feelings were not something to play around with, and I knew that if I did it, there would not be a way back. I wasn't ready…

…to make us both miserable by giving up on our happiness.

"Alright," I said, "I'll marry you."

I surprised him again. For a couple of seconds, he was looking at me in confusion and then seemed like he wanted to ask again but decided not to risk it.

"You're such a brave girl," he said, grinning, and pulled me onto his lap. "You won't regret it," he whispered.

I felt his hot lips on my neck and shivered, squeezing his hips with my legs and holding him tight, his body pressed against mine.

"I know…"

***

We didn't go back to his apartment. Aaron drove me straight to his parents' house. Amalia met us at the gates and went in for a warm embrace. This was the first time I realized I wasn't the only problem Aaron had to deal with. He also had a real danger of losing his brother pushing him to the edge, and I could feel his worry. He spent all night on his phone and made a new path on the lawn from walking back and forth so many times. I couldn't stop watching him from the window. I looked at the way he moved, the way he talked, the way he clenched his fists… When I caught his glare I felt an urge to hide behind the curtain.

I kept thinking about saying "yes" and felt nothing shake inside. I wasn't sure whether I was too used to the shock of the latest events or I just was in inner peace with this decision. I stopped trying to fight it and just went with it. We got there. He could do whatever he wanted because I was ready to adapt. I didn't want to run and fight him again. I had no more right to that.

It was hard to believe I was pregnant but I was sure I'd get there too.

When it was almost dark, he entered our room, put his phone on the table, and looked at me. I was sitting on the pillow next to the fireplace. It was impossible to not react to his attention even when I couldn't see him upfront.

"Sorry," he said. My chest filled with his doubts. "I'll take a shower…"

He was never taught to be with someone like me.

"Come here," I ordered, copying his tone. I didn't want us to act like strangers. It was a start, and we were not hopeless. "Are you going back to your feral ways?" I asked and chuckled.

Aaron smiled.

"You see right through me…" he told me and grabbed me into a hug. "I'm just afraid to do something wrong…"

"Well, it's too late for that…" I replied and wrapped my legs around his waist. I felt him tense in response. His hunger was in his every breath, every movement of his fingers on my neck. He didn't let himself go further, afraid of harming me.

"How much patience do you think you have?" I purred into his ear, moving my hips to his. "And what will happen when you're out of it?"

"We…"

"…can do whatever we want," I interrupted. "The ultrasound was okay. Everything is fine."

"We don't know if it was, because you ran away and I didn't ask!" he growled reproachfully, breathing heavily.

"Well, we only can do it if there is no danger to a baby, and there isn't any," I said. If he didn't make his move, I would certainly do everything myself. I didn't want to think about where this thirst came from. I wanted him to be mine again after everything that had happened between us. "I want you, Mr. Houwer, and you can't say "no" to a pregnant lady!"

He wasn't hesitating any longer. His capitulation looked like a victory. It was as though I was the one who had been refusing and he finally caught me. He took all these days of involuntary abstinence and made it worth it. I wasn't sure it was a good idea to moan, growl and scream so loudly in his parents' house, but it was safe to say everyone knew we were celebrating the engagement.

I was purring into his neck with one of my legs on his hip.

Finally! My head was delightfully empty, and my body was weak and at ease. The future didn't seem so grim anymore.

"We're going to the hospital tomorrow," Aaron said, trying to spoil the mood.

"Sure," I replied with a smile. "We can get permission for you to have sex with me... Maybe they'll even stamp it to make it official..."

"Thea," he called, "I can feel your fear... Talk to me."

I froze in his arms and held my breath. How could I explain that all we have are parts of the puzzle that would take an eternity to finally complete? It was whole for him but not for me. I didn't have his instincts to guide me, I didn't have his confidence.

"Are you afraid?" he asked again.

"Of course... What if I won't be a good mom, Aaron?"

"You will," he reassured and stroked my hair. "We will learn together. Also, my mom is always there to help..."

"I don't want this baby to be like me... to have parents who have no idea why they had him in the first place..."

He blinked slowly.

"Tell me how you want to do this."

I did. I told him how my childhood was, I told him about things I didn't want and things I dreaded. He was listening closely, not interrupting me, not touching me, and not distracting. It was something new for us. We were finally in the same room, we were talking and listening. Everything changed when we decided to stay together willingly.

"Okay," he concluded. "However, I can't promise you five dogs."

I chuckled. My thoughts were a mess, hormones were making me emotional and bringing me to the verge of tears for no reason, but I felt at ease. I gave him my all, and he took it.

"You'll have to give up your dream for now," he said, showing what his biggest concern was. I was thankful that he tried to take my life into consideration.

"Yeah, I know," I replied and shrugged. "I don't think they'll forget me any time soon."

"Oh, that's for sure," he commented and smiled. "You'll be on TV for a while..."

"And the wedding..."

"Yeah, only one week away."

"That's crazy."

"I'll make it happen, you just need to show up."

"So, am I not allowed to participate in planning?"

"Of course you are. You can do whatever you want with it. The process hasn't even started yet."

Well, changing the bride and nothing else was apparently not an option for Aaron Houwer. It also meant that he got himself a new set of problems to deal with.

"Preparing a wedding in a week? You seem to like risk, Mr. Houwer."

"That's the only way to do it with you, Thea."

"Can we just sign the papers quietly?" I suggested. "It's not like you have lots of time to deal with this..."

There was another surprised expression for my mental collection.

"Are you serious?" he asked.

"Yeah… I just thought we can't do that…"

"Well, we can…" he said and looked at me intently. "I want to give you everything. I know all girls dream of a perfect wedding…"

"I'm not like other girls," I said. "Considering everything that happened and your breakup with Grace, I don't want to rub my happiness in her face…"

"So you are happy?" he asked.

"Quite," I confirmed. "Let's do a quiet little thing."

It seemed that I had finally learned to make a human out of a beast. Aaron smiled, his smile open and relaxed, and pulled me closer.

"Whatever you want, Thea…"

"I like it when you say that," I replied. I smiled into his lips, we shared our first kiss that wasn't supported by passion and desire. It came from his sincere gratitude and our trust in each other. Our shared emotions told me we were on the right track. He was a part of me, and I was a part of him, and there was no way for us to run away from it. It was all worth it. Together we were something better than each of us ever was individually.

I was getting ready for dinner, feeling peaceful and happy. We were planning to tell his parents about our engagement because they obviously had already learned about the baby. Denver and Amalia were both happy, but worried, and I could see it in their eyes.

When Jaden walked in, I got goosebumps.

"Aaron," he said, walking to the table, "mom, dad… Thea." I got a special glare from him.

"Jay," Amalia sobbed and crashed into him. "Jay…"

"Mom," Aaron called and stood up, "you know it's not over. I won't allow them to hurt him…"

"Aaron," Jaden said through the teeth, "I'll take the responsibility... I'll deal with it myself."

"For my mistake? Really?" my Beast asked and narrowed his eyes.

"You protected me, and I will protect you," Jaden stated and looked at me again. "You wouldn't make it in time: Dewman had already got an injection... One more hour and you'd lose her."

I was listening and putting new pieces of the puzzle together. So, Jaden actually killed Dewman. Aaron couldn't possibly do it, he had told me that he was weak when he came into the office.

"Aaron, what is Melvis saying?" their father asked.

"That we can frame it as an official challenge."

"I had no grounds," Jaden noted skeptically.

"We'll find something," Aaron said. "I'm looking for it."

"Aaron, my job is to find grounds," Jaden replied and sat down, putting his hands on the table in front of him. I had an opportunity to study him closer, but I was always distracted by how fiercely he wasn't afraid of the future. He had an unbreakable core, just as Aaron did. He wasn't facing death right now how he was in the courtroom, but I saw that his eyes were the same. "There aren't any. If I couldn't find them, no one can. Dewman is clean. He bought Theana legally..."

"He had no right no challenge someone else's mark without learning who gave it and why," Aaron countered.

"Well, it's not something one gets murdered for," Jaden argued.

"Well, it will be a precedent then," Aaron snapped and grabbed Jaden's wrist. "I'll make it a precedent."

"It will put you in danger," Jaden said, looking up at his brother. "You will have to tell them about your connection with Thea."

"All I'll lose is the position, and you are about to lose your life," Aaron growled. "I have my priorities straight!"

"No one can take your job, and the family will suffer because of it!"

"You can take my job!"

The kitchen went silent. I didn't know how important Aaron's words were.

"Don't let the family down, Aaron," Jaden said and stood up.

Well, that was a first. I'd never met a man who was as stubborn as Jaden. Aaron's gaze sometimes made me want to run away, but Jaden's would probably make me want to shoot myself.

"Don't tell me what to do, I'm still your Prime," Aaron told him and stood up too.

"And it will stay this way."

"Jay," Amalia sobbed, standing up too. "Please... Don't do that... Don't leave me... I know it's hard, but don't go, please..."

"Jaden," Denver called. "I never had to make this choice, but I know yours is dictated by your weakness..."

Jaden swallowed and looked into the emptiness in front of him.

"... I know it's difficult to live through your loss, but she wouldn't be happy if you decided to follow her..."

"Well, I will be," Jaden said through his teeth, turned, and left.

Amalia squeezed her eyes shut. Aaron stroked my shoulders with his hand and turned to the exit.

"I'll be back in a second," he said and followed his brother.

Amalia and I started to clean up in heavy silence.

"He..." she sobbed, freezing next to the fridge. "He had a girlfriend... she was like us. They met at work, she was his assistant," she continued. "Jay... he has a dangerous job..."

I put glasses onto the table and stepped closer to Amalia. It was easy to hug this woman who was so dear to Aaron, even though just a short while ago I couldn't even imagine doing that. I was used to quick hugs at work, which meant nothing. Holding someone sincerely as a sign of support was only something I had experienced with Bunny. Then with Aaron... Now I opened my arms to someone I barely knew but wanted to make feel better.

"What happened to her?"

"She died not long ago," Amalia muttered. "Jaden... he is as good as dead after that."

"When was it?" I asked.

"The night Aaron tried to save them," she replied and hugged herself. "Jay was leading some investigation, and there were some serious authorities of our world involved. It's good Aaron always knows about his business... When Jaden got into a trap, Aaron managed to save him. But it was too late for Cami..."

Amalia started crying. I was just realizing at what a horrific time I entered Aaron's life. His emergency flight back from Apollynis, his exhaustion... I was only making it worse for him the whole time, and he was on edge the whole time, risking everything.

"You have two great sons," I whispered carefully. "I'm so sorry..."

"Well, at least I'm sure we're giving one of them to a good person," Amalia said and let out a sad smile. "Their race raises Primes from the strongest boys in the family. They have no chance to show feelings or be happy... Jaden is a Prime too. Aaron was right when he said he could take his place. I'm proud that they are choosing to feel something. Why are bastards like Alexander Shane considered to be the specimen of family heads? How can there even be a family without mutual love and support?!"

I was pretty sure her opinion didn't matter to those holding power. Maybe they were right, but it was not up to us to make this judgment.

"I'm so happy he met you. I'm sorry it was like that, but it would not work otherwise."

I knew she was right. Otherwise, I would be on a leash next to Dustin Dewman. Aaron and Jaden got me out of that, but it seemed like the price was too much to pay.

***

The next morning there were no text messages or flowers on the nightstand. However, there was a black diamond. I carefully picked up the chain made of white gold and felt the heaviness of the rock, which shone mysteriously in the dim light.

"I know you are not a fan of jewelry…"

I turned to the door. Aaron was there with a tray and was smiling.

"… but it's one of the Prime's traditions to give their women those things," he ended and walked into the room. "They say it made families stronger back in the old days."

"Did you really buy it for me?" I asked. I wanted to know if he chose me straight away. When I remembered the night in Dewman's office, I got goosebumps. Back then Aaron seemed to be a devil from hell who came to take my soul.

"I did," he confirmed and put the tray on the floor. "When I saw it on your neck I realized I was not going to give you up. I wanted to take something to remind me of you…" he said with a smirk. "You have an hour to get ready…"

"Are we going to the hospital?" I asked with a grimace of pain.

"You're going to work, Thea," he stated and surprised me. "You're not on a maternity leave yet…"

I lost my ability to speak for a second.

"How?" I muttered hoarsely, while he was setting up the breakfast before the fireplace.

"Shane is on the restraining order, and you need to complete your contract with the fashion house."

I narrowed my eyes.

"How did you make it happen?"

Aaron closed his eyes.

"They needed your diamond for the show. I told them there would not be a diamond without you to show it."

He seemed to be afraid of my reaction, but I was pleased that he was learning to tell the truth, even if it wasn't nice.

"Thank you," I said and smiled.

"Really?" he asked and sat next to me.

"Really, Aaron. I wanted to walk the runway on the opening night. Especially with the diamond that you refused to give me…" I explained and grinned.

He pulled me closer as if he was checking if I was okay. Maybe he wanted to make sure I wasn't hiding anything. The day before we had realized that we feel each other better when we're touching. This kind of connection wasn't available to many, even Aaron's parents didn't have it, so we had to learn along the way. It was good motivation to start taking baby steps towards each other.

"Give it to me," Aaron asked and sat me between his legs, touching my flat stomach. "I forgot to tell you that I'm extremely happy," he whispered.

It felt right. It wasn't something to say out loud. I knew he would probably prefer to not say it at all, but he learned his lesson of not telling me things.

"It makes me happy to know that you are," I noted, closing my eyes.

"I can feel that."

We were walking through a minefield, warning each other of our presence. It was scary. What if we ever got tired of being together? Being strangers who were so open was a challenge. We could do nothing, but accept it, stop ignoring it, take it for all it was and live with it.

At that moment I knew he wasn't expecting me to say it back. He was accepting me for who I was. He knew I needed more time.

"You'll be late," Aaron warned and smiled, distracting me from my thoughts. I grinned and turned, putting my hands on his shoulders.

"Thank you," I said, looked him in the eyes, and kissed him.

I saw him close his eyes. He was fighting the urge to grab me and sit me back down. He squeezed his fingers in my hair and pulled me closer.

"No, thank you," he whispered, before letting me go.

We both froze for a moment, looking each other in the eyes, and I suddenly realized we would make it work. He was worth trying and being the only one for him. He didn't simply enter my heart, but tore his way in with claws and fangs, leaving ugly bleeding scars, but I knew the scars would heal. He would be the one to lick them and heal them...

Aaron, as if thinking the same thing, gave me a questioning look.

"Want to stay home?"

"Can we?"

He slowly sighed, thinking.

"We can if you're not looking forward to going to work..."

"I want to stay with you..."

My monster got back into his human form, smiling.

"Great," he said with his sexy voice. "Then I'll bring some more coffee."

"And some sweet bread with spicy tomatoes, please. Yesterday I saw them..."

Aaron smirked and exited the room. His happiness, however, stayed with me. Or was it my own?

Well, we were certainly going to figure it all out.


Epilogue

My heart was beating fast in my chest. My breathing grew heavy as I watched the runway from behind the curtain. The music only made the anticipation worse. Organized chaos backstage was turning into a logical and impressive view for the audience. I knew that life was worth it when I was about to go on stage and be a part of this genius masterpiece of a show. However, it wasn't the only thing that made me nervous...

"Thea, ready?" the junior coordinator called, trying to raise his voice to overpower the cacophony of sounds. "A minute call."

I nodded.

The transitional music in the room switched off, the lights froze and shattered in pieces before falling to my feet. I walked onto the runway. With my every step the projections of glass cracked and fell down. It was so realistic, I felt I was actually walking of shattered glass.

It reminded me so much of the way I made not long ago.

A couple of hundreds of viewers were in the room, but I only saw one of them. He was the only one who mattered, he was the only one I saw watching my steps. He was the one I trembled for and he was the one whose opinion mattered. I knew Aaron was there. He came to watch me without telling me. I didn't ask him, although I really wanted to share this moment with him. He didn't disappoint. He came in, leaving everything behind, and I knew it wasn't easy for him to do.

Jaden's trial was in process... Every day Aaron came back home as if he just went through a war, and we sat in silence and looked at the city from the windows of his apartment. He always pulled me closer, healing his wounds, unable to tell me what was going on. I knew he was losing.

He came here anyway.

My face was now on the biggest screen in the city as well as many smaller screens all over the country. I heard orders in a small earpiece, and they directed me in the show's augmented reality. Virtual rocks and jewelry dropped down onto the glass dome and turned into my image. My every step was a part of this canvas of lights and music. I regretted nothing. Even if it was all part of someone else's evil plan, it turned out to be magical. The audience applauded in reassurance.

I saw Alexander. He was not far away before the show, and now he was waiting for me personally ten meters away. He wasn't allowed to come closer. He was standing there with his hands in his pockets, smiling in his usual manner. He got the diamond he wanted. The opening was popular, but I was hardly less well-known with my infamous reputation. It might be that they discussed me even more. The web was full of my and Aaron's pictures. Here he is picking me up from *Teyvalle*, here he is smiling, hugging me, kissing me, holding me tight. Everyone noticed how unusually affectionate Mr. Houwer became. I wasn't the only one who liked him more this way.

"Let's go," Knife reminded and walked me into my personal changing room.

There was a surprise — madam Duvalle herself.

"Miss Melory, can we talk?" she asked without her usual demeanor. "I would like to offer you a permanent contract with our fashion house."

The dress was tight enough to hold me from falling.

"Contract?" I repeated.

"Yes, our board would like to have you is one of our permanent models."

"I would love to," I said, watching Knife leave, and looked her in the eyes, "but I'm expecting…"

"I know," she replied. I started blinking fast because it could only mean one thing — she wasn't human either. Only beasts knew I was pregnant after Aaron's trial. "You're not planning to leave forever, are you? We are always short on maternity models, and let's face it, you were quite professional, considering everything that happened. We value that. I personally value that. Think about it. Your agent has the contract."

When she left, I stood in the middle of the room for a while before Knife came in and told me someone was waiting for me.

They were waiting for me in the parking lot. Bunny was dressed in a smart suit and had a huge bouquet of flowers, and Aaron was there too. The men were standing next to each other near the car.

"Thea, congratulations," my friend said, hugging me.

"You look amazing," I replied and hugged him back.

"Ugh, I should really step my game up to get to your level. You're far up now…"

"I just married well," I whispered into his ear.

Aaron and I got married in Apollynis without telling anyone. After another difficult week, my beast grabbed me and drove me to the airport. We entered the jet, where we knew the bedroom was strong enough to handle our appetites. He was not giving me any rest since doctors told him that it was safe. My own hunger for him got really strong too.

Whatever we did, however many days went by, there was still one thing bothering him. His fear for his brother was tangible, and although he didn't give me details, I saw despair grow in his eyes.

"Hi," I said, finally being in his arms. "Thank you…"

"I wouldn't miss it," he said and hugged me.

I knew that something was wrong from the moment I felt a slight tremble travel from him to me. I didn't know what it was, but I knew I needed to be the one to hold him. When my fingers squeezed his shoulders, he took a deep breath and clenched onto me tightly as if I was the last thing holding him from falling into his grief.

"Aaron," I whispered, letting his emotions in. They terrified me more than any fear. There was no more fear in him.

There was no one to be scared for.

"Death sentence," he muttered, tearing the words from his soul. I opened my eyes wide, gasping for air, unable to hold so much pain. "Shhh… Calm down… Breathe… You're my everything… Breathe…"

I breathed into his neck, squeezing his shoulders, sharing his anger and pain with every breath.

We would get through this…

We had no choice.

www.ingramcontent.com/pod-product-compliance
Lightning Source LLC
LaVergne TN
LVHW010505200726
843506LV00013B/2535